Doctored Evidence

Donna Leon

Doctored Evidence

ATLANTIC MONTHLY PRESS   *New York*

First published in the United Kingdom in 2004 by
William Heinemann

FIRST AMERICAN EDITION

Library of Congress Cataloging-in-Publication Data
Leon, Donna.
Doctored evidence : a Commissario Guido Brunetti mystery / Donna Leon.
p. cm.
ISBN 0-87113-918-9
1. Brunetti, Guido (Fictitious character)--Fiction. 2. Single women--Crimes
against--Fiction. 3. Police--Italy--Venice--Fiction. 4. Romanians--Italy--Fiction.
5. Venice (Italy)--Fiction. I. Title.
PS3562.E534D63 2004
813'.54--dc22   2003063941

Atlantic Monthly Press
841 Broadway
New York, NY 10003

04 05 06 07 08 10 9 8 7 6 5 4 3 2 1

for Alan Curtis

Signor dottore
Che si può fare

Honoured doctor
What can be done?

Così fan tutte

—Mozart

1

She was an old cow and he hated her. Because he was a doctor and she his patient, he felt guilty about hating her, but not so guilty as to make him hate her any the less. Nasty, greedy, ill-tempered, forever complaining about her health and the few people who still had the stomach for her company, Maria Grazia Battestini was a woman about whom nothing good could be said, not even by the most generous of souls. The priest had given up on her long ago, and her neighbours spoke of her with distaste, sometimes with open animosity. Her family remained connected to her only by means of the laws governing inheritance. But he was a doctor, so he had no choice but to make his weekly visit, even though it now consisted of nothing more than a perfunctory inquiry as to how she felt, followed by the speedy measuring of her pulse and blood pressure. He'd been coming for more than four years now, and his aversion had become so strong that he had lost the fight against his repeated disappointment at the continued absence of signs of illness. Just past eighty, she looked and acted a decade older, but she'd live to bury him; she'd live to bury them all.

He had a key and used it to let himself into the building. The whole place was hers, all three floors, though she occupied only half of the second. Spite and meanness caused her to maintain the fiction that she occupied all of it, for by so doing she kept her sister Santina's daughter from moving into either the floor above or the one below. He forgot how many times, in the years since the death of her son, she had hurled abuse upon her sister and told him how much pleasure it gave her perpetually to frustrate her family's designs upon the house. She spoke of her sister with malice that had gathered momentum ever since their shared childhood.

He turned the key to the right, and because it is in the nature of Venetian doors not to open at first try, he automatically pulled the door towards him as he turned the key. He pushed the door open, stepping into the dim entrance hall. No sunlight could penetrate the decades of grease and dirt that covered the two narrow windows above the door to the *calle*. He no longer noticed the dimness, and it had been years since Signora Battestini had been able to come down the steps, so the windows were unlikely to be cleaned any time soon. Damp had fused the wires years before, but she refused to pay for an electrician, and he had lost the habit of trying to switch the light on.

He started up the first flight of stairs, glad that this was his last call of the morning. He'd finish with the old horror and go and have a drink, then get some lunch. He didn't have to be at his surgery to see patients until five; had no plans after lunch and nothing he particularly wanted to do, so long as he could be free of the sight and sound of their wasted and bloated bodies.

As he started up the second flight, he found himself hoping that the new woman – he thought this one was Romanian, for that was how the old woman referred to her, though they never stayed long enough for him to remember their names – would last. Since her arrival, the old shrew was at least clean and no longer stank of urine. Over the years he'd watched them come and go; come because they were drawn by the prospect of work, even if it meant cleaning and feeding Signora Battestini and submitting to her unrelenting abuse; go because each had eventually been so worn down that even the most abject need could not resist the assault of the woman's nastiness.

From the habit of politeness, he knocked at her door, though he knew it a futile courtesy. The blaring of her television, which had been audible even from outside the building, drowned out the sound: even the younger ears of the Romanian – what *was* her name? – seldom registered his arrival.

He took the second key and turned it twice, then stepped into the apartment. At least it was clean. There had been a time, he thought it was about a year after her son died, when no one had come for more than a week, and the old woman had been left alone in the apartment. He still remembered the smell of the place when he'd opened the door for his then bi-monthly visit, and, when he'd gone into the kitchen, the sight of the plates of decomposing food left on the table for a week in the July heat. And the sight of her, body encased in layers of fat, naked and covered with the drips and dribbles of what she had tried to eat, hunched in a chair in front of the eternally blaring television. She'd ended up in hospital that time, dehydrated and disoriented, but they'd wanted quit of her after only three days, and since she demanded to be in her own home, they'd gladly taken the option and had her carried there. The Ukrainian woman had come then, the one who'd disappeared after three weeks, taking a silver serving plate with her, and his visits had been increased to once a week. But the old woman had not changed: her heart pounded on, her lungs pulled in

3

the air of the apartment, and the layers of fat grew ever thicker.

He set his bag on the table by the door, glad to see that its surface was clean, a sure sign that the Romanian was still there. He took the stethoscope, hooked it behind his ears, and went into the living room.

Had the television not been on, he probably would have heard the noise before he went in. But on the screen the much-lifted blonde with the Shirley Temple curls was giving the traffic report, alerting the drivers of the Veneto to the potential inconvenience of *traffico intenso* on the A4 and drowning the industrious buzzing of the flies at work on the old woman's head.

He was accustomed to the sight of death in the old, but deaths in old age were usually more decorous than what he saw on the floor beneath him. The old die softly or the old die hard, but because death seldom comes as an assault, few resist it with violence. Nor had she.

Whoever had killed her must have taken her completely by surprise, for she lay on the floor to the left of an undisturbed table on which stood an empty cup and the remote control of the television. The flies had decided to divide their attention between a bowl of fresh figs and Signora Battestini's head. Her arms were flung out in front of her, and she lay with her left cheek on the floor. The damage was to the back of her head, which reminded him of a soccer ball his son's dog had once bitten, deflating it on one side. Unlike her head, the skin of the soccer ball had remained smooth and intact; nothing had leaked from it.

He stopped at the door, looking around the room, too stunned by the chaos to have a clear idea of what he was looking for. Perhaps he sought the body of the Romanian; perhaps he feared the sudden arrival from some other room of the person who had done this. But the flies told him that whoever had done this had had more than enough time to flee. He glanced up, his staggered attention caught by the sound of a human voice, but all he learned was that there had been an accident involving a truck on the A3 near Cosenza.

He walked across the room and switched off the television, and silence, neither hushed nor respectful, filled the room. He wondered if he should go into the other rooms and look for the Romanian, perhaps try to help her if they had not succeeded in killing her, too. Instead, he went into the hall and, taking his *telefonino* from his pocket, dialled 113 and reported that there had been a murder in Cannaregio.

The police had little trouble finding the house, for the doctor had explained that the victim's home was at the beginning of the *calle* to the right of the Palazzo del Cammello. The launch glided to a halt on the south side of the Canale della Madonna. Two uniformed officers jumped on to the *riva*, then one of them leaned back into the boat to help the three men from the technical squad unload their equipment.

It was almost one. Sweat dripped from their faces, and their jackets soon began to cling to their bodies. Cursing the heat, wiping vainly at their sweat, four of the five men began to carry the equipment to the entrance to Calle Tintoretto and along to the house, where a tall, thin man waited for them.

'Dottor Carlotti?' the uniformed officer who had not helped in unloading the boat asked.

'Yes.'

'It was you who called?' Both men knew the question was unnecessary.

'Yes.'

'Could you tell me more? Why you were here?'

'I came to visit a patient of mine – I come every week – Maria Grazia Battestini, and when I went into the apartment, I found her on the floor. She was dead.'

'You have a key?' the policeman asked. Though his voice was neutral, the question filled the air around them with suspicion.

'Yes. I've had one for the last few years. I have the keys to the homes of many of my patients,' Carlotti said, then stopped, realizing how strange it must sound, his explaining this to the police, and made uncomfortable by the realization.

'Would you tell me exactly what you found?' the policeman asked. As the two men spoke, the others deposited the equipment inside the front door and went back to the launch for more.

'She's dead. Someone's killed her.'

'Why are you sure someone killed her?'

'Because I've seen her,' Carlotti said and left it at that.

'Have you any idea who might have done it, Dottore?'

'No, of course I don't know who he was,' the Doctor insisted, trying to sound indignant but managing only to sound nervous.

'He?'

'What?' said Carlotti.

'You said, "he," Dottore. I was curious to know why you think it was a man.'

Carlotti started to answer, but the neutral words he tried to pronounce slipped out of his control and, instead, he said, 'Take a look at her head and tell me a woman did that.'

His anger surprised him; or rather, the force of it did. He was angry not with the policeman's questions but at his own craven response to them. He had done nothing wrong, had merely stumbled upon the old woman's body, and yet his unthinking response to any brush with authority was fear and the certainty that it would somehow cause him harm. What a race of cowards we've become, he caught himself thinking, but then the policeman asked, 'Where is she?'

'On the second floor.'

'Is the door open?'

'Yes.'

The policeman stepped into the dim hallway, where the others had crowded to escape the sunshine, and made an upward motion with his chin. Then he said to the doctor, 'I want you to come upstairs with us.'

Carlotti followed the policemen, resolved to say as little as possible and not to display any unease or fear. He was accustomed to the sight of death, so the sight of the woman's body, terrible as it was, had not affected him as much as had his instinctive fear of being involved with the police.

At the top of the stairs, the policemen entered the apartment without bothering to knock; the doctor chose to wait outside on the landing. For the first time in fifteen years, he wanted a cigarette with a need so strong it forced the beat of his heart into a quicker rhythm.

He listened to them moving around inside the apartment, heard their voices calling to one another, though he made no attempt to listen. The voices grew softer as the policemen moved to the next room, where the body was. He moved over to the windowsill and half sat on it, heedless of the accumulated filth. He wondered why they needed him here, came close to a decision to tell them they could reach him at his surgery if they wanted him. But he remained where he was and did not go into the apartment to speak to them.

After a time, the policeman who had spoken to him came out into the corridor, holding some papers in a plastic-gloved hand. 'Was someone staying here with her?' he asked.

'Yes.'

'Who?'

'I don't know her name, but I think she was a Romanian.'

The policeman held out one of the papers to him. It was a form that had been filled in by hand. At the bottom left was a passport-sized photo of a round-faced woman who could have been the Romanian. 'Is this the woman?' the policeman asked.

'I think so,' Dottor Carlotti answered.

'Florinda Ghiorghiu,' the policeman read, and that brought the name back.

'Yes. Flori,' the doctor said. Then, curious, he asked, 'Is she in there?' hoping the police would not find it strange that he had not looked for her, and hoping they had not found her body.

'Hardly,' the policeman answered with barely disguised impatience. 'There's no sign of her, and the place is a mess. Someone's been through it and taken anything valuable.'

'You think . . .' Carlotti began, but the policeman cut him off.

'Of course,' the officer answered with anger so fierce it surprised the other man. 'She's from the East. They're all like that. Vermin.' Before Carlotti could object, the policeman went on, spitting out the words. 'There's an apron in the kitchen with blood all over it. The Romanian killed her.' And then, speaking the epitaph for Maria Grazia Battestini that Dottor Carlotti would perhaps not have given, the policeman muttered, 'Poor old thing.'

2

The police officer in charge, Lieutenant Scarpa, told Dottor Carlotti that he could go home but warned him that he was not to leave the city without police permission. So rich was Scarpa's tone with insinuations of undetected guilt that whatever resistance Carlotti might have offered died unspoken, and he left.

The next person to arrive was Dottor Ettore Rizzardi, *medico legale* for the city of Venice and thus officially responsible for declaring the victim dead and for making the first speculation as to the time of that event. Coolly, if somewhat excessively polite with Lieutenant Scarpa, Rizzardi stated that Signora Battestini had apparently died as the result of a series of blows to the head, a judgement he believed would be confirmed by the autopsy. As to the time of death, Dr Rizzardi, after taking the temperature of the corpse, said that, the flies notwithstanding, it had probably been between two and four hours earlier, thus some time between ten and noon. At the look on Scarpa's face, the doctor added that he could be more precise after the autopsy, but it was highly unlikely that she had been dead longer than that. As to the weapon that had killed her, Rizzardi would say no more than that it was some sort of heavy object, perhaps metal, perhaps wood, with grooved or rough edges. He said this unaware of the blood-smeared bronze statue of the recently beatified Padre Pio, already placed in a transparent plastic evidence bag and waiting to be taken to the lab for fingerprinting.

The body having been examined and photographed, Scarpa ordered it taken to the Ospedale Civile for autopsy, telling Rizzardi that he wanted it done quickly. He ordered the members of the crime team to begin searching the apartment, although from its wild disorder it was clear that this had already been done. After Rizzardi's silent departure, the lieutenant chose to search the small room at the back of the house that had apparently belonged to Florinda Ghiorghiu. Not much larger than a closet, the room appeared not to have suffered the attentions of whoever had searched the living room. It contained a narrow bed and a set of shelves curtained by a worn piece of fabric that had perhaps once been a tablecloth. When Scarpa pulled the cloth to one side, he saw two folded blouses and an equal number of changes of underwear. A pair of black tennis shoes stood side by side on the floor. On the windowsill beside the bed were a photograph in a cheap cardboard frame of three small children, and a book he didn't bother to examine. Inside a cardboard folder he found photocopies of official documents: the first two pages of Florinda Ghiorghiu's Romanian passport and copies of her Italian residence and work permits. Born in 1953, her occupation was given as 'domestic helper'. There was a second-class return train ticket between Bucharest and Venice, the second half still unused. Because there was no table and no chair in the room, there was no other surface to inspect.

Lieutenant Scarpa pulled out his *telefonino* and called the

Questura to get the number for the Frontier Police at Villa Opicina. Calling the number, he gave his name and rank and a brief account of the murder. He asked when the next train from Venice was expected to cross the border. Saying that their suspect might be on that train and firmly emphasizing that the killer was Romanian, he added that, should she manage to reach Romania, there was little chance of extraditing her, so it was of the utmost importance that she be removed from the train.

He said he'd fax her photo as soon as he got to the Questura, re-emphasized the viciousness of the crime, and hung up.

Leaving the scene of crime team to continue its examination of the apartment, Scarpa ordered the pilot to take him back to the Questura, where he faxed Ghiorghiu's form to the Frontier Police, hoping that the photo would come through clearly. That done, Lieutenant Scarpa went to speak to his superior, Vice-Questore Giuseppe Patta, to inform him of the speed with which violent crime was being pursued.

In Villa Opicina, the fax came through as the officer in charge of the Frontier Police, Captain Luca Peppito, was phoning the *capostazione* at the railway station, telling him that the Zagreb express would have to be halted long enough to allow him and his men to search for a violent killer who was attempting to flee the country. Peppito replaced the phone, checked that his pistol was loaded, and went downstairs to collect his men.

Twenty minutes later, the Intercity to Zagreb pulled into the station and slowed to a halt that normally lasted only long enough for the engines to be changed and the passengers' passports to be checked. In recent years, customs inspection between these two minor players in the game of a united Europe had become perfunctory and generally led to nothing more than the payment of duty on the odd carton of cigarettes or bottle of grappa which were no longer viewed as a threat to the economic survival of either nation.

Peppito had sent men to both ends of the train and placed two more at the entrance to the station; all were under orders to examine the passports of any female passengers alighting from the train.

Three men climbed on at the back of the train and started to work their way forward, examining the passengers in every compartment and checking that no one was in the toilets, while Peppito and a pair of officers began the same process, working backwards from the first carriage.

It was Peppito's sergeant who spotted her, sitting in a window seat in a second-class compartment, in the first carriage behind the engine. He almost overlooked her because she was asleep or pretending to be, her head turned towards the window and resting against it. He saw the broad Slavic planes of her face, her hair grown out white at the roots for lack of care, and the squat, muscular frame so common among women from the East. Two other people sat in the compartment, a large red-faced man reading a German-language newspaper, and an older man working on one of the word puzzles in *Settimana Enigmistica*. Peppito slid the door back, banging it against the frame. That shook the woman awake; she looked about her with startled eyes. The two men looked up at the uniformed officers, and the older one asked, '*Sì?*' expressing his irritation only in the tone.

'Gentlemen, leave the compartment,' commanded Peppito. Before either of them could protest, he allowed his right hand to wander over to the butt of his pistol. The men, making no attempt to take their suitcases, left the compartment. The woman, seeing the men leave, got to her feet, acting as though she thought the order was meant for her as well.

As she tried to squeeze past Peppito, he gripped her left forearm with a firm hand. 'Documents, Signora,' he spat out.

She looked up at him, her eyes blinking quickly. '*Cosa?*' she said nervously.

'*Documenti,*' he repeated, louder.

She smiled nervously, a placatory tightening of the muscles of her face, demonstrative of harmlessness and good will, but he saw the way her eyes shifted down the corridor towards the door. '*Sì, Sì, Signore. Momento. Momento,*' she said in an accent so strong the words were almost incomprehensible.

A plastic bag hung from her right hand. '*La borsa,*' Peppito said, indicating the bag, which was from Billa, and meant to hold groceries.

At his gesture, she whipped the bag behind her. '*Mia, mia,*' she said, stating possession but demonstrating fear.

'*La borsa, Signora,*' Peppito said and reached for it.

She turned halfway round, but Peppito was a strong man and managed to pull her back towards him. He released her arm and grabbed the bag. He opened it and looked inside: all he saw were two ripe peaches and a purse. He took the purse and let the bag fall to the floor. He glanced at the woman, whose face had grown as white as the hair showing at her roots, and flicked open the small plastic purse. He recognized the hundred-Euro notes instantly and saw that there were many of them.

One of his men had gone off to tell his colleagues that they had found her, and the other stood in the corridor, trying to explain to the two men that they would be allowed back to their seats as soon as the woman had been removed from the train.

Peppito snapped the purse shut and moved to put it in the pocket of his jacket. The woman, seeing this, reached for it, but Peppito batted her hand away and turned to say something to the men in the corridor. He was standing at the entrance of the compartment, and when she lunged towards him with her entire body, she drove him back into the corridor, where he lost his balance and fell on to one side. That was all it took for the woman to slip past him and run to the open door at the front of the carriage. Peppito called out and struggled to his feet, but by the time he was standing, she was down the steps and racing along the platform beside the train.

Peppito and the policeman closest to him ran to the door and jumped down on to the platform; both drew their pistols. The woman, still running and now clear of the engine, turned and saw the guns in their hands. At the sight of them she screamed aloud and leapt from the platform down on to the tracks. In the distance could be heard, at least by anyone not caught up in the panic and tension of this scene, the arrival of a through freight train on its way south from Hungary.

The policemen and their shouts followed the running woman. She looked up, saw the approaching train, glanced back to calculate the distance between herself and the policemen, and decided to risk it. She ran forward a few more steps, staying close to the tracks, then suddenly veered and jumped to the left, just metres before the train would reach her. The policemen shouted, the whistle of the train blared at the same moment as the shriek of the brakes filled the air. Perhaps it was one of these noises that caused her to falter; perhaps she merely put her foot down on the rail instead of the gravel. Whatever the reason, she fell to one knee, then instantly pushed herself up and lunged forward. But, as the policemen had seen from the greater distance, it was too late, and the train was upon her.

Peppito never mentioned it again, what happened then, at least not after he described it in his report that afternoon. Nor did the officer with him, nor the men in the engine of the freight train, though one of them had seen it happen before, three years ago, just outside Budapest.

Later, the papers reported that seven hundred Euros had been found in the woman's purse. Signora Battestini's niece, who held power of attorney for her aunt, declared that she had, the previous day, collected her aunt's pension at the post office and taken it to her: seven hundred and twelve Euros.

Given the state of the Romanian woman's body, no attempt was made to check for traces of Signora Battestini's blood. One of the men who had been in the compartment with her said that she had seemed very disturbed when she got on to the train in Venice but had grown noticeably calmer the farther they got from the city, and the other one said she had been careful to take the plastic bag with her when she went down the corridor to the toilet.

In the absence of other suspects, it was declared that she was the likely murderer, and it was decided that police energies could be better employed than in continued investigation of the case. It was not closed, merely left unattended: in the normal course of things, it would disappear for lack of attention and, after the sensational headlines which greeted the murder and the Romanian's flight had been forgotten, it would join them in oblivion.

The authorities attempted to establish at least the bureaucratic evidence relating to the murder of Maria Grazia Battestini. Her niece said that the Romanian woman, whom she had known only as Flori, had been with her aunt for four months before the crime. No, the niece had not hired her: that was all in the hands of her aunt's lawyer, Roberta Marieschi. Dottoressa Marieschi, it turned out, served as lawyer for a number of elderly persons in the city, and for many of them she procured maids and domestic helpers, primarily from Romania, where she had contacts with various charitable organizations.

Dottoressa Marieschi knew nothing more about Florinda Ghiorghiu than what was contained in her passport, a copy of which Dottoressa Marieschi had in her possession. The original was found in a cloth bag tied to the waist of the woman who had fallen under the train and, when cleaned and examined, it turned out to be false, and not even a very good forgery. Dottoressa Marieschi, when questioned about this, replied that it was not her job to recertify the validity of passports which the Immigration Police had accepted as genuine, merely to find clients for whom the persons bearing those passports – and here she took the opportunity to repeat the phrase, 'which the Immigration Police had accepted as genuine' – might be suitable.

She had met the Ghiorghiu woman only once, four months before, when she had taken her to Signora Battestini's home and introduced the two women. Since then, she had had no further contact with her. Yes, Signora Battestini had complained about the Romanian woman, but Signora Battestini was in the habit of complaining about the help that was sent to her.

Because the case remained in limbo, the niece could get no answer to her questions about the state of her aunt's apartment, whether it was still a protected crime scene or not. When she tired of the lack of response, she consulted with Dottoressa Marieschi, who assured her that the conditions of her aunt's will were sufficiently clear to guarantee her undisputed possession of the entire building. A week after Signora Battestini's death the two women met and discussed at length the legal status of the dead woman's estate. Assured by the lawyer's words, the niece went into the apartment the day after their conversation and cleaned it. Whatever she judged to be of potential value or importance was placed into cardboard boxes and taken up to the attic. The remainder of her aunt's clothing and personal possessions were put into large plastic garbage bags and left outside the door of the apartment. The next day the painters went in, Dottoressa Marieschi having convinced the heiress that it would be best to buy some new furniture and rent the apartment to tourists by the week. She would see to the business of finding suitable tenants, and no, if the arrangements remained informal and payment was made in cash, she saw no reason why it would be necessary to declare this income to the authorities. After consulting once again with Dottoressa Marieschi, the heiress agreed to restore the apartments, with a view to charging high rents for them.

And so things rested, as little as three weeks after the death of Maria Grazia Battestini. Her worldly possessions sat in the attic, tossed carelessly into boxes by someone with no interest in them beyond the vague hope that some day, when she got around to taking a closer look at them, something in one of them might prove to be of value; and her apartment, newly painted, was already the subject of a very serious inquiry from a Dutch cigar manufacturer, who was interested in renting it for the last week of August.

3

Thus things stood, contentment shared equally among them: the police, who had effectively closed, though they had not solved, the case; Signora Battestini's niece, Graziella Simionato, who anticipated a convenient and welcomed new income; and Roberta Marieschi, who applauded herself for having so successfully retained the Battestini family on her list of clients. No doubt things would so have remained had it not been for the dominant household god of Venice, indeed of all towns and cities: gossip.

Late in the afternoon of the third Sunday in August, the shutters were pushed open on the windows of a second-floor apartment just off the Canale della Misericordia, not far from the Palazzo del Cammello. The owner of the apartment, Assunta Gismondi, was a graphic designer who had lived in Venice all her life, though she now worked primarily for an architect's studio in Milano. After pushing back the shutters to allow some air into the stifling apartment, Signora Gismondi, from the habit of years, looked across the canal at the windows directly opposite and was surprised to see the shutters of the second-floor apartment closed. She was surprised, though hardly disappointed.

She unpacked her suitcase, hung up some clothes and stuffed others in the washing machine. She looked through the post that had accumulated during the three weeks she had been in London, checked her faxes and read them, but because she had been in email contact with her lover, as well as with the employers who had sent her to London on the training course, she did not bother to turn on her computer to check for new messages. Instead, she took her shopping bag and went out to the Billa on Strada Nuova, the only place where she would be able to get enough food to prepare a meal for herself that evening. The idea of eating in another restaurant filled her with horror. She would rather stay home and eat pasta with *olio e peperoncino* than sit alone again and eat among strangers.

Billa on Strada Nuova was open, and Signora Gismondi was able to fill her bag with fresh tomatoes, eggplant, garlic, salad, and, for the first time in three weeks, find decent fruit and cheese that did not require the payment of a week's salary for even the smallest of portions. Back in her apartment, she poured olive oil into a frying pan, chopped up two, then three, then four cloves of garlic and let them simmer slowly, breathing in the scent with a joy that was almost religious in its intensity, happy to be home, among the objects, the smells and the sights she loved.

Her lover called half an hour later and told her he was still in Argentina, where things were a mess and getting worse, but he planned to be back in a week or so, when he'd fly up from Rome for at least three days. No, he'd tell his wife he had to go to Torino for business; she wouldn't care, anyway. When she replaced the phone, Assunta sat in her kitchen and ate a plate of pasta with a sauce of tomatoes and grilled eggplant, then ate two peaches and finished a half-bottle of Cabernet Sauvignon. Glancing out the window at the house across the way, she whispered a silent prayer that the shutters would never open again, in which case she would never request another favour of life.

The next morning, on her way to her favourite bar for a coffee and a brioche, she stopped at the newsagent's for the paper.

'Good morning, Signora,' the man behind the counter greeted her. 'I haven't seen you for a while. Vacation?'

'No. In London. For work.'

'Did you enjoy it?' he asked, his tone making it clear that he had serious doubts as to whether that were possible.

She picked up the *Gazzettino* and read bold headlines that foretold imminent political collapse, ecological disaster, and a crime of passion in Lombardia. How sweet to be home. She shrugged in belated response to his question, as if to suggest the unlikelihood of enjoying work, no matter in what city, no matter in what land.

'It was all right,' she finally equivocated. 'But it's good to be home. And you? Anything new?'

'You haven't heard, then?' he said, face suddenly alight at the pleasure of being the first to pass on bad news.

'No. What?'

'The Battestini woman, the one across from you. You haven't heard?'

She thought of the shutters, suppressing the hope that sprang up inside her. 'No. Nothing. What?' She placed the newspaper on the counter and leaned towards him.

'She's dead. Murdered,' he said, caressing the word.

Signora Gismondi gasped her surprise, then demanded, 'No. What happened? When?'

'About three weeks ago. The doctor found her; you know, that one who goes in to see the old people. Someone'd beaten in her head.' He paused to see the effect of his news, judged her to be satisfactorily stunned, so went on, 'My cousin knows one of the cops who found her, and he said whoever did it must really have hated her. At least that's what my cousin said he said.'

He looked at his audience. 'But I guess she did, huh? Hate her, I mean.'

'What?' Gismondi said, confused by the unexpected news and then by this inexplicable remark. 'Who? I don't know who you're talking about.'

'The Romanian woman. That's who killed her.' He saw her surprise and launched himself into the second, and better, act of his drama. 'Yeah, she tried to get out of the country, but they found her on the train, the one that goes to Romania.'

Signora Gismondi looked suddenly pale, but that only increased his relish. 'They stopped her up there at the border. Villa Opicina, I think. On the train, just sitting there cool as ice, after killing that old woman. She hit one of the policemen and tried to push him under a train, but he got away, and it was her who got hit.' He saw the Signora's mounting confusion and, out of respect for his sources, if for nothing else, he added, 'Well, that's what the papers say and what I've heard from people.'

'Who got hit? Flori?'

'The Romanian? Was that her name?' he asked, suspicious that she should know it.

'Yes,' Signora Gismondi said. 'What happened to her?'

He seemed puzzled by her question. What else could happen to a person who got hit by a train? 'I told you, Signora,' he said with strained patience. 'The train hit her. Up there. In Villa Opicina or wherever it was.' He was not an intelligent man and lacked imagination, so those words meant next to nothing to him. That is, in saying them, he conjured up no image of the steel wheels, the rolling point of contact they made with the metal rails under them, was incapable of summoning up the image of what would happen to something, anything, caught inexorably between those two things.

She placed a hand on the newspapers as if to steady herself. 'She's dead?' she asked, as if the man had not spoken.

'Of course,' he answered, impatient at her slowness in understanding things. 'But so's that poor old woman.' His indignation was audible, and the sound of it seeped into Assunta Gismondi's mind.

'Of course,' she said softly. 'Terrible, terrible.' She took out some money and set it on the counter, forgot to pick up her paper, and left the shop, vowing never to go there again. Poor old woman. Poor old woman.

She went back to her apartment and, doing something she'd never done and wasn't even sure could be done, she went on to the Internet and called up the *Gazzettino* from the day after she had left for London. She regretted her decision to immerse herself in English during the time she had been there: no papers and no news from home, no seeking out of other Italians. It was as though the last three weeks had never taken place. Though, the *Gazzettino* rapidly informed her, they surely had.

She read only the stories that had to do with Signora Battestini's murder, and as the days and the editions passed, she followed the tale as it had evolved. The substance was much as the newsagent had said: old woman found dead by her doctor, Romanian servant missing, train stopped at the border, attempt to flee, death. False papers, no woman of that name, family devastated by murder of favourite aunt, quiet funeral of victim.

Assunta Gismondi switched off the computer and stared at the blank screen. When she tired of that, she turned her attention to the books that lined one wall of her studio and read through the names of the authors on the top shelf: Aristotle, Plato, Aeschylus, Euripides, Plutarch, Homer. Then she looked out the window, across the canal at the closed shutters.

She reached to the right of her computer and picked up the phone. She dialled 113 and asked to speak to a policeman.

As she walked through the door of the Questura half an hour later, she chided herself for her foolishness in having assumed that they would have sent someone to talk to her. She was a citizen, doing her civic duty, volunteering information that was of great importance, so of course a bored policeman, who refused to give his name, told her that she was obliged to come down to the Questura to talk to them. As soon as she heard his officious voice, she regretted having given her name when she called: had she not, she would have been tempted to forget the whole thing and let them worry about it. Only she knew they would not worry, knew that the last thing on their minds, assuming that they had minds, would be any desire to change their assumptions and then go to the trouble of working out new ones.

She turned to the right, to a window behind which sat a uniformed officer. 'I called half an hour ago,' she began, 'and said I had to talk to someone about a crime. They told me I had to come in here to do it, so here I am.' He remained unmoved, so she added, 'I'd like to speak to someone about the murder that happened a few weeks ago.'

He considered this for a moment, as though this were Dodge City and he had to work out which one she might be referring to. 'The Battestini woman?' he finally asked.

'Yes.'

'That would be Lieutenant Scarpa,' the officer said.

'May I speak to him?'

'I'll call and see if he's here,' the man said, reaching for his phone. He turned his back to her and spoke softly into the receiver, making Signora Gismondi wonder if he and Lieutenant Scarpa were planning a strategy that would get her to confess to involvement in the murder. After what seemed a long time, he came out of the small cubicle. Pointing towards the back of the building, he said, 'Down that corridor there, Signora. Turn right and it's the second door on your left. The lieutenant is expecting you.' He went back into the cubicle, closing the door behind him.

She started down the corridor, surprised that she should be allowed to walk around in the Questura so freely. Hadn't they ever heard of the Red Brigades?

She found the door, knocked, and was told to enter. A man of about her own age was seated behind a metal desk in a room hardly bigger than the cubicle downstairs. If he stood, he would be much taller than she. He had dark hair, and eyes that looked as though they would limit their work to seeing the surface of things. There was the uniformed man, his chair, the desk, and two armless chairs placed in front of it.

'Lieutenant Scarpa?' she asked.

He looked up at her and nodded, then looked down at the papers on his desk.

She gave her name and her address, then asked, 'Are you in charge of the investigation of the murder of Signora Battestini?'

'I was,' he said, again raising his eyes. He pointed to one of the chairs and said, 'Please sit down.'

One step brought her to the chair, and she sat, then, realizing that it was placed so that the sun from the small window shone into her face, she got up and moved to the other, angling it away from both his desk and the window before she sat down again.

Signora Gismondi had no direct experience of the police, but she had for six years been married to a very lazy and equally violent man, and she simply put herself back into that time and situation and acted accordingly. 'You said you *were* in charge, Lieutenant,' she said softly. 'Does that mean the investigation is being handled by someone else?' If so, she wondered, then why had she been sent to talk to this man?

He made a point of finishing whatever it was he was

reading and setting it aside before he looked up at her. 'No.'

She waited for an explanation, and when none was forthcoming, she repeated, 'Does that mean the investigation is closed?'

He paused a long time before repeating, 'No.'

Giving no sign of impatience or exasperation, she asked, 'May I ask what it does mean?'

'That the investigation is not currently being actively pursued.'

Hearing the tortured vowels the longer sentence revealed in his accent, she adjusted her response to the information that he was a southerner, perhaps Sicilian. Feigning indifference, she asked, 'To whom is it, then, that I might give information about this matter?'

'If the case were being investigated, you would give it to me.' He allowed her to grasp the implications of his statement and returned his attention to the papers on his desk. Had he told her to leave, he could have made it no clearer how little interest he had in whatever she had to tell him.

For a moment, she faltered. It would all lead, what she had to say, to trouble for her and, if they didn't believe her, possibly to actual risk. It would be so easy to push herself to her feet and leave, abandon the issue and this man with the indifferent eyes.

'I read in the *Gazzettino* that she was murdered by the Romanian woman who lived with her,' she said.

'That's correct,' he said, and then added, 'She did it.' His tone, like his words, brooked no opposition.

'It might be correct that I read it in the *Gazzettino*, and it might be correct that it was printed there, but it is not correct that the Romanian woman killed her,' she said, driven by the omniscience of his second remark to launch herself at the truth.

His indifference, however, was unassailable. 'Have you some evidence for that statement, Signora?' he asked, not for an instant suggesting that he might be interested in considering it, even if she had.

'I spoke to the Romanian woman the morning of the murder,' she said.

'I fear the same is probably true of Signora Battestini,' the lieutenant said, no doubt thinking it a clever thing to say.

'I also took her to the train station.'

That caught his interest. He put both hands on the front of his desk and leaned towards her, as though he wanted to leap across the desk and squeeze a confession from her. 'What?' he demanded.

'I took her to the train to Zagreb. That is, the one that passes through Villa Opicina. She would have to change in Zagreb for the train to Bucharest.'

'What are you talking about? Are you saying you helped her?' He half stood, then lowered himself back into his chair.

She didn't deign to answer his question and, instead, repeated, 'I'm saying that I took her to the station and helped her buy a ticket and a seat reservation for the train to Zagreb.'

He said nothing for a long time, studying her face, perhaps considering what he had just heard. He surprised her by saying, 'You're Venetian,' as though it were part of some case he had begun to make against her. Before she could ask what he meant by that, he went on, 'So have you just recovered from amnesia and come in to tell us all this, after three weeks?'

'I've been out of the country,' she answered, surprised to hear the guilt in her voice.

He pounced. 'Without a phone or a newspaper?'

'In England, taking an intensive language course. I decided not to speak Italian at all,' she explained, omitting mention of phone conversations with her lover. 'I got back last night and didn't find out about it until this morning.'

He changed theme, but the suspiciousness remained in his voice. 'Did you know her, this Romanian?'

'Yes.'

'Did she tell you what she had done?'

Signora Gismondi willed herself to keep her patience. It was the only weapon she had. 'She didn't do anything. I met her in the morning, just outside the apartment. It's directly across the *calle* from mine. She was locked out, and the old woman was upstairs.'

'Upstairs?'

'At her window. Flori was out in the street, ringing the doorbell, but the old woman wouldn't let her in.' Assunta Gismondi raised the first finger of her right hand and waved it slowly back and forth in the air in front of her, imitating the gesture she had seen the Battestini woman make.

Scarpa said, 'You called her "Flori". Was she a friend of yours?'

'No. I used to see her from the window of my apartment. Occasionally we waved to one another or said simple things. She didn't speak Italian at all well, but we understood one another.'

'What sort of things did she tell you?'

'That her name was Flori, that she had three daughters and seven grandchildren. That one of her daughters worked in Germany, but she didn't know where, in what city.'

'And the old woman? Did she say anything about the old woman?'

'She said that she was difficult. But everyone in the neighbourhood knew that.'

'Did she dislike her?'

Losing her patience for an instant, Signora Gismondi shot back, 'Everyone who knew her disliked her.'

'Enough to kill her?' Scarpa asked greedily.

Signora Gismondi smoothed the fabric of her skirt across her knees, brought her feet together neatly under her, took a breath, and said, 'Lieutenant, I'm afraid you haven't been paying attention to what I've been telling you. I met her on the street in the morning. The old woman was at the window, waving her finger at her and refusing to let her in. I took the woman – Flori – I took her to a café and tried to talk to her, but she was too upset to think clearly. She was in tears for much of the time we were there. She said the woman had locked her out, that her clothing and things were inside. But she had her passport with her. She said she never went anywhere without it.'

'It was false,' Scarpa declared.

'I don't see what difference that makes,' Signora Gismondi shot back. 'It would have got her out of Italy and back to Romania.' Rashness and anger made her add, 'It certainly proved sufficient to get her in.' Hearing her own anger, she paused, imposed calm at least upon her voice, and said, 'That's all she wanted to do, go home to her family.'

'You seem to have managed very well without her speaking any Italian, Signora,' Scarpa said.

Signora Gismondi bit back her response and said, 'There was very little for her to say: *"basta"*, *"vado"*, *"treno"*, *"famiglia"*, *"Bucaresti"*, *"Signora cattiva"*.' As soon as she heard herself say it, she regretted that last.

'So you say you took her to the train?'

'I don't only say it, Lieutenant. I declare it. It is true. I took her to the station and helped her buy a ticket and a seat reservation.'

'And this woman with a false passport who you say was locked out of the house, she just happened to be walking around with enough money on her to pay for a ticket to *Bucaresti*?' he asked, in a crass imitation of her own pronunciation of the word.

'I bought her ticket,' Signora Gismondi declared.

'What?' Scarpa asked, as though she'd confessed to madness.

'I bought her ticket. And I gave her some money.'

'How much?' Scarpa said.

'I don't know. Six or seven hundred Euros.'

'You're asking me to believe you don't even know how much you gave her?'

'It's the truth.'

'How is it the truth? You saw her there and you just snapped your fingers in the air and seven hundred Euros floated into your hand, and you thought how nice it would be to give them to the Romanian woman, seeing as she was locked out of the house and had nowhere to go?'

Signora Gismondi's voice was steel. 'I was on my way back from the bank, where I had just cashed a cheque sent to me by a client. I had the money in my purse, and when she told me she wanted to go back to Bucharest, I asked her if she'd been paid.' She looked across at Scarpa, as if to ask him to understand. She saw no evidence that he was capable, but she went on nevertheless. 'She said she didn't care about that; she just wanted to get home.' She paused, suddenly embarrassed to confess to such weakness to this man. 'So I gave her some money.' His look changed and she saw his contempt for her weakness, her gullibility. 'She'd been there for months, and the woman locked her out without giving her what she owed her or letting her come back in to get her things.' It came to her to ask him what he expected her to do in a situation like that, but she thought better of it and said, 'I couldn't let her work for months and get no money.' She chose to say no more.

'Then what?' he asked.

'I asked her what she was going to do, and as I told you, she said all she wanted to do was go home. She had calmed down by then and stopped crying, so I said I'd go to the station with her and find out about the trains. She said she thought there was a train for Zagreb around noon.' It seemed simple enough to her, all of this. 'So that's what we did, went to the station.'

'And her train ticket, you claim you paid for that, too?' he asked, intent on plumbing the full depths of her gullibility.

'Yes.'

'And then?'

'And then I went home. I had to leave for London.'

'When?'

She paused to consider this. 'The flight was at one-thirty. The taxi came to get me at noon.'

'And you were at the train station until what time, Signora?'

'I don't know, ten, ten-thirty.'

'And what time are you saying all of this began? When did you say you met this woman?'

'I'm not sure, nine-thirty, perhaps.'

'You were leaving the country for three weeks, you had a taxi coming, and yet you still had time to take this woman you say you barely knew to the station and buy her a ticket?'

She ignored his deliberate provocation. She wanted to explain how she always hated the final hours before leaving, how she hated walking around her apartment, checking and rechecking that the gas was off, the windows and shutters closed, the phone cable disconnected from the computer, but she did not want to tell any of this to him. All she said was, 'There was time.'

'Do you have any proof of this?' he asked.

'Proof?'

'That you were there?'

'Where?'

'London.'

She was tempted to demand what difference that would make but, recalling her husband and the way any sort of resistance had driven him to violence, said only, 'Yes.'

'And you left her there?' he demanded, abandoning London.

'Yes.'

'Where?'

'In the station, by the ticket windows.'

'How long did it take you?'

'What? To buy her a ticket?'

'No. To walk home.'

'Eleven minutes.'

He raised his eyebrows at this and pushed himself back in his chair. 'Eleven minutes, Signora? That seems very exact. Have you been planning this?'

'This what?'

'This story.'

Before answering, she took two deep breaths. 'Lieutenant, it is exact, not because it is a story, but because it takes eleven minutes. I've lived in that house for almost five years, and I go back and forth to the station at least twice a week.' She felt the anger mounting in her voice, tried to control it, and lost. 'If you are capable of simple arithmetic, that is more than five hundred times, back and forth. So if I say it takes eleven minutes, that's how many minutes it takes.'

Ignoring her anger entirely, he asked, 'So that's how long it would take her?'

'Take who?'

'The Romanian woman.'

She started to tell him that the Romanian woman had a name, Flori, but she stopped herself and said only, 'That's how long it would take anyone, Lieutenant.'

'And what time was it that you began to walk these eleven minutes, Signora?'

'I've told you. Ten-thirty, perhaps a bit after that.'

'And the train to Zagreb leaves at 11:45,' he said with the certainty of one who has checked the timetable.

'I think so, yes.'

As if speaking to a person who had reached adulthood without having learned to calculate time, he said, 'That's more than an hour, Signora.'

The absurdity of this forced her to say, 'That's ridiculous.

31

She wasn't the sort of person who would go back and kill someone.'

'And are you experienced in dealing with such people, Signora?'

She resisted the impulse to hit him. Instead, she took a quick breath and said, 'I've told you what happened.'

'Do you expect me to believe all this, Signora?' Lieutenant Scarpa asked in a half-mocking voice.

She knew that she had acted out of human decency; thus, no, she did not expect Lieutenant Scarpa to believe her. 'Whether you believe me or not, Lieutenant, makes no difference at all. What I've told you is true.' Before he could say anything, she added, 'I have no reason to lie about this. In fact, your response makes me realize it would have been far easier if I hadn't said anything. But I know the old woman would not let her into the apartment. I gave Flori the money, and I took her to the station.' He started to object, but she held up a hand and said, 'And it remains true, Lieutenant, whether you choose to believe it or not: she did not kill Signora Battestini.'

4

They sat opposite one another for some time, until finally Scarpa pushed himself out of his chair, came around behind hers, and left the room, careful to leave the door open behind him. Signora Gismondi sat and studied the objects on the lieutenant's desk, but she saw little to reflect the sort of man she was dealing with: two metal trays that held papers, a single pen, a telephone. She raised her eyes to the wall: Christ looked back at her from the crucifix as if equally unwilling to reveal whatever he might have learned from his proximity to Lieutenant Scarpa.

The room had only a small window, and it was closed, so after twenty minutes Signora Gismondi could no longer ignore how uncomfortable she felt, even with the door open behind her. It had grown unpleasantly warm, and she got to her feet, hoping it might be cooler in the corridor. At the moment she stood, however, Lieutenant Scarpa came back into the room, a manila folder in his right hand. He saw her standing and said, 'You weren't thinking of leaving, were you, Signora?'

There was no audible menace in what he said, but Signora Gismondi, her arms falling to her sides, sat down again and said, 'No, not at all.' In fact, that was just what she wanted to do, leave and have done with this, let them work it out for themselves.

Scarpa went back to his chair, took his seat, glanced at the papers in the trays, as if searching for some sign that she had looked through them while he was away, and said, 'You've had time to think about this, Signora. Do you still maintain that you gave money to this woman and took her to the train station?'

Though the lieutenant was never to know this, it was this flash of sneering insinuation that stiffened Signora Gismondi's resolve. She thought of her husband, who had been short and light-haired and looked nothing at all like Scarpa, and realized nevertheless how very similar the two men were. 'I am not "maintaining" anything, Lieutenant,' she said with studied calm. 'I am stating, declaring, asserting, proclaiming, and, if you will give me the opportunity to do so, swearing that the Romanian woman whom I knew as Flori was locked out of the home of Signora Battestini and that Signora Battestini was alive and standing at the window when I met Flori on the street. Further, I state that, little more than an hour later, when I took her to the station, she seemed calm and untroubled and gave no sign that she had the intention of murdering anyone.' Then, remembering his remark, she added, 'Whatever those signs might be.' She wanted to continue, to make it clear to this savage that there was no way that Flori, poor dead Flori, could have committed this crime. Her heart pounded with the desire to continue telling him how wrong he was; sweat accumulated between her breasts with the desire to embarrass him, but the habit of civilian caution exerted itself and she stopped speaking.

Scarpa, impassive, got up and, taking the folder with him, left the room again. Signora Gismondi sat back in her chair and tried to relax, told herself that she had had her say and it was finished. She forced herself to take deep breaths, then leaned back in the chair and closed her eyes.

After long minutes she heard a sound behind her, opened her eyes, and turned towards the door. A man as tall as Scarpa, though not dressed in uniform, stood there, holding what looked to be the same manila folder. He nodded when her eyes met his and gave a half-smile. 'If you'd be more comfortable, Signora, we can go up to my office. It has two windows, so I imagine it will be a little cooler.' He stepped aside, thus inviting her to approach.

She stood and walked to the door. 'And the lieutenant?' she asked.

'He won't trouble us there,' he said and put out his hand. 'I'm Commissario Guido Brunetti, Signora, and I'm very interested in what you have to tell us.'

She studied his face, decided that he was telling the truth when he said that he was interested in what she had to say, and took his hand. After this formal moment, he waved her through the door. When they got to the bottom of the staircase, a surprisingly elegant survivor in a building that had suffered indignities in the name of efficiency, he came up beside her.

'I think I know you,' she said.

'Yes,' he answered. 'And I think I know you, too. Do you work near Rialto?'

She smiled and relaxed. 'No, I work at home, over by the Misericordia, but I come to the market at least three times a week. I think that's where we've seen one another.'

'At Piero's?' Brunetti asked, naming the postage-stamp-sized shop where she bought *parmigiano*.

'Of course. And I think I've seen you in Do Mori,' she added.

'Less and less, though.'

'Since Roberto and Franco sold it?'

'Yes,' he said. 'I know the new guys are perfectly nice, but it's not the same, somehow.'

How maddening it must be to take over a successful business in this city, she thought. No matter how good you are and no matter how many improvements you might make, ten, twenty years after you take over, people will still be whining about how much better it was when Franco or Roberto or Pinco Pallino, for that matter, ran the place. These two new owners – she had never learned their names – were just as nice as the former ones, had the same wine, even had better sandwiches, but no matter how good anything they sold could be, they were doomed to spend their professional lives being held up to a long-forgotten standard, held up and found wanting, at least until all the old customers died or moved away, when they would become the new standard against whom the inadequacy of whoever replaced them would be measured.

At the top of the steps, Brunetti turned left and led her down the corridor and stopped outside one of the doors, inviting her to enter before he did. The first things she noticed were the tall windows that looked across to the church of San Lorenzo, and the large wardrobe that stood against one wall. Once again, there was a desk, a chair behind it, and two in front of it.

'May I offer you something to drink, Signora? A coffee? A glass of water?' He smiled, willing her to accept, but she was still bearing a grudge against Scarpa's behaviour, so she refused, though she did it politely. 'Perhaps later,' she said and took the chair nearer the window.

Choosing not to retreat behind his desk, he pulled the second chair around to face her and sat down. He set the folder down, smiled, and said, 'Lieutenant Scarpa has told me what you told him, Signora, but I'd like to hear it in your own words. I'd be grateful for as many details as you can give me.'

She wondered if he were going to turn on a tape recorder or take out a notebook: she had read crime novels. But he sat facing her, quiet, his elbow on the desk, and waited for her to speak.

She told him, then, everything she had told Scarpa: coming back from the bank after cashing the cheque; seeing Flori with the plastic bag in her hand; Signora Battestini up at the window, looking down at them, silent, waving her outstretched finger back and forth in a sign of absolute negation.

'Can't you remember how much money you gave her, Signora?' he asked when she was finished.

She shook her head. 'No, the cheque was for about a thousand Euros. I bought some things on the way home: cosmetics and some batteries for my Discman; some other things but I don't remember what they were. I recall that, when I took the money out to give it to her, I kept some of the bills – it was all in one hundred notes – then gave her the rest.' She thought back to the scene, tried to recall if she had counted the money when she got home. 'No, I don't remember exactly, but it must have been six or seven hundred Euros.'

'You're a very generous woman, Signora,' he said and smiled.

From Scarpa, she realized, the words would have been a sarcastic declaration of disbelief; from this man, they were a simple compliment and she felt flattered by his praise. 'I don't know why I did it,' Signora Gismondi said. 'She was out there in the street, wearing some sort of housedress made out of synthetic fabric, and canvas gym shoes. I remember one of them had a tear on the side. And she'd been working for her for months. I'm not sure exactly when she started, but I know she came when the windows were still closed.'

He smiled. 'That's a strange way to date things, Signora.'

'Not if you lived near her,' she said with some vehemence. Seeing his confusion, she said, 'The television. It's always on, all day long and all night long. During the winter, when we all have our windows closed, it's not so bad. But in the summer, from about May until September, it's enough to make me crazy. My windows are directly opposite hers, you see. She keeps it on all night, so loud I've had to call the police.' She realized the tense she was using and said only, 'Kept.'

He shook his head in sympathetic understanding, as would any Venetian, citizen of a city with some of the narrowest streets and one of the oldest populations in Europe.

Encouraged by this, she went on. 'I used to call you, that is, call the police and complain about it, but no one ever did anything. But then, last summer, one of the men I talked to said I should call the firemen. But when I did, they said they couldn't come just for the noise, not unless there was some danger or there was an emergency.' Brunetti's nod suggested that he found her explanation interesting.

'So if she left it on, even if I could see her asleep in her bed – I can see her bed from my own bedroom window,' she added parenthetically, unable to stop herself using the present tense – 'I'd call the firemen and say I couldn't see her and . . .' her voice took on the robotic sound of someone reading from a prepared text, 'and was afraid that something had happened to her.' She looked up, grinned, and then grinned even more broadly when she saw his own smile of understanding. 'And then they were obliged by law to come.'

Suddenly sobered by the return of reality, she added, 'And now something awful *has* happened to her.'

'Yes,' Brunetti said. 'It has.'

Silence fell between them until finally he asked, 'Could you tell me more about this woman called Flori? Did you ever learn her surname?'

'No, no. I didn't,' she said. 'It wasn't like that at all, not as though we'd ever been introduced. It's just that we saw one another at the window every so often, and, the way one does, we smiled and said hello, and then I asked how she was or she asked me. And then we'd talk. Not about anything at all, just to say hello.'

'Did she ever say anything about Signora Battestini?' he asked, his words revealing only curiosity, not suspicion.

'Well,' Signora Gismondi revealed, 'I had a pretty good idea of what sort of person she was. You know how it is in a neighbourhood: everyone knows everyone else's business, and I knew people didn't like her very much. And she'd had that television on for ever. So I asked how the Signora was, and all Flori did was smile and shrug and shake her head and say *"difficile"*, or something like that, just enough to let me know that she realized what the old woman was like.'

'Anything else?'

'Occasionally, I'd telephone and ask her to turn the television down,' she said, then explained, 'Flori, that is. I'd been calling Signora Battestini for years, and sometimes she'd be very nice and turn it down, and other times she'd scream at me. Once she even slammed down the phone and turned the television up louder, God knows why.' She glanced at him to see what he was making of all of this, nothing more than the worst sort of small town gossip, but he still seemed genuinely interested. 'But Flori would say *"Sì, Signora"* and turn it down. I suppose that's why I liked her, or I felt sorry for her, whatever it was.'

'I'm sure that was a great relief. Nothing's worse, is it, especially when you're trying to sleep?' His sympathy was audible.

'Sometimes, during the summer, it was impossible. I've got a house up in the mountains, near Trento, and I'd have to go up there just to get a good night's sleep.' She smiled and shook her head at the apparent lunacy of the situation. 'I know it sounds crazy that a person can drive you out of your own home, but that's the way it was.' Then, with a puckish smile, she added, 'Until I discovered the firemen.'

'How did they get in?' Brunetti asked.

She told him with evident pleasure. 'The downstairs door was always locked, and they couldn't open it. So they had to go to Madonna dell'Orto, or somewhere over there, and come back with a ladder. They'd lay it on the ground in front of her house and put it together, then raise it up to her windows . . .'

'Second floor?' he asked.

'Yes. It must have been, I don't know, seven or eight metres long. And then one or two of them would climb up and in her window and go into her bedroom and wake her up.'

'You saw all of this?' he asked.

'Yes. I watched it from my windows. When they got inside, I'd move into my bedroom. That's when I saw them wake her up.' She smiled at the memory. 'They were really very nice, the firemen. They're all Venetian, so she had no trouble understanding them. They'd ask her how she was and then they'd suggest she turn down the television. And then they'd leave.'

'How?'

'Excuse me?' she asked.

'How did they leave? Back down the ladder?'

'Oh, no,' she said with a laugh. 'They'd go out the door and down the stairs, and when they got outside, they'd take the ladder down and take it apart.'

'How many times did you do this, Signora?'

'Why? Is it illegal?' she asked, worried for the first time in her conversation with Brunetti.

'I don't see how it could be,' he answered calmly. 'Quite the opposite, in fact. If you couldn't see her from one of the windows in your apartment, then it seems to me you'd have every reason to be concerned that something had happened to her.'

He didn't repeat his question, but still she answered it. 'Four times, I think. They always got here in about fifteen minutes.'

'Hum,' he said appreciatively, and she wondered if he was surprised or pleased. Then he said, 'Did it stop when Flori came?'

'Yes.'

He allowed a long time to pass and then said, 'The lieutenant told me that you took her to the station, Signora, and left her there. Is this true?'

'Yes.'

'At about ten-thirty?'

'Yes.'

Changing the subject, he asked, 'Did Signora Ghiorghiu have any other friends here that you know of?'

Hearing him refer to Flori with such formality pleased her, but her smile was brief, more a tightening of her lips than a smile. 'I was hardly a friend, Commissario.'

'You behaved like one.'

Reluctant to try to speak about this, she returned to his question. 'No, not that I know of. We weren't really friends because we really couldn't talk. Just people who liked one another.'

'And when you left her at the station, how would you describe her behaviour or her mood?'

'She was still upset by what had happened but much less so than before.'

He looked down at the floor for a moment, then back at her. 'Did you ever see anything else from your window, Signora?' he asked, but before she could even think about defending herself from the suggestion of nosiness, he went on, 'I ask because, if we accept the premise that Flori didn't do this, then someone else must have, and anything you can tell me about Signora Battestini might help.'

'You mean, to find out who it really was?' she asked.

'Yes.'

So effortless had been his acceptance of the possibility of Flori's innocence that she didn't have time to register surprise. 'I've been thinking about this since I called you,' she said.

'I imagine you must have, Signora,' he said but didn't prod her.

'I've lived across from her for more than four years, since I bought the apartment.' She paused but he gave no indication of wanting or needing to hurry her. 'I moved in in February, I think; towards the end of winter, at any rate. So I didn't notice her, not until the spring, when it got warmer and we started to open our windows. That is, I might have seen her moving around the apartment, but I paid no attention to her.

'As soon as the noise started, though, I paid attention. I started by calling across the *calle*, but it didn't do any good. She was always asleep; never woke up. So one day I went over and looked at the doorbells, then I found her number in the phone book and called her. I didn't say who I was or where I lived or anything like that; I just asked her if she could, at night, try to keep her television turned down.'

'And how did she respond?' he asked.

'She said she always turned it off before she went to bed and hung up.'

'And then?'

'Then it started during the day, and I'd call and when she answered I'd ask her, always very politely, to turn it down.'

'And?'

'And most of the times she did.'

'I see. And at night?'

'Sometimes it wasn't on, for weeks at a time. I'd begin to hope something had happened, that she'd been taken away or gone away.'

'Did you ever think of getting her a pair of those earphones, Signora?'

'She'd never wear them,' she answered with absolute certainty. 'She's crazy. That's why. Mad as a horse. Believe me, Signore, I did my homework on this woman. I spoke to her lawyer, her doctor, her niece, the people at the psychiatric centre at Palazzo Boldù, to the neighbours, even to the postman.'

She saw his interest and went on. 'She was a patient at Boldù for years, when she could still manage the stairs and leave the house. But either she stopped or they threw her out – if a psychiatric centre can throw people out, that is.'

'I doubt they can,' he said. 'But I suppose they could encourage her to leave.' He waited a moment, then asked, 'The niece? What did she say?'

'That her aunt was "a difficult woman".' She snorted in scorn, 'As though I didn't know that. She didn't want to have anything to do with it. In fact, I'm not sure she really understood what I was talking about. Same with the police, as I told you, and with the *Carabinieri*.' She paused, then added, 'Someone in the neighbourhood – I can't remember who it was – told me her son died five or six years ago, and that's when the television began. For company.'

'So he died before you moved in?'

'Yes. But from what I've heard, I suspect she was always "a difficult woman".'

'And her lawyer?' Brunetti asked.

'She said she'd speak to Signora Battestini.'

'And?'

Signora Gismondi pushed her lips together as if in disgust.

'The postman?' he asked with a smile.

She laughed out loud. 'He had nothing good to say about her, as a matter of fact. He'd take everything up to her, whenever it came – he was always climbing those steps – and she never gave him anything. Not even at Christmas. Nothing.'

His attention was unwavering and so she went on. 'The

best story I heard about her was from the marble man, the one over by the Miracoli,' she said.

'Costantini?' he asked.

'Yes. Angelo,' she said, pleased that he knew whom she was talking about. 'He's an old friend of the family, and when I told him who I was having trouble with, he told me that she called him about ten years ago and asked him to come and give her an estimate for a new flight of steps. He said he already knew her or knew about her, so he knew it was pointless to go, but he went anyway. He measured the steps, did all the calculations, and went back the next day to tell her how many steps she needed and how high they would have to be, and how much it would cost.' Like anyone who enjoys telling a good story, she paused there, and he responded like any good listener.

'And?'

'And she said she knew he was trying to cheat her, and she wanted him to do it with fewer stairs and each of them lower.' She allowed the full idiocy of this to sink in, then added, 'It makes you wonder whether maybe Palazzo Boldù really did throw her out.'

He nodded at this. 'Did people visit her, Signora?' he asked after a moment.

'No, no one I can remember, well, not anyone I remember seeing more than a few times. There were all the women who worked for her, of course. Most of them were black, and once I spoke to a woman who said she was from Peru. But they all left, usually after only a few weeks.'

'But Flori stayed?' he asked.

'She said she had three daughters and seven grand-children, and I suppose she had to keep the job so she could send them money.'

'Do you know if she was paid, Signora?'

'Who? Flori?'

'Yes.'

'I think so. At least she had a little money.' Before he could ask her to explain, she said, 'I met her once on Strada Nuova. It was about six weeks ago and I was having a coffee in a bar, and she came in. It was that place just at the corner near the Santa Fosca *traghetto*. When I went over, she recognized me, you know, from the window, and she kissed me on the cheek, as if we were old friends. She had her purse open in her hands, and I saw that all she had were some coins. I don't know how much. I didn't look, you know, but I saw there wasn't much.' She stopped speaking, memory taking her back to that afternoon in the bar. 'I asked why she had come in, and she said she wanted an ice-cream. I think she said she loved ice-cream. I know the man who runs the place, so I told him I was offering and not to take her money, that I'd pay.'

It was only now that the possibility occurred to her: 'I hope I didn't hurt her feelings. By insisting I pay, I mean.'

'I don't think it would, Signora,' he said.

'I asked her what she wanted and she said chocolate, so I asked him to give her a double cone, and I could see from her face when he gave it to her that all she had been going to get for herself was a single, and that made me feel so sorry for her. She had to put up with that horrible woman all day and all night long, and she couldn't even afford a double ice-cream cone.'

For a long time, neither of them said anything.

'And the money you gave her, Signora?' he asked.

'It was an impulse, nothing more than that. The money I had was for a job I'd bid for and intentionally bid too high, hoping I wouldn't get it because it was very boring: designing packaging for a new range of light bulbs. But they gave me the job, and it turned out to be so easy that I felt a little bit guilty about being paid all that money. So I guess it was easier to give it away than it would have been if I'd really worked to get it.' She remembered the money and the impulse that had caused her to give it to Flori. 'It didn't do her much good, did it?' she asked. 'She never got to spend it.'

As the idea came to her, she said, 'Wait a minute; I've just realized something. I've still got three hundred Euros of that money. I left it here when I went to England. I knew I couldn't use it there. So I've still got the notes.'

The evident interest in his glance prompted her to continue, 'That's all you've got to do to prove that I did give it to her, that she didn't steal it from Signora Battestini.' When he didn't respond, she went on. 'The notes were all new and were probably in a series, so all I've got to do is give you the notes I've still got, and if you compare the serial numbers with the ones on the money she had with her on the train, you'll see that she didn't steal anything.'

Puzzled by his lack of enthusiasm and, she admitted to herself, hurt by his lack of appreciation, she asked, 'Well? Wouldn't it be proof?'

'Yes,' he said with evident reluctance, 'it would be proof.'

'But?' she asked.

'But the money is gone.'

5

'How can that be?' she asked. Enough time elapsed between her question and his response to render it, when it came, redundant. She had to consider only for a moment to realize that such a sum of money passing through a series of public offices and officials had as much chance of survival as would an ice cube passed from hand to hand on the beach at the Lido.

'There seems to be no record of the money after it left the police in Villa Opicina,' he said.

'Why are you telling me this, Commissario?'

'In the hope that you won't tell anyone else,' he answered, making no attempt to avoid her gaze.

'Are you afraid of the bad publicity?' she asked with more than a little of Lieutenant Scarpa's sarcasm, as if it were somehow contagious.

'No, not particularly, Signora. But I would like this piece of information not to be made public, just as I would like to keep everything you're telling me from becoming public knowledge.'

'And may I ask why?' The sarcasm had backed off, but there was still plenty of scepticism left in her voice.

'Because, the less the person who did this knows about what we know, the better it is for us.'

'You say, "the person who did this," Commissario. Does that mean you believe me, that Flori didn't kill her?'

He sat back in his chair and touched his lower lip with the forefinger of his left hand. 'From what you tell me, Signora, it doesn't sound likely that she was a killer, especially in that way.'

Hearing this and believing him, she relaxed, and he went on, 'And once she had a ticket home and some money, I find it unlikely that she'd go back and kill the old woman, no matter how difficult she had been.' He took a notebook from the pocket of his jacket and flipped it open. 'Could you tell me what she was wearing, please, when you took her to the train?'

'A housedress, the sort of thing you never see any more. Buttons down the front, short sleeves, made of something like nylon or rayon. Synthetic. Must have been terrible for her in this heat. It was grey or beige, some light colour, and had a small pattern on it; I don't remember what.'

'Was it something you saw her wearing in the house, when you saw her from your window?'

Signora Gismondi considered this, then answered, 'I think so. She had that and a light-coloured blouse and dark skirt. But most of the time she had an apron on, so I don't have a clear memory of her clothes.'

'Did you see any changes in her while she was there?'

'I don't know what you mean by changes.'

'Did she get her hair cut, or coloured? Start to wear glasses?'

She remembered the white roots of Flori's hair that last day, when she'd taken her to the café to try to calm her down. 'She stopped dyeing her hair,' she finally said. 'She probably couldn't afford it.'

'Why do you say that?' he asked.

'Do you have any idea of what it costs to have your hair dyed in this city?' she asked him, wondering if he had a wife and, if so, whether she was of an age to dye her hair. She guessed him to be somewhere in his fifties: he would have seemed younger than that, she realized, were it not for the thinning of the hair at the crown of his head and for the lines around his eyes. But, paradoxically, his eyes seemed those of a much younger man: astute, bright, quick to register what they saw.

'Of course,' he said, understanding the meaning of her question, and then, 'Is there anything else you can tell me about Signora Battestini? Anything at all, Signora, no matter how unimportant or inconsequential it might seem and, yes,' he went on with an easy smile, 'no matter how much it might sound like gossip.'

She responded easily to the invitation to be of help. 'I think I said that everyone in the neighbourhood knows her.' He nodded and she continued. 'And they know she's caused me so much trouble . . .' Here she stopped briefly to interrupt herself, 'You see, I'm the only person whose bedroom faces her apartment. I don't know whether other people's bedrooms were always at the back, or if they've changed their houses around over the course of the years to get away from the noise.'

'Or whether it's just recently that this has begun,' he suggested.

'No,' she responded immediately. 'Everyone I talk to tells me it's been going on since the son died. The people to my right have air conditioning, so they sleep with the windows closed, and the old people below me close their shutters and windows both. God knows why it is they don't suffocate during the summer.' She suddenly realized how stupidly garrulous she must sound and broke off, tried to remember what had started her on this subject, then, finding the thread, returned to it. 'Everyone knows her, and if I mention her name, everyone is ready to talk about her. I've heard her life story a dozen times.'

'Really?' he asked, obviously interested. He turned a page in his notebook and glanced at her with what she took to be an encouraging smile.

'Well, let's say I've heard bits and pieces of her life story.'

'And would you tell me what they are?'

'That she's lived there for decades. I'd guess from what people say that she was in her eighties, maybe older,' she said. 'There was the one son, but he died. People have told me it wasn't a happy marriage. I think her husband died about ten years ago.'

'Do you know what he did?'

She paused and tried to remember, dredging through half a decade of random gossip. 'I think he had some sort of job with the city or the provincial government, but I don't know what it was. People said he spent most of his time after work in the bar on the corner, playing cards. They also said that's the only thing that kept him from, er, from killing her.' She looked up nervously, hearing what she had said, but then went on. 'Everyone who ever mentioned him sounded like they thought he was a pleasant enough man.'

'Do you know the cause of his death?'

She paused for a long time. 'No, but I think someone told me it was a stroke or a heart attack.'

'Did it happen here?'

'I've no idea. They just said he died and left them everything, her and the son: the house, whatever money he had, another apartment on the Lido, I think. When the son died, she must have inherited it all.'

He nodded occasionally as she spoke, in acknowledgement that he understood what she was saying and in encouragement.

'I think that's all I ever heard about the husband.'

'And the son?'

She shrugged.

'What did people say about him?'

'They didn't,' she said, apparently surprised by her own answer. 'No one ever mentioned him to me, that is. Well, aside from the person who told me that he'd died.'

'And about her?'

This time, her answer was immediate. 'Over the years, she fought with all of the people who lived around her.'

'About what sort of things?'

'You're Venetian, aren't you?' she asked, but because this was so evident in his face and audible in his voice, she meant it as a joke.

Brunetti smiled, and she said, 'Then you know the sort of things we fight about: garbage left in front of someone's door, or a letter put in the wrong letter box and not passed on, a dog that barks all the time: it doesn't really matter what it is. You know that. All you've got to do is respond to it in the wrong way, and you've got an enemy for life.'

'And Signora Battestini sounds like the kind of person who responded in the wrong way.'

'Yes,' she said, with an assertive double nod.

'Was there any incident in particular?' he asked.

'Do you mean was there any incident that might have led someone to kill her?' Signora Gismondi asked, trying to make it sound like a joke and not really succeeding.

'Hardly. People like this don't get killed by their neighbours. Besides,' he said with a small, bold smile, 'from what you've told me, you were the most likely to have done it, but I hardly think you did.'

Hearing him say that, she was struck by an awareness that this was one of the strangest conversations she'd ever had, though no less enjoyable for that.

'Do you want me to continue to repeat things people said or try to tell you what I made of it all?' she asked.

'I think the second would be more helpful,' he said.

'And quicker,' she offered.

'No, no, Signora. I'm in no hurry at all; please don't think that. Everything you have to say interests me.'

From another man, these words might have sounded deliberately ambiguous, their flirtatiousness disguised by their apparent sincerity, but from him she took only their literal meaning.

She sat back in her chair, relaxed in a way she could not have been with the other policeman, as she knew she could never be with him or with men like him. 'I told you I've been in that apartment only four years. But I work at home, and so I'm usually willing to listen to people when they talk to me because I spend most of my time alone, working.' She considered, then added ruefully, 'That is, when the noise lets me.'

He nodded, having learned over the years that most people need to talk and how easy it was, with either the reality or the semblance of concerned curiosity, to get them to talk about anything at all.

With a wry smile she said, 'And you see, people in the neighbourhood have told me other things about her. No matter how much their stories showed how much they hated her, they always finished by saying she was a poor widow who had lost her only child, and it was necessary to feel sorry for her.'

Sensing her desire to be prodded into gossip, he asked, 'What other things did they tell you, Signora?'

'About her meanness, for one thing. I told you she never tipped the postman, but many people have told me she would always buy the cheapest thing on offer. She'd walk halfway across the city to save fifty lire on the price of a packet of pasta: things like that. And my shoemaker said he got tired of her always saying she'd pay him next time and then saying, when she came in again, that she already had, until he wouldn't let her into the shop any more.' She saw his expression and added, 'I don't know what's true in all of this. You know how it is: once a person gets a reputation for being one way or another, then stories begin to be told, and it no longer much matters whether the thing ever happened or not.'

Brunetti had long been familiar with this phenomenon. He'd known people who had been killed because of it, and he'd known people to take their own lives because of it.

Signora Gismondi went on. 'Sometimes I'd hear her screaming at the women who worked for her, hear it from across the *campo*. She'd shout terrible things: accuse them of lying or stealing. Or she'd complain about the food they made for her or the way they'd made the bed. I could hear it all, at least during the summer if I didn't use the Discman. Sometimes I'd see them at the window and I'd wave or smile at them, the way you do. Then if I saw one of them on the street I'd say hello or nod.' She looked to one side as if she'd never previously bothered to consider why she had done this. 'I suppose I wanted them to know that not all people were like her, or that not all Venetians were.'

Brunetti nodded again, acknowledging the legitimacy of this desire.

'One of them, she was from Moldavia, asked me one day if I had any work for her. I had to tell her I already had a cleaning woman, who had worked for me for years. But she looked so desperate that I asked around and found a friend whose cleaning woman had left, so she took her and she liked her, said she was honest and hard working.' She smiled and shook her head at her own garrulousness. 'Anyway, Jana told her that all she was being paid was seven thousand lire – that was before the Euro – an hour.' Failing to keep the indignation from her voice, she said, 'That's less than four Euros an hour, for God's sake. No one can live on that.'

Admiring her for her anger, Brunetti asked, 'Do you think this is what she was paying Signora Ghiorghiu?'

'I've no idea, but I wouldn't be surprised.'

'What was her response when you gave her all that money?' he asked.

Embarrassed, she said, 'Oh, she was pleased, I think.'

'I'm sure she was,' Brunetti said. 'How did she react?'

Signora Gismondi looked down at her hands, clasped in her lap, and said, 'She started to cry.' She paused, then added, 'And she tried to kiss my hand. But I couldn't have that, not there on the street.'

'Certainly not,' Brunetti agreed, trying not to smile. 'Can you remember anything else about Signora Battestini?'

'She used to be a secretary, I think, in one of the schools, I'm not sure which one, elementary, I think. But she must have retired more than twenty years ago. Maybe even more than that, when it was so easy to retire.' Brunetti wasn't sure, but he thought there was more reproach than regret as she said this.

'And her family? You said you spoke to a niece, Signora.'

'Yes, and she didn't want to have anything to do with her. There was a sister in Dolo, presumably the mother of the niece, but the last time I called, I got the niece, and she told me her mother had died.' She considered all of this and added, 'I got the feeling she didn't want to hear anything about her aunt until she was dead, too, and she could inherit the house.'

'You said you spoke to a lawyer, didn't you, Signora?'

'Yes, Dottoressa Marieschi. She has an office, at least it's listed in the phone book, down in Castello somewhere. I've never met her, just spoken to her on the phone.'

'How did you locate all these people, Signora?' he asked.

Detecting only curiosity in his tone, she answered, 'I asked around and I looked them up in the phone book.'

'How did you learn the name of the lawyer?'

She considered this for a long time before saying, 'I called her once, Signora Battestini, and I said I was from the electric company and had to talk to her about a bill that hadn't been paid. She gave me the name of the lawyer and told me to call her, even gave me the number.'

Brunetti gave her an admiring smile but stopped himself from praising her for what was no doubt a crime of some sort. 'Do you know if this lawyer handles all of her affairs?'

'She made it sound like that when I spoke to her,' she answered.

'Signora Battestini or the lawyer herself?'

'Oh, I'm sorry. Signora Battestini. The lawyer was, well, she was the way lawyers always are: she gave very little information and made it sound as though she had very little control over her client.'

That sounded as good a description of the ways of lawyers as Brunetti had ever heard. Instead of complimenting her on her sagacity, however, he asked, 'In all you've learned, is there anything you think might be important?'

Smiling, she said, 'I'm afraid I have no idea of what might be important or not, Commissario. All the neighbours really said was that she was terrible, and if any of them mentioned the husband, it was to say he was an ordinary man, nothing special at all, and that they were not happy together.' He waited for her to comment on the unlikelihood of anyone's finding happiness with Signora Battestini, but she did not.

'I'm sorry I haven't been very helpful,' she said, signalling her desire to end the conversation.

'On the contrary, Signora, I'd say you've been immensely helpful. You've stopped us from closing a case before we had investigated it sufficiently, and you've given us good reason to suspect that our original conclusions were wrong.' He left it to her to understand that he at least believed there was no need to corroborate her story before accepting it.

He got to his feet and stepped back from his chair. He extended his hand, saying, 'I'd like to thank you for coming to talk to us. Not many people would have done as much.'

Taking this as an apology for Lieutenant Scarpa's behaviour, she shook his hand, and left his office.

6

After the woman had gone, Brunetti went back to his desk, considering what he had just heard, not only from Signora Gismondi, but from Lieutenant Scarpa. What the first had told him seemed an entirely plausible story: people left the city and events continued in their absence. Often enough, people chose to have no contact with home, perhaps the better to savour the sense of being away or, as she had told Scarpa, to immerse themselves totally in a foreign language or culture. He tried to think of a reason why a woman as apparently sensible and honest as Signora Gismondi should invent such a story and hold to it in the face of what he was sure must have been Scarpa's opposition. He came up with no convincing explanation.

It was far easier to speculate about Scarpa's motives. To accept her story was to accept that the police had acted with unwonted haste in accepting a convenient solution to the crime. It was also to require an explanation of the whereabouts of the money that had disappeared while in police custody. Both matters had been in the hands of Lieutenant

Scarpa. More importantly, to accept her story would demand a re-examination of the case, or rather, it would demand that, more than three weeks after the murder, the case finally be examined for the first time.

Brunetti had been on vacation when Signora Battestini's body was discovered and had returned to Venice only after the case had been set aside, when he had continued with the investigation of the baggage handlers at the airport. Since the accused had been repeatedly filmed rifling through and stealing from passengers' luggage and since some of them were willing to testify against the others in the hope of receiving a lighter sentences, there was very little for Brunetti to do save to keep the papers and files straight and interview those who had not yet confessed but who might perhaps be persuaded to do so. He had read about the murder while he had been away and, foolishly lulled into believing what he read in the papers, had been convinced that the Romanian woman was guilty. Why else should she try to leave the country? Why else that panicked attempt to flee from the police?

Signora Gismondi had just provided him with alternative answers to these questions: Florinda Ghiorghiu left the country because her job was gone, and she tried to escape the police because she was a citizen of a country where the police were believed to be as corrupt as they were violent and where the thought of falling into their hands was enough to drive a person to flee in maddened panic.

When Brunetti had seen Scarpa in Signorina Elettra's office an hour before, the lieutenant was stiff with anger at what he insisted were a witness's lies. Sensing his rage, Signorina Elettra suggested to the lieutenant, 'Perhaps someone else could get the truth out of her.'

Brunetti was astonished by Signorina Elettra's civility to the lieutenant and by her apparent willingness to believe him. Her craft became evident only when she turned to him and said, 'Commissario, it seems the lieutenant has laid the groundwork by seeing through this woman's story. Maybe someone else could try to find out what's motivating her.' Turning back to the lieutenant and raising her hands in a gesture rich with deferential uncertainty, she added, 'If you think that might help, Lieutenant, of course.' He noticed that she was wearing a simple white cotton blouse: perhaps it was the tightly buttoned collar that made her seem so innocent.

Atavistic suspicion of Signorina Elettra flashed across Scarpa's face, but before he could speak, Brunetti interrupted, saying to Signorina Elettra, 'Don't look at me. I've got the airport to worry about, so I don't have time to be bothered with something like this.' He turned to leave.

Brunetti's reluctance prompted Scarpa into saying, 'She's just going to keep telling me the same story. I'm sure of that.'

It was a statement, not a request, and Brunetti held firm. 'I've got the airport case.' He continued towards the door.

That was enough to provoke Scarpa. 'If this woman's lying about a murder, it's more important than petty theft at the airport,' he said.

Brunetti stopped just short of the door. He turned towards Signorina Elettra, who said, with resignation, 'I think the lieutenant's right, sir.'

Brunetti, a man of sorrows and afflicted with grief, said, with perhaps too much resignation, 'All right, but I don't want to get involved. Where is she?'

Thus it was that he had spoken to Signora Gismondi, and everything she said led him to believe that he had indeed done as Signorina Elettra suggested and got the truth out of her.

Now he went downstairs to Signorina Elettra's office and found her talking on the phone. She raised a hand and held up two fingers to signal that it would take but a moment to finish the call, bent and took a few notes, then said thank you and hung up.

'How did that happen?' he asked, nodding with his chin to the point where Lieutenant Scarpa had stood.

'Know thy enemy,' she answered.

'Meaning?' he asked.

'He hates you, but he's only deeply suspicious of me, so all I had to do was offer him the chance to force you to do something you didn't want to do, and the desire to do that was enough to overcome his distrust of me.'

'You make it sound so easy,' he said, 'like something in a textbook.'

'The carrot and the stick,' she said, smiling. 'I offered him the carrot, which he thought he could turn into a stick he could use to beat you.' Then, suddenly serious, she asked, 'What did the woman say?'

'That she took the Romanian woman to the train station, bought her a ticket to Bucharest, and left her there.'

'How long before the train left?' she asked instantly.

He was pleased that she too could see the weakest link in Signora Gismondi's story. 'About an hour before the train left.'

'The newspapers said it happened over by the Palazzo del Cammello.'

'Yes.'

'There would have been more than enough time, then, wouldn't there?'

'Yes.'

'And?'

'Why bother?' he asked. 'This woman, Assunta Gismondi, says she gave the Romanian woman about seven hundred Euros,' he began, and when he saw Signorina Elettra raise her eyebrows he continued, 'and I believe she did.' Cutting off her question, he said, 'She's impulsive, the Gismondi woman, and I think generous.' Indeed, he was convinced that these were two of the qualities that had brought her to the Questura this morning, those and honesty.

Signorina Elettra pushed her chair back from her desk and crossed her legs, revealing a short red skirt and a pair of shoes with heels so high they would have raised her above even the worst *acqua alta*.

'If you will permit me a seemingly impertinent question, Commissario,' she began, and at his nod she continued, 'is this your head or your heart speaking?'

He considered for a moment, then answered, 'Both.'

'Then,' she said, getting to her feet, a process which raised her almost to his height, 'I think I'd better go down to Scarpa's office and make a copy of the file.'

'Isn't it in there?' he asked, waving a hand towards her computer.

'No. The lieutenant prefers to type up his reports and keep them in his office.'

'Will he give them to you?'

She smiled. 'Of course not.'

Feeling not a bit foolish, he asked, 'Then how will you get it?'

She bent down and opened a drawer. From it she took a thin leather case, and when she opened it he saw a set of picks and tools frighteningly similar to the ones he sometimes used. 'I'll steal it, Commissario. And make a copy. Then put it back where I found it. And, as the lieutenant is a suspicious man, I shall be especially careful when I replace the half-toothpick which he leaves between the seventh and eighth pages of files he thinks are important and which he fears other people will try to see.'

Her smile broadened. 'If you'd like to wait for me in your office, Commissario, I'll bring the copy up as soon as I've made it.'

He had to know. 'But where is he?' What he really wanted to ask was how she knew that Scarpa was not in his office.

'On one of the launches, on his way to Fondamenta Nuove.'

Brunetti was put in mind of the stand-off scenes he'd seen in so many of the westerns he'd watched while growing up, where the good guy and the bad guy stood face to face, each trying to stare the other down. Here, however, there was no question of good guy and bad guy; unless, of course, one were to take the narrow-minded view that breaking into a room at the Questura to make an unauthorized copy of state documents was in any way reprehensible. Brunetti's vision of the law was far too lofty to accept such a view, so he went to hold the door open for her. As she passed in front of him, she said, smiling, 'I won't be long.'

How did she do it? he found himself asking as he walked back to his office. He wasn't curious about the means at Signorina Elettra's command, the computer and the friends at the other end of the phone, always willing to do a favour and break a rule, or a law. Nor did he particularly care about the techniques she used to learn as much as she did about the life and weaknesses of her superiors. What puzzled him was how she found the courage to oppose them so consistently and so openly and to make no attempt to disguise where her loyalties lay. She had once explained to him how it was that she had given up a career in banking and accepted what must be, in the eyes of her family and her friends, a vastly inferior job with the police. She had acted on principle in leaving the bank, and he supposed she was acting on principle now, but he had never had the courage to ask her just what those principles were.

Back at his desk, he made a list of the information he needed: the extent of Signora Battestini's estate; to what degree Avvocatessa Marieschi was involved in Signora Battestini's affairs and what those affairs were; whether the dead woman's name had ever appeared in police files; same with her husband; what the people in the neighbourhood knew of bad feelings between her and anyone else; and, unlikely after three weeks, whether anyone remembered having seen someone other than the Romanian woman entering or leaving her apartment that day and would be willing to tell the police about it. He would also need to speak to the woman's doctor.

By the time he finished making this list, Signorina Elettra was back, careful to knock on his door before coming in.

'Did you make one for Vianello?' he asked.

'Yes, sir,' she said, placing a thin file on his desk and holding up an identical one.

'Do you know where he is?' he asked, careful to place no special emphasis on 'he' and thus avoid suggesting that she'd somehow had computer chips placed behind the ears of everyone in the Questura and was now able to keep tabs on them all by means of a satellite hook-up to her computer.

'He should be here this afternoon, sir.'

'Have you looked at this?' he asked, nodding at the folder.

'No.'

He believed her.

'Why don't you take a look at Vianello's copy before you give it to him?' He didn't need to explain why he wanted her to do this.

'Of course, sir. Would you like me to start checking the most obvious things?'

Years ago, he would have asked her what she had in mind, but familiarity had taught him that the 'things' were probably identical to the notes on his desk, and so he said only, 'Yes. Please.'

'Very well,' she said and left.

First in the file was the autopsy report. Long experience made Brunetti turn immediately to the signature; the same experience underlay his relief at seeing the scrawled letters indicating that Rizzardi had performed it.

Signora Battestini was eighty-three at the time of her death. She might well, the doctor suggested, have lived another ten years. Her heart and other organs were in excellent shape.

She had given birth at least once but had had a hysterectomy at some time in the past. Apart from that, there was no evidence of her ever having had a major illness or a broken bone. Because of her weight, more than a hundred kilos, her knees showed signs of excessive wear to such a degree that walking would have been very difficult for her, climbing stairs impossible. The slackness of her muscle tissue confirmed a general lack of activity.

Death was caused by a series of blows — Rizzardi estimated five – to the back of the head. Because the blows were all clustered at or near the same place, it was impossible to determine which of them had killed her: more likely it was the result of accumulated trauma. The killer, probably right-handed, was either much taller than the victim or had been standing behind the seated woman. The enormous damage wrought by the repeated blows suggested this second possibility, for the difference in height would have created an arc of almost a metre for the descending blows.

As to the weapon, Rizzardi refused to speculate, and it was impossible to know if he had been told about the statue found near the body. His report said only that the weapon was a rough-edged object weighing anywhere from one to three kilos. It could have been wood; it could have been metal: beyond that the pathologist stated only that the pattern of shattered skull was indicative of an object with a series of edges or ridges running along it horizontally.

Attached to this page was the laboratory report stating that the ridges on the bronze statue matched the shatter pattern on Signora Battestini's skull and that the blood found on it was the same type as hers. There were no fingerprints.

Death had resulted from trauma and loss of blood; the extensive damage to brain tissue had caused so much neurological impairment that the affected organs would soon have ceased to function, even had she been found before she bled to death.

The police examination of the scene of death appeared to have been, at best, cursory. Only one room had been dusted for prints, and there were just four photos in the file, all of Signora Battestini's body. These gave little evidence of whatever else might have been in the room and none at all of the 'hurried search' the report said appeared to have taken place. Brunetti had no idea if this laxity resulted from the rapid conclusion that the Romanian woman must have been guilty: he hoped it had not become standard procedure. He checked for the signatures at the bottom of the written report describing the scene, but the initials were illegible.

Next was the passport Florinda Ghiorghiu had been carrying. If the document was false, then what was the real name of this woman buried in Villa Opicina? He didn't even know that much, since nothing in the report actually said where she had been buried. The photo showed dark eyes and dark hair, the face utterly devoid of a smile: she stared at the camera as though she feared it was going to harm her. In a way, it had: the photo had led to the passport, leading to the job, leading to the scene on the train and her doomed flight across the tracks.

The next sheet of paper was a photocopy of Florinda Ghiorghiu's residence and work permits. Repeated on them both was the information on the passport. She had been granted permission to remain in Italy for six months, though the date of entry into Italy stamped on her passport was more than a year ago. Signora Gismondi had said the woman had appeared in the late spring: that left eight or nine months unaccounted for.

That was all. There was no information about how Florinda Ghiorghiu had come to be working for Signora Battestini. There were no receipts acknowledging that she had been paid, neither from employer nor employee. Brunetti knew that this was standard and that most of these women worked in the black economy – indeed, most of those who took care of the steadily ageing population were undocumented women, either from Eastern Europe or the Philippines – so the absence of such papers did not surprise him.

He picked up the file and went downstairs, conscious of how unprofessional his behaviour was going to be. When he entered her office, Signorina Elettra glanced up calmly, as if expecting him.

'I checked the records at the Ufficio Stranieri for the Veneto,' she began, then added, 'Don't worry. I did it legally. All that information is here in our computer.'

He ignored this. 'What did you find?'

'That Florinda Ghiorghiu had a completely legitimate work permit,' she said, but then she looked up at him and smiled.

'And what else?' he asked in response to her smile.

'That there are three women using the same passport.'

'What?'

'Three,' she repeated. 'One here in Venice, another in Milano, and a third in Trieste.'

'But that's impossible.'

'Well,' she conceded, 'it should be impossible, but apparently it's not.' Before he could ask if it was the same woman, applying for work in different cities, she explained, 'One of them started working in Trieste while the one registered here was working for Signora Battestini.'

'And the other?'

'I don't know. I have trouble with Milano.'

Rather than ask her to unravel the enigma of this remark, he said, 'Isn't there some central office or register for these things?'

'There's meant to be,' she agreed, 'but there's no cross-referencing between provinces. Our records include only the Veneto.'

'Then how did you find out?' he asked with real curiosity

and without a hint of uneasiness as to the legality of her methods.

She gave his question long consideration and finally answered, 'I think I'd rather not say, Commissario. That is, I could easily invent an answer so technically complex you'd never understand it, but I think it would be more honest simply to say that I'd rather not tell you.'

'All right,' he agreed, knowing she was right. 'But you're sure?'

She nodded.

As if she'd read his mind, she said, 'The fingerprints,' referring to the government's boast that, within five years, it would have a complete fingerprint register of everyone living in the country, foreign or Italian. Brunetti had laughed when he first heard about the proposal: the railways can't keep the trains on the tracks, schools collapse at the faintest tremors of the earth, three people can use the same passport; and they want to collect more than fifty million sets of fingerprints.

An English friend of his had once remarked that living here was like living in something he called 'the loony bin'. Brunetti had had no idea of what the loony bin actually was, nor where it was located, but that hadn't prevented him from believing that his friend was correct: further, he thought it as precise a description of Italy as any he had ever heard.

'Do you know where they are, these other women? Do you have their addresses?'

'I do for the woman living in Trieste, but not for the one in Milano.'

'Have you checked the other provinces?'

'No. Just the North. It's not really worth the time to check the rest. No one much troubles with things like residence or work permits down there.'

As always, when his own prejudices were expressed he heard how they sounded and felt no small chagrin. 'Down there,' 'The South.' How many times had he heard those phrases, how many times had he used them? He thought he had been careful and never spoken like that in front of the kids, at least not in the tone of contempt and distaste that he still so often heard. But Brunetti could not deny that he had long since come to the conclusion that the South was a problem with no solution, that it would remain a criminal netherworld long after he had ceased to have any professional interest in it.

These reflections were interrupted by his sense of fair play and by intruding memories of some of the things he'd recently witnessed here in the oh-so-superior North. He was pulled from these reflections by Signorina Elettra's voice, saying, '. . . can go and look at her apartment'.

'What was that?' he asked, 'I was thinking about something else. What did you say?'

'That it might be an idea to see if you can have a look at the things in her apartment to try and get a sense of what might have happened.'

'Yes, by all means,' he agreed. He pointed to the file he'd placed on her desk and asked, 'Were her keys in the original?'

'No. Nothing.'

'There's no reference to them, either. Scarpa didn't say whether the apartment was still sealed, did he?'

'No.'

Brunetti considered this. If there were no keys, then he'd have to ask Scarpa for them, which he did not want to do. To request them from Signora Battestini's next of kin would alert people, who might well fall into the category of suspects, that the police were taking a renewed interest in the case, and that would be enough to alarm them into caution.

At last he turned to Signorina Elettra and asked, 'Could I borrow your picks?'

7

It was almost lunchtime and Brunetti, long familiar with his wife's insistence on knowing how many people would be home for any meal, called to tell her he would not be.

'Wonderful,' she responded.

'I beg your pardon,' he said, not disguising his surprise.

'Oh, don't be a such baby, Guido. The kids are both at friends' houses for lunch, so I can read while I eat.'

'What are you going to eat?' he asked.

'Don't you want to know what I'm going to read?'

'No. I want to know what you're going to eat.'

'So you'll know what you're missing?'

'Yes.'

'And sulk?'

'No.'

There was a long pause and, even down the line, he could all but hear her mind working. Finally she asked, 'If I promise to eat only *grissini* and cheese and then eat the peach that has the spot on it, will you feel better?'

'Oh, don't be silly, Paola,' he insisted but he did so with a laugh.

'Done,' she declared. 'And in order to reward you for the lunch you miss, I promise to cook you swordfish steaks and shrimp for dinner.'

'In the tomato sauce?'

'Yes. And if I have time, I'll use the rest of the peaches and make ice-cream.'

'And maybe a little less garlic than you usually use?' he asked, taking advantage of what he thought was a strong bargaining position.

'In the ice-cream?'

He laughed and hung up, telling himself to remember when he got home to ask her what she was reading.

That left him free to go over to Signora Battestini's apartment, which he thought would be best done just after lunchtime, when most people would be in their houses, and the heat would have driven the tourists from the streets. As a reluctant alternative to a proper meal, he decided to have some *tramezzini*, and after serious reflection decided that Boldrin was the best place. Besides, it was more or less on the way if he decided to walk and would get him to the apartment at about one.

Olga, the boy cat, was lying asleep in his usual place on the floor in front of the bar, and Brunetti was pleased to see that his hair had finally grown back, though it lacked the grey silkiness of years before. The illness that had struck down the neighbourhood cat three years ago was already urban myth: one story claimed someone had poured acid on him, while another blamed his shocking baldness on a sudden allergy. Regardless of their belief, many people had helped pay the veterinary bills during Olga's long convalescence, Brunetti among them. Brunetti stepped over him and approached the bar.

Two *tramezzini* with prosciutto and zucchini, however

excellent, and two glasses of white wine could not, even in a moment of delirium, be called lunch, but the thought of their superiority to Paola's bread sticks, cheese and mouldy peach allowed him to consider them as something less rigorous than a penance.

When he reached the address, he saw that the shutters were closed. The single doorbell bore the name 'Battestini', so he couldn't employ his ordinary ruse of ringing a bell at random and saying he was visiting someone else whose name was listed by the bells. If he spoke Veneziano, this always worked. Now, instead, he would have to use the picks. Resisting the urge to look around to check if anyone could see him, he put his hand in the pocket of his jacket and pulled out the smallest of the picks. It was a simple lock and he was quickly inside, again careful not to look behind him as he pushed the door open.

The entrance was pleasantly cool after the heat outside: the walls were freshly whitewashed, and light streamed in from the windows above the door. He started up towards the second floor and found that the walls of the staircase were equally clean, the marble steps gleaming. The door to the apartment had no name beside it, though this would hardly be necessary if she owned the entire building. He bent to study the lock, saw that it was a simple Cisa, a model he'd opened a number of times before. He chose the medium-sized pick this time, inserted it into the lock, closed his eyes to give his full attention to his fingers, and started hunting for the first tumbler.

It took him less than a minute to turn the lock. He pushed open the door, felt on the wall until he found the light, and when he switched it on was at first puzzled that a woman such as Signora Battestini would have chosen to live in such cool simplicity: a pale, machine-made carpet on the floor, two spotless white easy chairs, a dark blue sofa that looked as though it had never been sat upon, and a low glass table with a shallow wooden platter at the centre. He realized then what must have happened: the crime scene tape had been removed, either by complacent police or eager relatives, and the place had been speedily redecorated. He took a closer look at the furniture and saw that what looked like maple was really cheap laminate, the sort of thing a landlord would put in an apartment meant to be rented by the week.

He walked towards the back of the apartment, and in all the rooms he saw the same cool hand at work: everywhere white furniture and walls and always one contrasting dark piece of furniture. Only the bathroom displayed any signs of what the apartment might once have been: new fixtures had been installed, but the pink tiles remained, some of them dull and opaque with age.

He opened closets and found new sheets and towels, some still in their plastic packaging; in the kitchen new dishes and cutlery. He looked under the beds and on the top shelves of the closets, but he found no evidence of the former owner. For fear of alerting the neighbours that someone was in the apartment, he left the shutters closed, and the trapped heat crawled over his body.

He left the apartment and went up the next flight of stairs. Ignoring the door he found at the landing, he climbed on up to the next floor. At the top was a door, the wood dry and splintery with age. Twin flanges were screwed into the door and jamb, and a padlock joined the metal rings on either side. He went back down the stairs and into what had been Signora Battestini's apartment, but no matter where he looked, he could find no tools. Finally he went into the kitchen and took one of the new, apparently unused, stainless steel kitchen knives and went back up to the attic door.

Though the wood of the door jamb was dry, it still took some effort to unscrew the flange and jerk it free. He pulled open the door and looked into the low attic. Luckily, there were two windows, neither very clean, at the other end, and they provided enough light to give some idea of the dimensions of the room and the objects scattered in it.

A double bed with a carved wooden frame, the sort he remembered from his grandmother's home, stood against one wall, beside it a matching marble-topped dresser, a leprous mirror attached to the back. Two easy chairs stood sideways to the wall, looking at one another, with between them a pink Formica clothing hamper.

A number of cardboard boxes were stacked just below the windows; as he crossed the room towards them, grime crunched under his feet. He pulled open the one on top of the first pile, relieved it was not taped shut, and found nothing but old shoes. He lifted it off the pile and set it on the floor, then opened the second. This seemed to hold the detritus of kitchen drawers: a carving knife with a mould-flecked bone handle, a corkscrew, a jumble of unmatched silverware, two dirty potholders, and pieces of metal the purpose of which he could not fathom. The third, heavier than the other two, was filled with small clumps of newspaper. He unwrapped one and saw that the date was from two weeks before. Inside, nestling in the sports pages, was a badly painted statue of the Madonna, appearing displeased that she was destined to spend at least the immediate future wrapped up in the latest cycling drug scandal. Beside her, in the first page of the Economy section of the *Gazzettino*, he found another triumph of what Paola called 'ChiesaKitsch', a Plexiglas sphere in which snow fell on a plastic Nativity scene. He rewrapped the ball and set the box aside.

The next box contained doilies and antimacassars, all bearing faint stains, cloths that must have come from the kitchen, as well as tea towels he was reluctant to touch. The one below that held a dozen or so cotton shirts, all white and all meticulously ironed and folded. Beneath them were six or seven dark coloured striped ties, each in a separate cellophane envelope. The next box was heavier and when he opened it he found papers of all sorts: old magazines, newspapers, envelopes that appeared still to contain letters, postcards, receipts for bills, and other pieces of paper he could not make out in the dim light. There was no way Brunetti could hope to carry it all away with him, so he had no choice but to sort through it and take what looked interesting.

The heat covered him, pressed against his skin, crawled up his nose, carrying dust with it. He dropped the papers back into the box and started to remove his jacket, which clung to him through his shirt, both of them soaked. Just as he pulled it clear of his shoulders, he heard the sound of a door closing below him, and he froze, the jacket halfway down his upper back.

He heard voices, one high-pitched – either a woman or a child – and the deeper resonance of a man. The voices drowned out whatever noise their feet made on the steps. He tried to remember if he had turned off the light and closed the door to the apartment behind him. It had the kind of lock that clicked shut without the key. He knew he'd left it open when he first came up to the attic and could only hope he'd thought to close it the second time.

The voices grew nearer, each answering the other with sufficient frequency for him to abandon the idea that the first voice was that of a child. He heard a door open, then close, and the voices stopped. He closed his eyes, the better to hear them. He had no idea which apartment they had entered, the one directly below him or Signora Bettestini's one floor down. He had not been at all conscious of the noise his feet made on the wooden floor, but now he tested it by shifting minimally to one side and froze again at the protest from the boards.

He pulled his jacket back on and leaned forward to set the papers back in the box. He looked at his watch and saw that it was five minutes before two. At five past, he leaned over to pick up the papers and turned them to the light to try to read them. He soon realized the impossibility of concentrating on the papers, not with two people in the apartment downstairs, so he placed them in the box once more. Before long, his back began to stiffen, and he swivelled around at the waist a few times to relieve tension.

Another quarter of an hour passed before he heard the voices again, the door having opened silently. What story could he give, should they decide to come up the stairs and find him in the attic? Technically, it was still a crime scene, so he could argue his right to be there. But the picked lock and the jemmied door to the attic suggested something beyond regular police procedure and were sure to cause trouble.

The voices remained at the same level for a while, then gradually grew fainter. Finally, he heard the front door close, and as the silence spread through the building, Brunetti took two steps backward and stretched his arms high above his head, catching his right hand in a spider's web. He pulled it back instantly, wiping it on the front of his jacket. He turned and walked to the door of the attic and then back to the boxes, shaking his hands in front of him to rid himself of accumulated stress.

Something caught in his memory, and he went back to the box of kitchen linens, opened it and pulled out a plastic string shopping bag of a kind that had been popular in his childhood but had long since disappeared. He slipped the large round handles over his left wrist, wiped his hands on a towel, and tossed it into one of the boxes.

He went back to the box of papers and quickly sorted through them, leaving behind magazines and newspapers and choosing only what looked like letters or documents. He pulled open the mouth of the bag and put the papers inside carelessly, suddenly overwhelmed by the desire to be free of this enclosed space, this heat, and the permeating smell of dust and unwashed objects.

Outside the attic, he used the kitchen knife to screw the flange back into place, then slipped the knife into the pocket of his jacket. On the landing, he tried the door of the apartment, but it was shut: he didn't bother to use the picks to see if it was double-locked.

Downstairs, he pulled open the outside door and stepped into the full heat of the afternoon sun, soothed by the sense that its rays would burn him clean of the smell and dirt of the attic.

When he arrived at the Questura, shortly after three, the first person he saw was Lieutenant Scarpa, just pulling up in one of the police launches. Because they could not avoid reaching the entrance at the same time, Brunetti prepared some innocuous greeting, keeping the string bag to the side away from Scarpa.

'Have you been in a fight, Commissario?' Scarpa asked with seeming concern when he saw the stains on Brunetti's jacket and shirt.

'Oh, no. I tripped when I was walking past a building site and fell against a wall,' Brunetti said with equally false sincerity. 'But thank you for asking.'

Holding the string bag so that it remained largely out of sight behind him, Brunetti nodded to the guard who opened the door for them, nodded to him in return and snapped out a crisp salute for the lieutenant. Not thinking it necessary to say anything further to Scarpa, Brunetti walked across the foyer and started up the steps. From behind him, he heard the lieutenant say, 'I haven't seen a bag like that for ages, Commissario. It's just like the ones our mothers used to use,' and then, after a long pause, he added, 'when they could still do the shopping.'

The faltering of Brunetti's step was so slight as not to be evident, as had been the first signs of the madness which had seized his mother a decade ago and still held her prisoner. He had no idea how Scarpa had learned about her, indeed, had no proof that he knew, but then why else the lieutenant's frequent references to their mothers? And why his repeated, and falsely humorous, suggestion that any lapse of memory or efficiency on the part of anyone at the Questura must be a sign of senility?

Ignoring the remark, Brunetti continued up to his office. He closed the door, set the bag on his desk, removed his jacket and held it up to look at the front. Grey linen and one of his favourites, it had broad black stains running horizontally across the front; he doubted that any cleaning could remove them. He draped it on the back of his chair and loosened his tie. It was only then that he noticed how filthy his hands were, so he went down to the bathroom on the floor below and washed them, then splashed water on his face and ran his wet hands around the back of his neck.

Seated at his desk, he pulled the bag towards him, spread it open, and drew the stack of papers from it. Abandoning the idea of trying to sort them into categories, he began to read them over as they lay in the pile. Gas bills, ENEL, water and garbage bills, all paid through her account at Uni Credit: these were clipped together according to utility and arranged in chronological order. There was a sheaf of letters of complaint from neighbours, Signora Gismondi among them, about the noise of her television. They dated back seven years and had all been sent *raccomandate*. There was a photocopy of her marriage certificate, a letter from the Ministero dell' Interno to her husband, acknowledging receipt of his report of 23 June 1982.

There followed a stack of letters, all addressed to either Signora Battestini or her husband, sometimes to both. He opened them and read quickly through the first paragraph of each, then glanced quickly through the rest of the letters to see if there was anything that might be important. Some were painfully pro forma letters from a niece, Graziella, written in a very unschooled hand, each thanking her for a Christmas gift, though the gift was never specified. Over the course of the years, Graziella's handwriting and painfully simple grammar remained unchanged.

One of the envelopes bearing Graziella's name and return address contained no letter: instead, he found a sheet of paper written in the sharp, spiky letters of a different hand. Along the left margin ran a list of four sets of initials, and to the right of each of them a series of numbers or, in some cases, numbers preceded by or followed by a letter or letters. A voice spoke his name from the door, and he looked up to see Vianello. Instead of a greeting, Brunetti surprised him by asking, 'You like crossword puzzles, don't you?'

Nodding, the inspector came across the room and sat in one of the chairs in front of Brunetti's desk. Brunetti passed him the sheet of paper and said, 'What do you make of this?'

Vianello took the sheet, laid it flat on the surface of his superior's desk, and, propping his chin in both palms, looked down at it. Brunetti continued to go through the other papers, leaving Vianello to it.

After a number of minutes but without taking his eyes from the paper, Vianello asked, 'Do I get a clue?'

'It was in the attic of the old woman who was murdered last month.'

A few more minutes passed and finally Vianello asked, 'Have you got a phone book, sir? The yellow pages.'

Curious, Brunetti bent down and pulled the Venice yellow pages out of his bottom drawer.

The inspector opened the book at the front and flipped through a few pages. Then he picked up the sheet of paper and laid it on top of the open book. He placed his right forefinger on the first item on the list and ran his left down a page of the book which Brunetti could not see. Apparently finding what he was looking for, Vianello moved his right finger to the second, and the left again hunted down the page of the phone book. Satisfied with whatever he was finding, Vianello grunted and moved his right finger. This process continued until he got to the fourth item on the list, at which he looked up at Brunetti and smiled.

'Well?' Brunetti asked.

Vianello turned the book around and pushed it across the desk. On the right-hand page Brunetti saw, in capital letters, BAR, followed by the first few dozen names of the alphabetical listing of the hundreds of bars in the city. Vianello's broad forefinger passed into his field of vision and drew his attention to the left-hand page. He understood instantly: BANCHE. Of course, banks. So the list was a series of abbreviations of their names, followed by the account numbers.

'I also know a three-letter Cambodian monetary unit beginning with K, sir,' Vianello said.

8

After a few minutes' discussion, Brunetti went downstairs
and made a few photocopies of the paper. When he came
back, he and Vianello wrote out the full names of the banks
beside each of the abbreviations. When they had them all,
Brunetti asked, 'Are you good enough to get into them?'
leaving it to Vianello to infer that he meant with a computer
and not with a pickaxe and crowbar.

Regretfully, Vianello shook his head and said, 'Not yet, sir.
She let me try it once, with a bank in Rome, but I left a trail so
broad that a friend of hers sent her an email the next day to
ask her what she thought she was doing.'

'He knew she did it?' Brunetti asked.

'The man told her he recognized her technique in the way
I first entered the system.'

'Which was?' Brunetti asked.

'Oh, you wouldn't understand, sir,' Vianello said in a
haunting echo of the cool, objective tone Signorina
Elettra used and which the inspector had probably learned
from her. 'She started me off using an opening code,

then she let me try to find a specific piece of information.'

'Which was?' Brunetti said, adding, 'if I might ask.'

'She wanted me to see if I could discover how much money had been transferred into a particular account from a numbered account in Kiev.'

'Whose account?' Brunetti asked.

Vianello pressed his lips together, considering, and then named the Assistant Minister in the Department of Commerce who had been most active in arranging government loans to the Ukraine.

'Did you find out?'

'Alarm bells,' Vianello began, then explained, 'figuratively, that is – began to sound. So I got out as quickly as I could, but not before I'd left very obvious signs that I'd been in there.'

'Why would she want to know something like that?' Brunetti mused.

'I think she already knew, sir,' Vianello said, then added, 'In fact, I'm sure she did. That's how she knew how to help me get in.'

'Did she explain to her friend?' Brunetti asked.

'Oh, no, sir. That would just have made it worse, if he knew she was helping the police.'

'You mean none of these people she asks for help knows where she works?' asked an astonished Brunetti.

'Oh, no. That would be the end of it, if they did.'

'Then where do they all think she's working?' He had some vague idea that any messages she sent must be traceable to the Questura. They all had email addresses: he'd even used his a few times, and he knew it was perfectly clear that it was at the Venice Questura.

'I think she reroutes things, sir,' Vianello said cautiously.

Though Brunetti wasn't clear how this could be done, the verb made it clear that it had been done. 'Reroutes it how, through what?'

'Probably her last working address.'

'The Banca d'Italia?' asked an astonished Brunetti. At Vianello's nod, Brunetti demanded, 'Do you mean she's sending and getting information via an address at a place where she hasn't worked for years?' At the second nod, Brunetti raised his voice. 'It's the national bank, for God's sake. How can they allow a person who hasn't worked there for years to use their address as if she still did?'

'I don't think they would allow it, sir,' Vianello agreed, then explained, 'that is, if anyone there knew she was using it.'

To continue with this conversation, Brunetti suddenly realized, would lead either to madness or, more dangerously, to criminal knowledge which, at some time in the future, he might have to deny under oath. But, unable to control his curiosity, he asked, 'Did you find out?'

'Find out what?'

'How much was deposited?'

'No.'

'Did she?'

'I assume so.'

'Why? Did she tell you?'

'No. She said it was privileged information, and I couldn't have it unless I found it out myself.'

Hearing this, the expression, 'Honour among thieves', did flit through Brunetti's mind, but his admiration and respect caused him to swat it aside and return his attention to the matter at hand. 'Then we have to ask her to do this?'

'I think so. Yes.'

Together they got to their feet and, Vianello carrying the sheet of paper with the deciphered initials, they went downstairs to see if Signorina Elettra was in her office.

She was, but unfortunately so was her immediate superior, Vice-Questore Giuseppe Patta, today wearing a cream linen suit with a black shirt, also of linen. His tie, of slate-coloured silk, had threads of the same colour as the suit running diagonally across it. Brunetti noticed, as he had failed to do earlier, that Signorina Elettra was wearing a black linen suit and a cream-coloured silk blouse. It occurred to him that, had the two of them planned this, Patta would probably have been motivated by emulation, she by parody.

Seeing Vianello with a sheet of paper in his hand, Patta demanded, 'What's that, Inspector? Something to do with the Commissario's nonsensical idea that that woman was not murdered by the Romanian?'

'No, Vice-Questore,' a humbled Vianello said. 'It's a code I use for choosing teams for the Totocalcio.' He brought the paper out from behind him and made as if to show it to Patta, saying, 'You see, this first column is the code for the team name, and then here are the numbers of the players I think are going to . . .'

'That's enough, Vianello,' Patta said with undisguised irritation. Then, to Brunetti, 'Unless you're busy choosing your winning teams, too, Commissario, I'd like to have a word with you.' He turned towards the door to his office.

'Of course, sir,' said Brunetti and followed him, leaving Vianello to talk to Signorina Elettra.

Patta went to his desk but didn't invite Brunetti to sit, a good sign, for it meant the Vice-Questore was in a hurry. It was almost five: Patta would barely have time for the police launch to take him over to the Cipriani for a swim and get him home in time for dinner.

'I won't keep you, Commissario. I want to remind you that this case is settled, regardless of what your ridiculous ideas about it might be,' he began, not bothering to specify which of Brunetti's ideas he found ridiculous and thus allowing himself the option of considering them all to be so. 'The facts speak for themselves. The Romanian killed that poor old woman, tried to escape the country, and then gave clear proof of her guilt by trying to escape from a routine police inspection at the border.' He put his hands together, making a steeple out of his fingers, and covered his mouth for a second with his forefingers, then separated them and said, 'I don't want the work of this police department called into question by a suspicious and irresponsible press.'

He raised his chin and devoted his full attention, and gaze, to Brunetti. 'Have I made myself clear, Commissario?'

'Excellently clear, sir.'

'Good,' he said, taking Brunetti's affirmation as agreement that he would do as he was told. 'Then I won't keep you any longer. I have a meeting to attend.'

Brunetti murmured polite words and left the office. Outside, Signorina Elettra sat at her desk, reading a magazine; there was no sign of Vianello. When she looked up, Brunetti raised a finger and pointed at his nose, then upwards in the direction of his office. He heard Patta's door open behind him. Signorina Elettra glanced back at her magazine, ignoring Brunetti, and idly flipped a page. He left and went up to his office to wait for her.

Vianello was by the window of Brunetti's office when he arrived, standing on his toes and leaning out of the window, looking down at the dock in front of the Questura. Brunetti heard the motor of one of the launches start up, then listened as it pulled away and started down towards the Bacino and, presumably, off towards the Cipriani. Saying nothing, Vianello drew his head back inside and moved towards a chair.

A moment later Signorina Elettra came in and closed the door behind her. She took the chair next to Vianello; Brunetti leaned back against his desk.

He hardly thought it necessary to ask her if Vianello had told her what had to be done. 'Will you be able to check them all?' he asked.

'Only this one will be difficult,' she said, pointing to a name halfway down the list. 'Deutsche Bank. They've taken over two other banks, but their office here is new, and I've never had to ask them for anything, so it might take me some time, but I can make the requests to the others this afternoon: I should have the answers by tomorrow.' The way she phrased it, one not familiar with her tactics would assume that all of this would be done according to strict banking procedure: all information given in compliance with court orders which, in turn, had been supplied in response to police inquiries filed through the proper channels. Since this was a process which ordinarily took months and which new laws made increasingly difficult, if not impossible, the reality was that the information would be plucked from the files of the banks as effortlessly as the wallet from the back pocket of an unsuspecting Belgian tourist on the Number One vaporetto.

Looking at Vianello, Brunetti asked, 'What do you think?'

With a polite nod at Signorina Elettra to show that she had told him about Brunetti's conversation with Signora Gismondi, Vianello said, 'If the woman you spoke to is telling the truth, then it's not likely that Signora Ghiorghiu killed the old woman. Which means that someone else did, and I agree that these bank records are a good first place to look for a reason why.'

Signorina Elettra interrupted here. 'Do you think there's any chance that she might have been the murderer?'

Vianello glanced at him, equally curious, and Brunetti said, 'If you've seen the photos of Signora Battestini's body, you've seen what the blows did to her head.' Taking their silence for assent, he went on, 'It doesn't make any sense to me that the Ghiorghiu woman would go back and do that in cold blood. She had a lot of money, she had a train ticket home, and she was already at the station. And from what Signora Gismondi said, it sounds as though she'd had time to calm down. I can't see any reason why she'd go back and kill the old woman, and if she did, not in that way. That was rage, not calculation.'

'Or calculation disguised as rage,' suggested Vianello.

This opened vistas of malice Brunetti preferred not to contemplate, but he nodded in reluctant assent. Rather than speculate about the possible, however, he wanted them to discuss the actual, and so he turned his attention to Signorina Elettra. 'I'll talk to her lawyer tomorrow and to the relatives.' Turning to Vianello, he said, 'I'd like you to go and see if people in the neighbourhood remember seeing anything that day.'

'Is this official?' Vianello asked.

Brunetti sighed. 'I think it would be better if you managed to make your questions casual, if such a thing is possible.'

'I'll ask Nadia if she knows anyone who lives over there,' Vianello said. 'Or maybe we'll go over there for a drink or have lunch in that new place on the corner of Campo dei Mori.'

Brunetti acknowledged Vianello's plan with a grin, then turned to Signorina Elettra and said, 'The other thing I'd like checked is any possible involvement she might have had with us.'

'Who? The Romanian?'

'No. Signora Battestini.'

'A master criminal in her eighties,' she chortled. 'How I'd love to discover one.'

Brunetti named a former Prime Minister and suggested she might begin by searching the files for information about him.

Vianello laughed outright and she had the grace to smile.

'And her husband and her late son while you're about it,' Brunetti said, returning them to the business at hand.

'Shall I have a look for the lawyer?'

'Yes.'

'I love to hunt for lawyers,' Signorina Elettra could not prevent herself from saying. 'They think they're so clever at hiding things, but it's so easy to flush them out of the undergrowth. Almost too easy.'

'Would you prefer to give them a sporting chance?' Vianello asked.

The question brought her back to her senses. 'Give a lawyer a sporting chance? Do you think I'm mad?'

9

Because he still had to read witness statements in the airport case and because he was not eager to talk to a lawyer, Brunetti contented himself with calling Avvocatessa Marieschi's office and making an appointment to speak to her the following morning. When the secretary asked what he wanted to discuss, Brunetti said only that it concerned a question of inheritance, gave his name, but made no mention of the fact that he worked for the police.

He spent an hour reading through contradictory and mutually exclusive statements. Luckily, a small photo was attached to each of them, so he could identify the person making the statement or answering the questions with the people he had observed on the videos from cameras hidden in the baggage hall of the airport. To the best of his under-standing, only twelve of the seventy-six people arrested were telling the whole truth, for it was only their testimony that was confirmed by the hours of video he had watched in the last week, film which captured all of the accused taking part in thefts of some sort.

Brunetti was reluctant to invest much time in the investigation, especially since the defence was arguing that, since the cameras had been placed there without the knowledge of the people being filmed, they represented an invasion of the 'privacy' of the accused, that all-purpose word that had been hijacked from English to fill a need in a language which had no term of its own for the concept. If this argument were upheld, and he realized it might well be, then the state's case collapsed, for all those who had admitted guilt, with the disappearance of the primary evidence against them, would instantly retract their confessions.

Besides, they were all still at work, it having been argued that, since the Constitution guaranteed everyone the right to work, it would be unconstitutional to fire them. 'The loony bin, the loony bin,' he whispered to himself and decided it was time to go home.

When he got there, he found that Paola had been as good as her word, for the aromas that met him as he entered the apartment were a rich blend of seafood, garlic, and something he wasn't sure about, perhaps spinach. He set the COIN bag in which he had folded his dirty jacket by the door and went down the hall to the kitchen. She was already seated at the table, a glass of white wine in front of her, reading.

'All right,' he said, 'I'll ask you what you're reading.'

She glanced at him over her reading glasses and said, 'A book that should be of great interest to us both, Guido: Chiara's textbook on religious doctrine.'

Little good could come of this, Brunetti realized instantly, but still he asked, 'Why to us?'

'Because of what it tells us about the world we live in,' she said, setting the book down and taking a sip of wine.

'For example?' he asked, going to the refrigerator and taking out the open bottle. It was the good Ribolla Gialla they'd bought from a friend in Corno di Rosazzo.

'There's a chapter here,' she said, pointing at the page she had been reading, 'on the Seven Deadly Sins.'

Brunetti had often thought that it was convenient that there should be one for each day of the week, but he kept this thought to himself for the moment. 'And?' he asked.

'And I started thinking about the way our society has ceased to think of them as sins or, if not all of them, has managed at least to remove most of the scent of sin that was once attached to them.'

He pulled out a chair and sat opposite her, not really interested in this latest observation but willing to listen. He raised his glass in her direction and took a sip. It was as good as he remembered its being. Thank God, then, for good wine and good friends, and thank God even for a wife who could find reason for polemic in a middle school textbook of religious doctrine.

'Think of lust,' she continued.

'I often do,' he said and leered.

Ignoring him, she went on. 'When we grew up, it was, if not a sin, at least a semi-sin, or at least something that one did not discuss or present in public. Now you can't look at a film or television or a magazine without seeing it.'

'Do you think that's bad?' he asked.

'Not necessarily. Just different. Maybe a better case is gluttony.'

Ah, that was to strike a blow close to home, Brunetti thought, and pulled in his stomach a little.

'We're encouraged to it all the time. Every time we open a magazine or a newspaper.'

'Gluttony?' he asked, puzzled.

'Not gluttony for food, necessarily,' she said, 'but the taking 'in or consumption of more than we need. After all, what is owning more than one television or one car or one house but a form of gluttony?'

'I'd never thought of it that way,' he temporized and went back to the refrigerator for more wine.

'No, neither did I, not until I started to read this book. They define gluttony as eating too much and leave it at that, but I started thinking about what it would or could mean in larger terms.'

That, it seemed to Brunetti, was the essence of Paola, this woman he still loved to the point of distraction, that she was always thinking about things – everything, it sometimes seemed to him – in larger terms.

'Do you think you could start thinking about dinner in larger terms?' he asked.

She looked across at him, then at her watch, and saw that it was well after eight. 'Ah,' she said, as if surprised at being called back to such mundane things. 'Of course. I heard the kids come in.' Then, it seemed, she took her first look at him and asked, 'What did you do to your shirt? Wipe your hands on it?'

'Yes,' he said, and at her surprise added, 'I'll tell you after dinner.'

Both Chiara and Raffi were there, a rare enough event during the summer, when one or both of them was often away with friends for dinner, sometimes to spend the night. Raffi had reached an age when his puppy love for Sara Paganuzzi had taken on a far more adult tone, so much so that Brunetti had taken him aside one afternoon some months before and tried to talk to him about sex, only to be told that they'd learned all about that sort of thing at school. It was Paola who had made it clear, declaring the following night that, regardless of what his friends did or thought, she'd spoken to Sara's parents and they were all in agreement that he would not, under any circumstances, be allowed to spend the night at Sara's home, and Sara would not stay at theirs.

'But that's medieval,' Raffi had whined.

'It's also final,' Paola had said, putting an end to argument.

Whatever arrangement Raffi had worked out with Sara seemed to satisfy them both, for whenever she came to dinner she was polite and friendly to them all, and even Raffi seemed to bear his parents no ill-will for a policy most of his friends would certainly concur was 'medieval.'

Raffi and Chiara had both spent the day at the Alberoni, though with different groups of friends, and after a day of swimming and playing on the beach, they ate like field hands. It seemed, from the size of the platter Paola had covered with fish and shrimp, that she'd bought an entire swordfish. 'Are you going to eat a third portion?' Brunetti asked Raffi when he saw his son eyeing the almost empty platter.

'He's a growing boy, *Papà*,' Chiara surprised him by saying, thus suggesting that she was full.

Brunetti glanced at Paola, but she was busy helping herself to more spinach and missed the chance to appreciate the greatness of soul he displayed by failing to ask her if their son were guilty of gluttony. Turning back her attention, Paola said, 'Finish it, Raffi. Nobody likes cold fish.'

'If we were speaking English, would that be a pun, *Mamma*?' Chiara asked. Along with Paola's nose and lanky frame, Chiara had inherited her mother's passion for language, Brunetti knew, but this was the first time she'd branched out into making jokes in her second language.

By the time the ice-cream was finished, Chiara was almost asleep, so Paola sent both children to bed and started to gather the dishes. Brunetti carried the empty ice-cream bowl into the kitchen and stood at the counter, licking the serving spoon, then running it around the bottom of the bowl to pick up the last bits of peach. When there was no hopeful prospect of more, he set the bowl to the side of the sink and went back to the table to get the glasses.

When the dishes were soaking, Paola said, 'Do you think we should remain with the fruit theme and have a drop of Williams out on the terrace?'

'I'd probably starve to death without you to protect me,' Brunetti said.

'Guido, my dove,' she said, 'I worry a great deal about the things that could happen to you because of your job, but, believe me, starving to death is not one of them.' She went out on to the terrace to wait for him.

He decided to bring only two glasses and leave the bottle behind. Besides, he could go back and get more if he chose. Outside, he found her in a chair, her feet propped up on the lowest rung of the railing, her eyes closed. As he drew near, she stretched out her hand, and he put the glass into it. She sipped, sighed, sipped again. 'God's in His heaven, all's right with the world,' she said in English.

'Perhaps you've already had enough to drink, Paola,' he observed.

'Tell me about the shirt,' she said, and he did.

'And you believe this woman, this Signora Gismondi?' she asked when Brunetti had finished telling her about the events of the day.

'I think I do,' he said. 'There's no reason for her not to be telling the truth. Nothing she said suggested that she was anything but the old woman's neighbour.'

'With a grudge,' Paola suggested.

'Because of the television?' he asked.

'Yes.'

'You don't kill people because of the noise of a television,' he insisted.

She reached out and put her hand on his arm. 'I've been listening to you talk about your work, Guido, for decades, and it seems to me that there are a lot of people who are ready to kill for a lot less than the noise of a television.'

'For example?' he asked.

'Remember that man, was it in Mestre, who went outside to tell the guy in the car in front of his house to turn the radio down? When was it, about four years ago? He got killed, didn't he?'

'But that was a man,' Brunetti said. 'And he had a history of violence.'

'And your Signora Gismondi doesn't?'

That made Brunetti remember that he had not bothered to ask Signorina Elettra to see what she could find out about Signora Gismondi. 'I hardly think that's likely,' he said.

'You probably wouldn't find anything, anyway,' Paola said.

'Then why doubt her?'

She sighed silently, then said, 'It's disappointing at times that after all these years you still don't understand the way my mind works.'

'I doubt I'll ever understand that,' Brunetti admitted with no attempt at irony. Then, 'What is it I don't understand now?'

'That I believe you're right about Signora Gismondi. There'd be no sense in it: a person who is embarrassed when someone tries to kiss their hand in public.' It might be an inexact description of Signora Gismondo's remarks, and it seemed he might have few occasions to apply it, but this seemed as good a rule about human behaviour as Brunetti had ever heard.

'But I want you to be able to give proof to people like Patta and Scarpa and whoever else doesn't want to believe this.'

Paola still had her eyes closed, and he studied her profile: straight nose, perhaps too long, a faint tracing of lines around her eyes, lines he knew had been put there by humour, and just the first faint sagging of the flesh under her chin.

He thought of the kids, how tired they had been at dinner, while his eyes travelled down her body. He set his glass down on the table and leaned towards her. 'Could we return to our examination of the seven deadly sins?' he asked.

93

10

His appointment with Avvocatessa Roberta Marieschi was set for ten the next morning. Because her office was in Castello, just at the beginning of Via Garibaldi, Brunetti took the Number One and got off at Giardini. The trees in the public gardens looked tired and dusty and greatly in need of rain. Truth to tell, much the same could be said of most of the people in the city. He found the office with no difficulty, next door to what had once been a very good pizzeria, now transformed into a shop selling fake Murano glass. He rang the bell and went into the building, then up the stairs to the first-floor office.

The secretary with whom he had spoken the previous day looked up when he came in, smiled and asked if he were Signor Brunetti. When he said that he was, she asked him if he would mind waiting a few minutes because the Dottoressa was still with another client. Brunetti took a seat on a comfortable grey sofa and studied the covers of the magazines on the table to his left. He chose *Oggi* because he seldom got to read it, refusing to buy it and embarrassed to be seen reading it. He was deep into an account of the nuptials of a minor Scandinavian princeling when the door to the left of the secretary opened and an elderly man came into the waiting room. He had a black leather briefcase in one hand, a silver-headed walking stick in the other.

The secretary got to her feet and smiled. 'Would you like to make another appointment, Cavaliere?'

'Thank you, Signorina,' he said with a gracious smile. 'I'll read through these papers first and then call about making one.'

They exchanged polite goodbyes, and then the secretary approached Brunetti, who rose to his feet. 'I'll take you in, Signore,' she said and went to the door the old man had closed behind him. She knocked once and went in, Brunetti a step or two behind her.

The desk stood on the far side of the room, between two windows. No one sat there, but Brunetti's eye was automatically drawn to a sudden movement on the floor. As he looked, something flashed from under the desk, then instantly disappeared: light brown, it could have been a mouse or perhaps a dormouse, though he thought they lived in the country, not the city. He pretended not to have seen anything and turned at the sound of his name spoken by a woman's voice.

Roberta Marieschi was about thirty-five, tall, erect, and very pretty; she stood at a bookcase that covered one wall of the office, slipping a thick volume back into its place. 'Excuse me, Signor Brunetti,' she said. 'I'm sorry to have kept you waiting.' She came over to him, hand extended, and greeted his own outstretched hand with a firm grasp. Turning to the desk, she said, 'Please, have a seat.' The secretary left.

He studied the lawyer as she walked behind the desk and sat down. She was a bit shorter than he, but her athletic slimness made her look taller than she was. Her suit was dark grey raw silk, the skirt coming to just below the knee. She wore simple black leather shoes with a low heel, shoes for the office or shoes for walking. Her skin was lightly tanned, just enough to give a glow of health but not so much as to suggest that the next step would be leather. No single feature of her face called for special attention, but the composite did: brown eyes, thick lashes, lips full and soft.

'You said you had some questions about inheritance, Signor Brunetti?' she said, but before he could confirm this, she surprised him by saying, her voice filled with patient exasperation, 'Oh, stop that.'

He had been looking at the papers on her desk, and when he glanced up at her, she had disappeared, or at least her head had disappeared. At the same moment, the light brown thing appeared from under the desk, something between a frond and a fan, and began to move slowly from side to side.

'Poppi, I told you to stop that,' the lawyer's voice came from under the desk.

Uncertain what to do, Brunetti remained where he was and watched the dog's tail wag back and forth. After what seemed a long time, Avvocatessa Marieschi's head, her dark hair ruffled, re-emerged, and she said, 'I'm sorry. I usually don't bring her to the office, but I just got back from vacation, and she's angry with me for having left her alone.' She pushed her chair back and spoke to the dog. 'Isn't that right, Poppi? You're sulking and punishing me by trying to eat my shoe?'

The dog shifted around under the desk, and after Brunetti heard it flop on to the floor, a considerably greater length of tail emerged. The lawyer looked at him, smiled, perhaps even blushed, and said, 'I hope you don't mind dogs.'

'No, not at all. I like them quite a lot.'

A low growl sounded in response to his voice, and she bent down again and said, 'Come out of there, you fake. Come out and see there's nothing to be jealous about.' She reached under the desk, then lower, and then leaned back in her chair.

Slowly there emerged from beneath the desk the head and then the body of the most beautiful dog Brunetti had ever seen. Poppi was a golden retriever, and even though he knew this was the current fashionable dog, nothing could prevent his admiration. Tongue lolling from her mouth, Poppi had broad-spaced eyes that had only to turn their gaze on Brunetti to conquer him. She stood as high as the lawyer's chair, and as he watched, she laid her head in her owner's lap and gazed up at her with adoration.

'I hope you really do like dogs, Signor Brunetti, because if you don't, this is a very embarrassing situation,' the lawyer said. Unable to resist the automatic response, she put a hand on the dog's head and began to pull gently at her left ear.

'She's beautiful,' Brunetti said.

'Yes, she is,' Avvocatessa Marieschi said. 'And she's just as sweet tempered as she is beautiful.' Still busy with the dog's ear, she said, looking at Brunetti, 'But you didn't come here to listen to me talk about my dog, I know. Could you tell me what I can help you with?'

'Actually, I'm not sure your secretary understood me properly yesterday, Avvocatessa. I'm not a client, though there is something you can help me with.'

Smiling, her hand still busy with Poppi's ear, she said, 'I'm afraid I don't understand.'

'I'm a commissario of police, and I'm here to ask you some questions about one of your clients, Signora Maria Battestini.'

Poppi's lips pulled back and, turning to look at Brunetti, she made a deep rumbling noise, but her owner's voice drowned out the growl as she bent down over the dog's head and said, 'Did I pull your ear too hard, angel?' Briskly, she moved the dog's head aside with her hand and said, 'All right, back down you go. I've got to work.'

With no resistance at all, the dog disappeared under the desk, moved around a bit, and then flopped down, presenting Brunetti with another view of her tail.

'Maria Battestini,' the lawyer said. 'Terrible, terrible. I found that woman for her. I interviewed her and took her over and introduced her to Maria. Ever since I heard, I've felt responsible.' Her lips disappeared as she pulled them tight from inside, a gesture Brunetti recognized as one that often preceded tears.

Hoping to avert that, he said, 'You're hardly responsible, Avvocatessa. The police let her into the country, and the Ufficio Stranieri gave her a *permesso di soggiorno*. It would seem to me that, if anyone is responsible, it is the officials, not you.'

'But I'd known Maria so long, almost all my life.'

'How is that, Dottoressa?'

'My father was her lawyer, her and her husband's lawyer, and so I knew her ever since I was a little girl, and then when I finished university and came to work for my father, she asked if I could be her lawyer. I think she was my first client, that is, the first one who was willing to trust me as a lawyer.'

'And what did that entail, Dottoressa?' Brunetti asked.

'I'm afraid I don't understand,' she said, but she was talking now and not getting ready to cry.

'With what sort of things did she trust you?'

'Oh, nothing really, not then. A cousin had left her husband an apartment on the Lido, and some years after his death, when she wanted to sell it, there was a dispute about ownership of the garden.'

'Disputed ownership of property,' he said, rolling his eyes towards heaven, as if he could think of no crueller fate. 'Was that the only problem she had?'

She started to speak but stopped herself. 'Before I answer any more questions, Commissario, could you tell me why you're asking them?'

'Of course,' he agreed with an easy smile, recalling that she was a lawyer. 'It would seem that the crime has been solved, and we want to close the case formally, but before we do that we would like to exclude any other possibility.'

'What does that mean, "other possibility"?'

'That there might have been someone else responsible for the crime.'

'But I thought the Romanian woman . . .' she began, and then sighed. 'I honestly don't know whether to be happy or sad at the idea,' she finally admitted. 'If she didn't do it, then I can stop feeling so guilty about it.' She tried to smile, failed, and went on, 'But is there any reason why you, that is, the police, think that it might have been someone else?'

'No,' he said with the facility of the accomplished liar, 'not really.' Then, using Patta's favourite argument, he added, 'But in this climate of press suspicion of the police, we need to be as sure as we can be before we declare a case closed. The stronger the evidence, the less likely it is that the press will call our decisions into question.'

She nodded, understanding this. 'Yes, I see. Of course I'd like to help, but I don't really see any way I can.'

'You said you helped her with other problems. Could you tell me what they were?' When he saw her hesitation, he said, 'I think her death and the circumstances surrounding it, Dottoressa, allow you to speak to me without worrying about your responsibility to your client.'

She accepted his argument. 'There was her son, Paolo. He died five years ago, after a long illness. Maria was . . . she almost died from grief, I think, and she was incapable of doing anything for a long time afterwards. So I took care of the funeral for her and then of his estate, though that was all straightforward: everything went to her.'

Hearing her use the expression, 'a long illness', Brunetti realized how seldom he had ever heard anyone say that another person had died of cancer. It was always 'a long illness', 'a tumour', 'a terrible disease', or simply 'that disease'.

'How old was he when he died?'

'Forty, I think.'

The fact that his estate passed to his mother presumably

meant he was not married, so Brunetti asked only, 'Did he live with her?'

'Yes. He was devoted to her.'

Brunetti's language receptors filed that one in with 'a long illness', and he made no comment.

'Are you at liberty to reveal the contents of her will?' he asked, changing the subject.

'It was all completely standard,' she said. 'Her only living relative is a niece, Graziella Simionato: she inherited everything.'

'Was it a large estate?' he asked.

'Not particularly. There was the house in Cannaregio, another one on the Lido, and some money Maria had invested at the Uni Credit.'

'Have you any idea how much?'

'I'm not sure of the exact amount, but it's about ten million,' she said, then immediately corrected herself, 'old lire, that is. I still think in lire and have to translate.'

'I suppose we all still do,' Brunetti confessed, then added, 'One final thing, about this matter of the television. Can you tell me anything about that?'

She smiled and shook her head. 'I know, I know. I received a number of letters from people in the neighbourhood, complaining about the volume. Every time I'd get one, I'd go by and talk to Maria and she'd promise to keep the volume down, but she was old and she'd forget, or she'd fall asleep with it on.' She raised her shoulders in a sigh of resignation. 'I don't think there was any solution, not really.'

'Someone told us the Romanian woman kept the volume turned down,' he said.

'She also murdered her,' the lawyer shot back with real anger.

Brunetti nodded in acknowledgement and acceptance of the reprimand. 'I'm sorry,' he said, 'my remark was thoughtless.' Then, 'Could you give me the address of the niece?'

'My secretary has it,' Marieschi said in a voice that had suddenly grown cooler. 'I'll come with you and ask her to give it to you.'

That seemed to leave Brunetti no option but to leave, so he got to his feet and leaned towards the desk. 'Thank you for your time, Dottoressa. I hope none of my questions has disturbed you.'

She tried to smile and said in a lighter voice, 'If you had, Poppi would know it and wouldn't be asleep like a baby down there.' A sweep of the tail possibly belied the statement that Poppi was asleep, and Brunetti found himself distracted by the question of whether Chiara, if he told her about this scene, would ask if this were a sleeping-dog-lie.

He held the door open for the lawyer, waited while the secretary wrote down the address of Signora Battestini's niece, thanked them both, shook hands with the lawyer, and left.

11

To walk back to the Questura along the Riva degli Schiavoni at this hour would have melted him, so he cut back into Castello in the direction of the Arsenale. As he passed in front of it, he wondered, as he usually did whenever he looked at the statues, whether the men who had carved them had ever seen a real lion. One of them bore a greater resemblance to Poppi than it did to any lion he had ever seen.

The water in the canal in front of the church of San Martino was exceptionally low, and Brunetti paused to glance down into it. The slopes of viscous mud on either side gleamed in the sunlight, and the stench of corruption rose towards him. Who knew the last time the canal had been dredged and cleaned?

When he got to his office, the first thing he did was to open the window to let some air into the room, but what came in seemed only to bring humidity and made no difference to the temperature. He left the window open in the hope that some passing zephyr would find it and slip through it. He hung up his jacket and took a look at the papers on his desk, though he knew Signorina Elettra would never leave anything on his desk save the most innocuous material that could be read by anyone. The rest would be kept in her desk or, more securely still, in her computer.

On the boat going down to Castello that morning, the *Gazzettino* had informed him that the judge in the airport case had ruled that the tapes from the hidden cameras in the baggage hall did indeed constitute an invasion of the privacy of the baggage handlers under accusation and thus the videos could not be produced as evidence against them. Reading the story, Brunetti had been swept by the absurd desire to go into the Questura, collect all of the witness statements that had been carefully accumulated during recent months and carry them off to the paper garbage drop at the Scuola Barbarigo. Or even more dramatically, he pictured a funeral pyre on the dock of the Questura, with blackened scraps of carbonized paper carried up into the air by those same reluctant zephyrs he had been wishing for.

He knew what would happen: the judge's ruling would be appealed, and then the whole thing would start again and drag on and on, rulings and counter-rulings until the statute of limitations expired and the whole thing was sent to the archives. His career had been spent watching this same slow gavotte: so long as the music could be played slowly enough, with frequent pauses to change the members of the orchestra, then sooner or later people would get so tired of listening to the same old tune that, when time was called and it stopped, no one would notice.

It was reflections such as these, he realized, that made it sometimes difficult for him to listen to Paola's criticism of the police. He knew that the justification for the judicial system under which he worked was that the endless appeal process guaranteed the safety of the accused from false conviction, but as years passed and those guarantees became broader and stronger and more encompassing,

Brunetti began to wonder just whose safety the law was guaranteeing.

He shook himself free of these thoughts and went downstairs in search of Vianello. The inspector was at his desk, talking on the phone. When he saw Brunetti come in, he held up an outspread palm to indicate he would be at least five minutes and then raised his index finger in the general direction of Brunetti's office to show he would come up when he was finished.

Upstairs Brunetti found his office somewhat cooler than when he had first arrived. To pass the time until Vianello came up, he pulled some papers from his in-tray and began to read through them.

It was fifteen, not five, minutes before Vianello came up. He sat and, without preamble, said, 'She was a vicious old cow, and I couldn't find anyone who cared in the slightest that she's dead.' He paused, as if hearing what he had just said, and added, 'I wonder what's on her headstone – "Beloved wife"? "Beloved mother"?'

'I think the inscriptions are usually longer,' Brunetti observed. 'The carvers get paid by the letter.' Then, more to the point, he asked, 'Whom did you speak to and what else did you learn?'

'We stopped in two of the bars and had a drink. Nadia said she used to live over there. She didn't, but a cousin of hers did, and she used to visit her when they were kids, so she knew some names and could talk about a few of the stores that have gone out of business, so people believed her.

'In fact, she didn't even have to ask about the murder: people were eager to tell her. Biggest thing that's happened over there since the floods in '66.' Reading Brunetti's expression, he became less discursive. 'There was general agreement that she was greedy, troublesome and stupid, but invariably someone would remind everyone that she was a widow whose only son had died, and people would pull themselves up short and say that she really wasn't that bad. Though I suspect she was. We talked about her in the bars and then with the waitress at the restaurant, who lives around the corner from her, and there wasn't one person who had a good word to say about her. In fact, enough time has passed for there even to be a little bit of sympathy for the Romanian woman: one woman said she was surprised it took so long for one of the women to kill her.' Vianello considered this, then added, 'It's almost as if the residual sympathy she earned for the death of her son, well, a small part of it, has passed to Signora Ghiorghiu.'

'And the son? What did they say about him?' Brunetti asked.

'No one had much of anything to say. He was quiet, lived with her, went to work, minded his own business, never caused anyone any trouble. It's almost as if he didn't have a real existence and was only a means to enable people to feel sorry for her. His dying, that is.'

'And the husband?'

'The usual stuff; "*una brava persona*".' But then Vianello warned, 'That might just be amnesia talking.'

'Did anyone say anything about the other women who worked for her in the past?'

'No, not much. They came and cleaned or bought her food and cooked, but the Romanian was the first one who lived there with her.' Vianello paused, then added, 'My guess is that the others didn't have papers and didn't want to become known in the neighbourhood for fear that someone would report them.'

'Did she have much contact with her neighbours? The old woman, that is,' Brunetti asked.

'Not for the last few years, especially since her son died. She could still get up and down the steps until about three years ago, when she had a fall and did something to her knee. After that, it looks like she didn't go out again. And by then any friends she'd had in the neighbourhood were gone, either died or moved away, and she'd caused so much trouble that no one wanted anything to do with her.'

'What sort of trouble?'

'Leaving bars without paying, complaining that the fruit wasn't good enough or fresh enough, buying something and using it and then trying to take it back to the store: all the things that make people refuse to serve you. I'm told there was a period when she threw her garbage out the window, but then someone called the police, and they went in and talked to her, and she stopped. But the main complaint was the television.'

'Did anyone say they'd ever met her lawyer?'

Vianello thought about this for a moment, then shook his head and said, 'No, no one ever met her, but a few people said that they'd written to her, especially about the television.'

'And?'

'No one ever received an answer.'

That didn't surprise Brunetti: until a case was brought against the old woman, the lawyer would not be legally involved in the private behaviour of her client. But her refusal to respond to these complaints seemed at odds with Avvocatessa Marieschi's assertions of regard and concern for Signora Battestini. Then again, a lawyer did not write a letter and then not charge for doing it.

'And the day she was killed?'

'Nothing. One man thinks he remembers seeing the Romanian come out of the house, but he wouldn't swear to it.'

'What was he uncertain about, that it was the Romanian or that she was coming out of that house?'

'I don't know. As soon as I showed any interest in what he was saying, he clammed up.' Throwing up his hands, Vianello admitted, 'I know it's not a lot, but I don't think there's much else to be got by asking around.'

'That's nothing new, is it?' Brunetti asked, making no attempt to disguise his disappointment.

Vianello shrugged. 'You know what it's like. No one seems to remember much about the son; they all disliked her, and since the husband's been dead for a decade, all anyone can say is that he was *una brava persona*, how he liked to have a drink with his friends, and how they didn't understand how he could stay married to a woman like that.'

Would people say the same things about him after he died? Brunetti wondered.

'What about you?' Vianello asked.

Brunetti told him about his conversation with the lawyer, not omitting mention of the dog.

'Did you ask her about the bank accounts?' Vianello asked.

'No. She said that Signora Battestini had about five thousand Euros at the Uni Credit. I didn't want to ask about the other accounts until we know something more about them.'

As if the thought were mother to the deed, Signorina Elettra chose that moment to appear in the doorway. She wore a green skirt and a white blouse, and at her neck she had a necklace of large cylindrical amber beads. As she came towards them, the sun fell on the necklace, turning the beads a flaming red and in the process bedecking her in the colours of the flag, as if she were a walking personification of civic virtue. Coming closer, she passed out of the sunlight and turned again into herself. She held out a folder and put it on his desk.

Pointing to it, she said with appealing self-effacement, 'It turned out to be easier than I thought, sir.'

'And Deutsche Bank?' Vianello asked.

She shook her head in stern disapproval. 'It was so easy you could have done it, Ispettore,' she said by way of explanation and then added with even greater asperity, 'I think it's all this Europeanization: in the past, German banks were reliable; now it's as if they go home in the afternoon and leave the door open. I tremble at the thought of what will happen to the Swiss if they join Europe.'

Brunetti, unimpressed by her concern for the financial security of the continent, asked, 'And?'

'They were all opened the year before the husband died,' she explained, 'over a period of three days, each with an initial deposit of half a million lire. Ever since then, deposits of a hundred thousand lire were made every month into each account, except for the period right after the son died, when no deposits were made.' She smiled at their response to this and went on. 'But that was made up for when they began again after two months.' She left them to consider all this for a moment before adding, 'The last deposits – normal deposits, I suppose one could call them – were made at the beginning of July, bringing the total in the accounts, with interest, to almost thirty thousand Euros. But no deposits were made this month.'

All three of them considered the meaning of this, but it was Brunetti who gave voice to it. 'So the need for the payments died with her.'

'So it would seem,' agreed Signorina Elettra, and then added, 'But the strange thing is that the money was never touched: it sat there, just gathering interest.' She opened the file and, holding it so that both men could see the figures, said, 'Those are the totals in the accounts. They were all in her name.'

'What happened to them when she died?' Brunetti asked.

'She died on a Friday; on Monday all of it was transferred to the Channel Islands,' she said, and then added a suggestive, 'and . . .' that successfully captured the attention of both men before she continued, 'though no name is given for the person authorizing the transfers, all of the banks have powers of attorney on file in the names of both Roberta Marieschi and Graziella Simionato.'

'I asked Marieschi this morning how much money Signora Battestini had left, but all she mentioned was an account at the Uni Credit with about ten million lire.'

'Taxes?' Vianello gave voice to the obvious. By moving the accounts instantly out of the country and then trusting to general bureaucratic incompetence, it was not unlikely that the transfer would pass unobserved by the tax authorities, especially if they were in different banks.

'And the niece?' Brunetti asked.

'I've begun that,' was all she answered.

'It's more than sixty million,' Vianello said, like most people, still calculating in old lire.

'A nice sum to be in the hands of a widow who lived in three rooms,' Signorina Elettra commented, not that this needed to be said.

'And a nice sum to slip past the hands of the taxman,' Vianello added, not without audible admiration. Looking at Signorina Elettra, he asked, 'But can that be done?'

It was impossible for Brunetti to observe her tilted chin and expression of fierce concentration without wondering if there existed limits to her familiarity with the unlawful. Certainly years of employment in the national bank would be superb preparation, but he feared her craft had been raised to new heights by her years at the Questura.

Like Santa Caterina returning from contemplation of the Divine Presence, Signorina Elettra left the world of theoretical malfeasance behind and came back to Brunetti and Vianello. 'Yes,' she declared, 'if whoever did it counted on incompetence at the *Finanza* and played the odds that the transfer wouldn't be noticed, then it would be easy enough, I think.' Vianello and Brunetti began to calculate the odds of this until Signorina Elettra interrupted them by asking, 'But why would she leave the money there and never touch it?'

Brunetti, who had read Balzac's descriptions of the cunning and avidity of peasants, had no doubts about this.

'To watch it accumulate,' he said. Vianello's past did not include much in the way of French novels, but he had spent time in the countryside and instantly recognized the truth of this.

'I was up in the attic, and I saw the things she kept,' Brunetti said, remembering a pair of felt slippers so worn that not even Caritas would have dared to offer them to the poor and tea towels with tattered edges and worn-in stains. 'She'd have enjoyed looking at the numbers and watching them grow, believe me.'

'But where are the original records?' Vianello asked.

'Who packed up the apartment?' countered Brunetti.

'The niece inherited, so it would have been her job,' Signorina Elettra supplied. 'But it would be easy enough for the dead woman's lawyer to go into the apartment before that and take them.' Then, as an afterthought, she added, 'Or her killer.'

'Or they could have been what the killer was looking for,' Vianello said. His face brightened and he suggested, 'But we have the computer records if we ever want proof.'

Like Lachesis and Atropos, turning their blind eyes to an errant Clotho, Brunetti and Signorina Elettra turned and stared at Vianello. 'The government has seen to that, Ispettore,' Signorina Elettra said with a voice that stopped just short of reproach, as though he were responsible for the law that stipulated that only original bank records, not photocopies and not computer records, could be introduced as evidence.

Did Brunetti see the inspector blush? 'I hadn't thought,' Vianello confessed, realizing instantly that the information would have legal weight only when and if bank officials produced the original records of accounts that had slept unobserved for more than a decade, until their mysterious flight to a tax haven so famous as surely to be known even to a lawyer in a sleepy provincial town such as Venice.

Brunetti moved them away from finance and asked, 'The husband? Did you find anything?'

'Nothing very interesting,' she said. 'He was born here, in 1925, and died at the Ospedale Civile in January of 1993. Lung cancer. For thirty-two years he worked in various city offices, lastly at the schools department – specifically, the personnel office, than which I can imagine no greater tedium. His son worked for the school board, too, until his death five years ago. They overlapped there for a few years.'

'Anything else?' Brunetti asked, amazed that a man could spend three decades and more working in the city bureaucracy and, at the end, have only these few facts to show for it.

'That's all I can find, sir. It's very difficult to find anything from more than ten years ago: they haven't got around to computerizing those records yet.'

'When will they?' Vianello asked.

Signorina Elettra's shrug was so strong that it caused the amber beads to click together as though they, too, wanted to tsk away the very idea.

12

Brunetti refused to see this as an impasse. Turning to Vianello, he said, 'There should still be people working in the office who would remember them. I'd like you to go over and see if there are and what they can remember.'

Vianello's expression showed how unlikely he thought this, but he voiced no objection.

Signorina Elettra said she still had work to do in her office and left the room with the inspector.

Brunetti, thinking it unfair to ask them to work on this while he sat at his desk, picked up the file and found the name of Signora Battestini's doctor. His call was transferred to the doctor's *telefonino*, and when he answered, the doctor told him that he could talk to Brunetti in his *ambulatorio* either before or after he saw his afternoon patients. Convinced that it would be wiser to speak to the doctor before he had spent two hours listening to and tending to his patients, Brunetti said that three-thirty would be fine, asked where the office was, and hung up. That done, he dialled the number of Signora Battestini's niece, but no one answered.

There was to be no weekly staff meeting that day, a fact explained by the weather. During summer months, the meetings, which Vice-Questore Patta had initiated some years ago, were often either suddenly cancelled or postponed and then eventually cancelled, depending upon the weather. Sun cancelled the meeting instantly, thus allowing the Vice-Questore to have a swim before lunch as well as in the late afternoon. On rainy days, the meetings were held, though a sudden improvement in the weather often led to their postponement, and one of the police launches would take the Vice-Questore across the Bacino to his undoubtedly well-earned relaxation. Thus the staff conference became another of the secrets of the Questura, like the door to a cabinet that had to be kicked at the bottom before it would open. Brunetti envisioned himself and his colleagues as not unlike augurs, whose impulse, before planning or accepting any engage-ment, was first to consult the heavens. Brunetti thought it much to their credit that they could so seamlessly adjust their schedules to the vagaries of the Vice-Questore's.

At home, where he took himself for lunch, he arrived just as the family was sitting down. Paola, he noticed, had the lean and hungry look she often had after a bad day at the university, though the children were far too concerned with sating their hunger to pay much attention.

There was, the setting of plates on the table suggested, to be no first course, but before he could protest at this omission, however mildly, Paola appeared, holding an immense bowl from which rose fumes so fragrant as to soothe his soul. Before his powers of prediction could name the dish, Chiara cried with undisguised glee, 'Oh, *Mamma*, you made the lamb stew.'

'Is there polenta?' Raffi asked, his voice poignant with hope.

When he saw the smile that spread over Paola's face at the sound of their avidity, Brunetti thought of baby birds and the way their chirping forced their parents to behave in genetically determined ways. Paola offered only token resistance to that instinct by saying, 'Just as there has been each of the six hundred times we've eaten this, Raffi, yes, there is polenta,' but Brunetti could hear that her heart was in the tone and not the words.

'*Mamma*,' Chiara offered, 'if there are fresh figs for dessert, I'll do the dishes.'

'You have the soul of a merchant,' Paola said, setting down the bowl and going back into the kitchen to get the polenta.

Indeed there were figs, and with them *esse*, the S-shaped biscuits that a friend of Paola's father still sent them from Burano. And after that, Brunetti had no choice but to repair to bed to sleep for an hour.

When he woke, dry-mouthed and sweating in the stifling heat, he was conscious of Paola beside him. Because she never slept in the afternoon, he knew before he opened his eyes that she would be lying with her head on the pillow, reading. He turned his head and was proven right.

Recognizing the book, he asked, 'Are you still reading the catechism?'

'Yes,' she said, not removing her eyes from the page. 'I'm reading a chapter a day, though it's not called a catechism any more.'

Rather than inquire as to its new title, Brunetti asked, instead, 'And where are you now?'

'On the Sacraments.'

By rote, the words swam up from his youth: 'Baptism, communion, confirmation, marriage, ordination, confession . . .' and then his voice trailed off. 'There's seven of them, aren't there?' he asked.

'Yes.'

'What's the seventh? I can't remember. It's just gone.' As happened every time he failed to remember something simple and ordinary, he had a moment's panic that this was the same beginning no one had wanted to recognize in his mother.

'Extreme unction,' Paola said, glancing aside at him. 'Perhaps the most subtle of them all.'

Brunetti failed to understand what she meant and asked, 'Why "subtle"?'

'Think about it, Guido. Just at the time a person is approaching death, usually when it's generally agreed that there is little or no hope, the priest arrives.'

'Yes. Exactly. But I still don't understand why that's so subtle.'

'Think about it. In the past, the only people who could read and write were priests.'

Because he was hot and thirsty and because he usually woke up cranky if he slept in the afternoon, Brunetti said, 'Isn't that a bit of an exaggeration?'

'Yes, all right. It is. But priests could, and most people could not, at least not until the last century.'

'I still don't see where you're going with all of this,' he said.

'Think eschatologically, Guido,' she enjoined, further confusing him.

'I strive to do so every moment of every day,' he said, having forgotten the meaning of the word but already regretting that he'd snapped at her.

'Death, judgement, heaven and hell,' she said. 'Those are the four last things. And at the point when people are about to encounter the first and know they cannot escape the second, they start to think about the third and the fourth. And there is the priest, all too ready to talk about the fires of hell and the joys of heaven, though I've always been of a mind that people are far more concerned with avoiding the former than with experiencing the latter.'

He lay still, beginning to suspect where this was going.

'So there he was, the local priest – who incidentally often happened to be the notary – and then he no doubt started to talk about the fires of hell that would consume a person in the flesh, unspeakable pain to be prolonged for all eternity.'

She could have been an actress, he thought, so powerfully was her voice a testament to belief in every word she spoke.

'But there exists a way for the good Christian to achieve forgiveness,' switching to the present tense, she went on in her most syrupy voice, 'to free themselves from the fires of hell. Yes, my son, you have but to open your heart to the love of Jesus, your purse to the needs of the poor. You have but to put your name or, if you cannot write, your mark on this paper, and in exchange for your generosity to Holy Mother Church, the gates of heaven themselves will swing open to receive you.'

She let the book fall open on her chest and turned to face him. 'So the last-minute will was signed, leaving this or that, or everything, to the Church.' Her voice turned savage. 'Of course they wanted to get in there when they were sick or dying or out of their minds. What better time to suck them dry?'

She picked the book up again, turned a page, and said in an entirely conversational tone, 'That's why it is the most subtle.'

'Do you say these things to Chiara?' asked an appalled Brunetti.

She turned to him again. 'Of course not. Either she'll realize these things when she's older, or she won't. Please don't forget that I agreed never to interfere in the religious education of the children.'

'And if she doesn't realize these things?' he asked, quotation marks of emphasis around the last three words and expecting Paola to say that she would then be disappointed in her daughter.

'Then her life will probably be a lot more peaceful,' Paola said and returned her attention to the catechism.

*

Dottor Carlotti's *ambulatorio* was on the ground floor of a house in Calle Stella, not far from Fondamente Nuove. Brunetti had found the address in his *Calli, Canali, e Campielli* and recognized it when he saw two women with small children in their arms standing outside the door to the building. Brunetti smiled at the mothers and rang the bell to the right of the door. A grey-haired man of middle age answered, asking, 'Commissario Brunetti?'

When Brunetti nodded, the doctor put out his hand and, half shaking, half pulling, brought Brunetti into the building. He pointed to the door to his office, then stepped outside the door and invited the two women in, explaining that he would be busy for a time and asking them to come into the waiting room where they could at least escape the heat. He led Brunetti through the room so quickly that all Brunetti was aware of was the usual glossy-covered magazines and furniture that looked as if it had been taken from some relative's parlour.

The office was a copy of all the doctors' offices Brunetti had passed through in his life: the paper-covered examining table, the glass-topped counter holding packets of gauze-wrapped bandages, the desk covered with papers and files and boxes of medicine. The single difference from the offices of the doctors of his youth was the computer, which stood to the right of the desk.

He was an invisible man, Dottor Carlotti: look at him once, indeed, look at him five times, and the memory would register nothing save brown eyes behind dark-framed glasses, dry hair of an indeterminate colour retreating from the forehead, and a mouth of average size.

The doctor leaned back against his desk, arms folded, and waved Brunetti towards a chair. But then, as though he realized how unwelcoming his posture was, he went and sat behind his desk. He moved aside some papers, shifted a tube of something to the left, and folded his hands in front of him.

'How may I help you, Commissario?' the doctor asked.

'By telling me about Maria Battestini,' Brunetti began without introduction. 'You found her, didn't you, Dottore?'

Carlotti looked at the surface of his desk, then across at Brunetti. 'Yes. I ordinarily went to see her once a week.'

When it seemed the doctor was going to say nothing more, Brunetti asked, 'Was there an ongoing condition you were treating, Dottore?'

'No, no, nothing like that. She was as healthy as I am, perhaps even more so. Except for her knees.' Then he surprised Brunetti by saying, 'But you probably know that already, if it was Rizzardi who did the autopsy. Probably know more about her health than I do.'

'You know him?'

'Not really. We belong to the same medical associations, so I've spoken to him at dinners or at meetings. But I know his reputation. That's why I say you'd know more about her state of health than I do.' His smile was shy for a man Brunetti guessed must be well into his forties.

Brunetti said, 'Yes, he did the autopsy, and he told me exactly what you've said, that she was extraordinarily healthy for a woman her age.'

The doctor nodded, as if pleased that his opinion of Rizzardi's skill had been confirmed. 'Did he say what killed her?' Carlotti asked. Brunetti was surprised that anyone who had seen the woman's body could ask the question.

'He said it was trauma of the blows to her head.'

Again that nod, again a diagnosis confirmed.

Brunetti took out his notebook and opened it to the pages where he'd made some notes of what Signora Gismondi had told him.

'How long was she a patient of yours, Dottore?'

Carlotti's response was immediate. 'Five years, ever since the death of her son. She insisted that the doctor they both went to was responsible for his death, so she refused to go to him after the son died and asked to join my practice.' He said it with a hint of regret.

'And was there any basis to her claim that this other doctor was responsible?'

'It's nonsense. He died of AIDS.'

Suppressing his surprise, Brunetti asked, 'Did she know this?'

'Better to ask if she believed it, Commissario, because she didn't believe it. But she must have known it.' Neither found this difficult to make sense of.

'Was he gay?'

'Not publicly and not to the knowledge of my colleague, though that doesn't necessarily mean that he was not. Nor was he a haemophiliac, nor a drug user, and he'd never had a transfusion, at least not that he could remember or the hospital had any record of.'

'You tried to find out?'

'My colleague did. Signora Battestini accused him of criminal negligence, and he tried to protect himself by finding out the source of the infection. He also wanted to know if there was any chance of Paolo's having passed it on, but she refused to answer any questions about him, even when someone from the Public Health went to talk to her. When she became my patient, she said only that he had been murdered by the "doctors". I made it clear I would not listen to such things and suggested she find another doctor. So she stopped saying it, at least she stopped saying it to me.'

'And you never heard anything that suggested he might be gay?'

Carlotti shrugged. 'People talk. All the time. I've learned not to pay much attention to it. Some people seemed to believe he was, others not. I didn't care, so they stopped talking about him to me.' He glanced at Brunetti. 'So I don't know. My colleague believes he was, but that's because there seems no other way to explain his having the disease. But I repeat: I never met him, so I don't know.'

Brunetti left it there and asked, 'About Signora Battestini, then, Dottore. Is there anything you could tell me that might explain why someone would do this to her?'

The doctor pushed his chair back and stuck his legs out, unusually long legs in a man so much shorter than Brunetti. He crossed his ankles and scratched the back of his head with his left hand. 'No, not really. I've been thinking about this since you called, in fact, since I found her, but I can't think of anything. She was a person of a certain character . . .' the doctor began, but before he could continue with this platitude, Brunetti interrupted him.

'Please, Dottore. I've spent my life listening to people speak well of the dead or find ways to avoid speaking the truth about them. So I know about "a certain character", and I know about "difficult", and I know about "wilful". I'd like you to remember that this is a murder investigation, and because it is, Signora Battestini is far beyond any harm your words might do to her. So could you please forget politeness and tell me honestly about her and about why someone might want to kill her?'

Carlotti grinned at this, then glanced towards the door to the waiting room, from which the voices of the two women could be heard speaking in soft, nervous voices. 'I suppose it's a habit we all have, doctors especially, always afraid we'll be caught saying something we ought not to say about a patient, caught telling the truth.'

At Brunetti's nod, he went on. 'She was a nasty old shrew, and I never heard a good word said about her.'

'Nasty in what way, Dottore?' Brunetti asked.

The doctor considered before answering, as though he'd never stopped to think about why this woman was nasty or in what particular ways she was. His hand moved to his head and went back to scratching at the same spot. Finally he looked at Brunetti and said, 'Maybe all I can do is give you examples. Like the women who worked for her. She never stopped complaining about them or telling me, or them, that the things they did weren't done the right way. They used too much coffee to make her coffee, or they left lights on, or they should wash the dishes in cold water, not hot. If they tried to defend themselves, she'd scream at them, telling them they could go back where they came from.'

There was a cry from one of the children in the waiting room, but it stopped. Carlotti went on. 'It doesn't sound like a lot, I realize now, when I hear myself saying it, but it was terrible for them. They were probably all illegal, the women, so they couldn't complain, and the last thing any of them wanted to do was go back to where they came from. And she knew it.'

'Did you know any of them, Dottore?'

'Know them how?' he asked.

'Speak to them about where they came from, about what they did before they came here.'

'No. She wouldn't let me, probably wouldn't let anyone. If the phone rang while I was there, she demanded to know who it was, made them hand over the phone. Even if their *telefonini* rang, she wanted to know who was calling them, told them they couldn't talk on the phone while she was paying them to work.'

'And the last one?'

'Flori?' the doctor asked.

'Yes.'

'Do you think she killed her?' Dottor Carlotti asked.

'Do you, Dottore?'

'I don't know. When I found her, the first thing I did was look for Flori's . . . for her body. It never occurred to me that she could have done it: the only possibility I could think of was that she might have been another victim.'

'And now, Dottore?'

The man seemed genuinely pained. 'I read the papers, and I spoke to that other officer, and everyone seems sure she did it.' Brunetti waited. 'But I still can't believe it.'

'Why is that?'

The doctor hesitated for a long time, glancing at Brunetti's face as if to see if this man who also spent his time with human weakness would understand. 'I've been a doctor for more than twenty years, Commissario, and it's part of my profession to notice things in people. It might seem as though all I need to pay attention to are physical things, but I've seen enough sick people to know that what's wrong with the soul is often also wrong with the body. And I'd say that there was nothing wrong with Flori's soul.' He looked away, looked back, and said, 'I'm afraid I can't be more precise or professional than that, Commissario.'

'And Signora Battestini? Do you think there was something wrong with her soul?'

'Nothing more than greed, Commissario,' Carlotti answered instantly. 'The ignorance and stupidity, they didn't come from the soul. But the greed did.'

'Many old people have to be careful with their money,' Brunetti suggested, playing devil's advocate.

'This wasn't being careful, Commissario. This was obsession.' Then he surprised Brunetti by slipping into Latin. ' "Radix malorum est Cupiditas". Not money, Commissario. That's not the root of all evil. It's the *love* of money. *Cupiditas*.'

'Did she have much money to be greedy about?' Brunetti asked.

'I've no idea,' the doctor answered. One of the children in the outer room began to cry, that high-pitched wail that cannot be faked. Carlotti looked at his watch. 'If you have no more questions, Commissario, I'd like to get on with seeing my patients.'

'Certainly,' Brunetti said, getting to his feet and returning his notebook to his pocket. 'You've been more than generous with your time.'

As they walked towards the door, Brunetti asked, 'Did Signora Battestini ever receive visitors while you were there?'

'No, no one ever came to see her that I can recall,' the doctor said. He stood still as he searched his memory. 'Once or twice, as I said, she'd get phone calls, but she'd always say she was busy and tell whoever it was to call back.'

'Did she speak Veneziano to these people, do you remember, Dottore, when she talked to them?'

'I don't remember,' Carlotti answered. 'Probably Veneziano. She'd almost forgotten how to speak Italian. Some of them do.' Then, for the sake of clarity, he added, 'At least I never heard her speak it.' He put his hand back to his head. 'Once, about three years ago, she was on the phone when I came in. I had a key by then, you see, and I could let myself in if she didn't hear the bell. The television was on – I could hear it down in the street — so I knew she wouldn't hear me if I did ring, so I didn't bother. I opened the door, but the sound had been lowered. The phone must have rung while I was coming up the steps, and she was talking to someone.' He paused for a moment, then added, 'I suppose that whoever it was had called her. She often said it cost too much to make phone calls. At any rate, she had turned the television down a bit and was talking to someone.'

Brunetti waited beside him, saying nothing, allowing him space and time for memory.

'She said something about having hoped to hear from the person, whoever it was, but her voice was ... oh, I don't know ... cruel or sarcastic or something between the two. And then she said goodbye and called the person something. I can't remember now what it was. *Dottore* maybe, or *Professore*, something like that, and because she used a title, you'd think she would have spoken respectfully, but it was just the opposite.' Brunetti watched him as he spoke, saw the memory take shape. 'Yes, it was *Dottore*, but she was speaking in Veneziano. I'm sure of that.'

When it was clear that the doctor had no more to say, Brunetti asked, 'Did you say anything about the conversation to her?'

'No, no, I didn't. In fact, the moment was so strange, perhaps because of her voice, or just some feeling I had about the way she was talking, that I stayed just outside the doorway and didn't go in. There was something so strange in the air that I pulled the door closed and then made a business of putting the key in the lock and making a lot of noise with it when I opened the door. And I called her name and asked her if she was there before I went in.'

'Could you explain why you did this?' Brunetti asked, puzzled that this seemingly practical man should have had such a strong reaction.

The doctor shook his head. 'No. It was just a feeling, something I picked up from the way she was speaking. I felt as though I'd come into the presence of . . . of something evil.'

The child's screams had intensified while they had been talking. The doctor opened the door. He put his head through the opening and said, 'Signora Ciapparelli, you can bring Piero in now.'

He stood back to let Brunetti leave and shook his hand; by the time Brunetti reached the door of the waiting room, the door to the office was closed and the child had stopped crying.

13

Back in his office, Brunetti dialled the number for Signorina Simionato, but again there was no answer. What puzzled him was the money in the four accounts. Not the total sum: many apparently poor people managed to accumulate hidden fortunes during long lives of daily privation: lira by lira, renunciation by renunciation, they amassed something to pass on to their relatives or to the Church. They must spend their lives counting, Brunetti realized, counting and saying no to anything that was not fundamentally necessary to physical survival. Pleasures went untasted, desires unheeded, as life passed by. Or worse, pleasure was transformed and could be had only by negation and the resultant accumulation, and desire was satisfied only by acquisition.

He'd observed this phenomenon sufficient times no longer to be surprised by it: what did surprise him was the sophistication of the money's removal from the banks and then from the country. The sophistication and the speed. The transfers had been made on the Monday after her death, long before any legal action could have been taken regarding the will. This suggested that one – or both – of the women had only to learn of Signora Battestini's death to make a move, and that in its turn suggested that the old woman had kept a close eye on the accounts and would have noticed any withdrawal when the monthly statements arrived.

He made a note to question the postman and check if the statements were delivered to her home. Though Brunetti had found no sign of them in the attic, four statements from different banks – five if he included her normal account at the Uni Credit – could certainly not have passed unobserved by even the most negligent of postmen.

In his youth, Brunetti had considered himself an intensely political man. He had joined and supported a party, rejoiced in its triumphs, convinced that its accession to power would bring his country closer to social justice. His disillusionment had not been swift, though it had been hastened by the presence of his wife, who had reached a state of political despair and black cynicism well before he allowed himself to follow her lead. He had denied, both in word and in belief, the first accusations of dishonesty and endemic corruption against the men he had been sure would lead the nation to a bright and just future. But then he had looked at the evidence against them, not as a true believer, but as a policeman, and his certainty of their guilt had been immediate.

Since then, he had stayed clear of politics entirely, bothering to vote only because to do so set an example for his children, not because he now believed it could make any difference. In the years during which his cynicism had grown, his former friendships with politicians had languished, and his dealings with them had become formal rather than cordial.

He tried to think of someone in the current administration whom he could trust and came up with no name. Shifting his attention to the magistracy, he did come up with one name, the judge in charge of the investigation into the environmental damage caused by the petrochemical complexes in Marghera. Not a young man, Judge Galvani was currently the object of a well-orchestrated campaign to force him into retirement.

Brunetti found his number in the list of city employees he had been issued some years ago and dialled it. A male secretary answered, said the judge was not available, then, when Brunetti informed him that it was a police matter, said he might be. When Brunetti said he was calling at the request of the Vice-Questore, the secretary admitted that the judge was there and transferred the call.

'Galvani,' a deep voice said.

'Dottore, this is Commissario Guido Brunetti. I'm calling to ask if you could spare some time to speak to me.'

'Brunetti?'

'Yes, sir.'

'I know your superior,' Judge Galvani surprised him by saying.

'Vice-Questore Patta, sir?' Brunetti asked.

'Yes. He seems to have no good opinion of you, Commissario.'

'That's unfortunate, sir, but I fear it's out of my control.'

'Indeed,' the judge answered. 'What would you like to talk to me about?'

'I'd prefer not to say that on the phone, sir.'

Brunetti had often read the phrase 'a pregnant pause' in novels. This seemed to be one. At last Galvani asked, 'When would you like to see me?'

'As soon as possible.'

'It's almost six,' Galvani said. 'I'll leave here in about half an hour. Shall we meet at that place on the Ponte delle Becarie?' he asked, describing an *enoteca* not far from the fish market. 'At six-thirty?'

'That's very kind of you, sir,' Brunetti said. 'I'm wearing . . .' he began but Galvani cut him off.

'I know who you are,' the judge said and replaced the phone.

When Brunetti walked into the bar, he recognized Judge Galvani instantly. The older man stood at the counter, a glass of white wine in front of him. Short, squat, dressed in a suit that was greasy at neck and cuffs, with the enlarged nose of the heavy drinker, Galvani looked like anything other than a judge: a butcher, perhaps, or a stevedore. But Brunetti knew that he had only to open his mouth and speak, in a beautifully modulated voice from which Italian flowed in the well-articulated consonants and vowels most actors only dream of pronouncing, for the real man to step forth from behind the physical disguise. Brunetti went to stand beside him and said, putting out his hand, 'Good evening, Dottore.'

Galvani's grip was firm, warm and brisk. 'Shall we try to find a place to sit?' he asked, turning towards the tables at the back of the room, most of them occupied at this hour. Just as he turned, three men got up from a table on the left, and Galvani headed for it quickly, Brunetti staying behind to order a glass of Chardonnay.

When he got to the table, Galvani was already seated, but he got halfway to his feet when Brunetti reached him. Though curious about the case against the petrochemical factories in Marghera, where two of his uncles had worked before dying of cancer, Brunetti said nothing, knowing that the judge could not and would not speak of it.

Galvani raised his glass to Brunetti, and took a sip. He set his glass down on the table and asked, 'Well?'

'It's connected with the woman who was murdered last month, Maria Battestini. It seems that, at her death, she had a number of bank accounts with a total of more than thirty thousand Euros on deposit. The accounts were opened about ten years ago, when both her husband and son worked for the school board, and deposits were made until she died.' Brunetti paused, picked up his glass but set it down untasted. He took the stem between thumb and forefinger and rotated it nervously. Galvani said nothing.

'I am of the opinion that the woman accused of the murder of Signora Battestini did not kill her,' Brunetti continued, 'though I do not have any physical evidence to offer in support of that belief. If she didn't kill her, then someone else did. So far the only anomaly in what we know about the dead woman is the existence of these bank accounts.' Again he paused, but still he did not taste the wine.

'And where do I come into this, if I might ask?' Galvani asked.

Brunetti glanced at the judge. 'The first thing we need to do is establish the source of these payments. Since both men worked at the school board, that's the first place I would like to look.'

Galvani nodded, and Brunetti continued. 'You've been on the bench for decades here, sir, and I know you've had reason during those years to examine the workings of some of the city bureaucracies,' Brunetti said, not a little proud of his delicacy in describing what the conservative press often described as Galvani's 'mad crusade' against city administrations. 'So I hoped you would have some familiarity with the school board and the way it works.' Galvani met this remark with a cool, appraising glance, and Brunetti added, 'Really works, that is.'

The judge's nod was minimal, but it was sufficient to encourage Brunetti to go on. 'Or if you could suggest some reason, or perhaps some person, that might be able to explain these payments. Or perhaps the existence of some irregularity that might be better left undetected.'

'"Irregularity?"' Galvani asked. At Brunetti's nod, the judge smiled. 'How elegantly you put it.'

'For want of a better word,' Brunetti explained.

'Of course,' the judge said, sat back in his chair, and smiled again. On a face so ugly, Galvani's smile was strangely sweet. 'I know very little about the school board, Commissario. Or, more accurately, I know but do not know, which seems to be the way most of us go through life: believing things because someone has hinted at them or suggested them, or because such an explanation is the only one that corresponds with other things we know.' He took another small sip from his glass and set it down.

'The school board, Commissario, is the equivalent of the dead-letter office for civil servants, or, if you prefer, the elephants' graveyard: the place where the hopelessly incompetent have always been sent or, on the other hand, a place to stick someone until a more lucrative position can be found for them. At least it was that way until four or five years ago, when even the administration of this city had to acknowledge that certain positions there should be given to professionals with some understanding of the way children can be helped to learn. Before that time, positions there served as political plums, though they were relatively small plums. And that was a reflection of how little . . . how can I say this without saying it? . . . how little opportunity there was for the people who worked there to augment their salaries.' It seemed to Brunetti that Galvani's phrasing was no less elegant than his own.

The judge raised his glass but set it down untouched. 'If you're thinking that Signora Battestini's bank accounts could have been created to receive bribes paid to her husband or son in connection with the place where they worked, I'd suggest you reconsider your hypothesis.' He sipped, set the glass down, and added, 'You see, Commissario, the accumulation of such a relatively small sum over such a long period hardly speaks of the sort of graft I'm used to encountering in this city.' Leaving no time for Brunetti to register the implications of this remark, the judge went on, 'But, as I said, it is a department in which I have never had to involve myself, so perhaps it is merely that things are done on a smaller scale there.' Again, that smile. 'And one must always keep in mind that corruption, like water, will always find a place, however insignificant, to collect.'

For an instant, Brunetti found himself wondering if his own basilisk-eyed observations on local government would sound so profoundly dark to someone less well versed in their workings than he. Turning from this reflection as well as from the opportunity to comment on the judge's remarks, Brunetti asked only, 'Do you know who was in charge of the department during those years?'

Galvani closed his eyes, propped his elbows on the table, and lowered his forehead on to his palms. He remained like that for at least a minute, and when he looked up and across at Brunetti, he said, 'Piero De Pra is dead; Renato Fedi now runs a construction firm in, I think, Mestre; and Luca Sardelli has some sort of job in the Assessorato dello Sport. To the best of my memory, they were the men who ran the office up until the professionals were brought in.' Brunetti thought he had finished, but then Galvani added, 'No one ever seems to stay in the job for more than a few years. As I said, it's either a dumping ground or a launching pad, though in the case of Sardelli, he certainly wasn't launched very far. But in either case, there seems to be very little to be had from the position.'

Brunetti made a note of the names. Two of them rang familiarly in his memory: De Pra because he had a nephew who had gone to school with Brunetti's brother and Fedi because he had recently been elected as a deputy in the European Parliament.

Brunetti resisted the temptation to pose other offices and names to the judge and said only, 'You've been very generous with your time, sir.'

Again, that childlike smile transformed the judge's face. 'I was glad to. I've wanted to meet you for some time, Commissario. It was my belief that anyone who provided so much discomfort to the Vice-Questore must be a man worth knowing.' Telling Brunetti that he had already paid for their wine, the judge excused himself by saying it was time he was home for dinner, said goodbye, and left.

14

Brunetti was at the *ufficio postale* at seven-thirty the next morning, located the person in charge of the postmen, showed his warrant card, and explained that he wanted to speak to the *postino* who delivered mail to the area in Cannaregio near the Palazzo del Cammello. She told him to go to the first floor and ask in the second room on the left, where the Cannaregio *postini* sorted their mail. The room was high-ceilinged, the entire space filled with long counters with sorting racks behind them. Ten or twelve people stood around, putting letters into slots or pulling them out and packing them into leather satchels.

He asked the first person he encountered, a long-haired woman with a strangely reddened complexion, where he could find the person who delivered the mail to the Canale della Misericordia area. She looked at him with open curiosity, then pointed to a man halfway along her table and called out, 'Mario, someone wants to talk to you.'

The man called Mario looked at them, then down at the letters in his hands. One by one, merely glancing at the names and addresses, he slipped them quickly into the slots in front of him then walked over to Brunetti. He was in his late thirties, Brunetti guessed, his own height but thinner, with light brown hair that fell in a thick wedge across his forehead.

Brunetti introduced himself and started to take his warrant card out again, but the *postino* stopped him with a gesture and suggested they talk over a coffee. They walked down to the bar, where Mario ordered two coffees and asked Brunetti what he could do for him.

'Did you deliver mail to Maria Battestini at Cannaregio . . .'

Mario cut him off by reciting the number of the house, then raised his hands as if in fake surrender. 'I wanted to, but I didn't do it. Believe me.'

The coffees came, and both men spooned sugar into them. While he stirred his, Brunetti asked, 'Was she that bad?'

Mario took a sip, put the cup down and stirred in a further half-spoonful of sugar, and said, still stirring, 'Yes.' He finished the coffee and set the cup back on the saucer. 'I delivered her mail for three years. I must have taken her, in that time, thirty or forty *raccomandate*, had to climb all those steps to get her to sign for them.'

Brunetti anticipated his anger at never having been tipped and waited for him to give voice to it, but the man simply said, 'I don't expect to be tipped, especially by old people, but she never even said thank you.'

'Isn't that a lot of registered mail?' Brunetti asked. 'How often did they come?'

'Once a month,' the postman answered. 'Regular as a Swiss watch. And it wasn't letters, but those padded envelopes, you know, the sort you send photos or CDs in.'

Or money, thought Brunetti, and asked, 'Do you remember who they came from?'

'There were a couple of addresses, I think,' Mario answered. 'They sounded like charity things, you know, Care and Share, and Child Aid. That sort of thing.'

'Can you remember any of them exactly?'

'I deliver mail to almost four hundred people,' he said by way of answer.

'Do you remember when they started?'

'Oh, she was getting them already when I started on that route.'

'Who had the route before you?' Brunetti asked.

'Nicolò Matucci, but he retired and went back to Sicily.'

Brunetti left the subject of the registered packages and asked, 'Did you bring her bank statements?'

'Yes, every month,' he said, and recited the names of the banks. 'Those and the bills were the only things she ever got, except for some other *raccomandate*.'

'Do you remember who those were from?'

'Most of them came from people in the neighbourhood, complaining about the television.' Before Brunetti could ask him how he knew this, Mario said, 'They all told me about them, wanted to be sure that the letters were delivered. Everyone heard it, that noise, but there was nothing they could do. She's old. That is, she was old, and the police wouldn't do anything. They're useless.' He looked up suddenly at Brunetti and said, 'Excuse me.'

Brunetti smiled and waved it away with an easy smile. 'No, you're right,' Brunetti went on, 'there's nothing we can do, not really. The person who complains can bring a case, but that means that people from some department – I don't know what its name is, but it takes care of complaints about noise – have to go in to measure the decibels of the noise to see if it's really something called "aural aggression", but they don't work at night, or if they get called at night, they don't come until the next morning, by which time whatever it was has been turned down.' Like all policemen in the city, he was familiar with the situation, and like them, he knew it had no solution.

'Did you ever bring her anything else?' Brunetti went on.

'At Christmas, some cards; occasionally – but I mean only once or twice a year – a letter, as well as the letters about the noise. But, aside from them, only bills and the statements from the banks.' Before Brunetti could comment, Mario said, 'It's pretty much like that for all old people. Their friends have died, and because they've always lived here, their family and friends are here, too, so there's never any reason to write. I bet some of the people I bring mail to are illiterate, anyway, and have their children take care of the bills for them. No, she wasn't much different from the other old people.'

'You pretended to think I thought you'd killed her,' Brunetti said as they drifted towards the door of the bar.

'No reason, really,' the *postino* said in response to Brunetti's unasked question, 'except that there were so many people who couldn't stand her.'

'But that's a stronger reaction than for her just not saying thank you,' Brunetti said.

'I didn't like the way she treated the women who worked for her, especially the one who killed her,' he said. 'She treated them like slaves, really, seemed happy if she could make one of them cry; I saw her manage that more than once.' Mario stopped at the entrance to the sorting room and put out his hand. Brunetti thanked him for his help, shook his hand, and went downstairs and out towards Rialto. He was almost at the front entrance when he heard his name called from behind and, turning, saw Mario walking towards him, his leather bag pulling heavily on his left shoulder, the young woman with the red face close behind him.

'Commissario,' he said, coming up to Brunetti and reaching behind to take the young woman by the arm and all but pull her forward. 'This is Cinzia Foresti. She had that route before Nicolò did, up until about five years ago. I thought maybe you'd like to talk to her, too.'

The young woman gave a nervous half-smile, and her face, if possible, grew even redder.

'You delivered to Signora Battestini?' Brunetti asked.

'And to the son,' answered Mario. He patted the young woman on the shoulder and said, 'I've got to get to work,' then continued walking towards the front door.

'As your colleague told you, Signorina,' Brunetti said, 'I'm curious about the mail that was delivered to Signora Battestini.' Seeing that she was reluctant to talk, perhaps from shyness, perhaps from fear, he added, 'Particularly about the bank statements that came every month.'

'About them?' she asked with what seemed like nervous relief.

Brunetti smiled. 'Yes, and about the *raccomandate* that used to come from the neighbours.'

Suddenly she asked, 'Am I allowed to talk to you about this? I mean, the mail is supposed to be private.'

He pulled out his warrant card and held it out for her to examine. 'Yes, Signorina, it is, but in a case like this, where the person is dead, you may speak about it.' He didn't want to overplay his hand and suggest that she was obliged to; besides, he wasn't sure if he could force her to speak to him without a court order.

She chose to believe him. 'Yes, I took her the things from the banks, every month. And I was on that route for three years.'

'Did you deliver anything else?'

'To her? No, not really. Occasionally a letter or a card. And the bills.'

Prompted by her question, he asked, 'And to the son?'

She shot him a nervous glance but said nothing. Brunetti waited. Finally she said, 'Bills, mainly. And sometimes letters.' After a very long pause, she added, 'And magazines.'

Sensing her growing uneasiness, he asked, 'Was there anything unusual about the magazines, Signorina? Or about the letters?'

She glanced around the vast open hall, moved a bit to the left to take them farther away from a man who was making a telephone call from the pay phone near the entrance, and said, 'I think they were about boys.'

This time there was no mistaking her nervousness: the blush set her face aflame.

'Boys? Do you mean little boys?'

She started to speak but then looked at her feet. From his greater height, he saw the top of her head shake in slow negation. He decided to wait for her to explain but then realized it would be easier for her to answer while she was not looking at him.

'Young boys, Signorina?'

This time her head nodded up and down in affirmation.

He wanted to be sure. 'Adolescents?'

'Yes.'

'May I ask how you know this, Signorina?'

At first he thought she wouldn't answer but finally she said, 'One day it rained, and my bag wasn't completely under my slicker, so when I got to the house their mail was wet: the things on the top, that is. When I pulled it out of the bag, the cover came off the magazine and it fell on to the ground. I picked it up, and when I did, it opened and I saw a photo of a boy.' She looked firmly at the ground between their feet, refusing to look at him when she spoke. 'I have a little brother who was fourteen then, and that's what he looked like.' She stopped, and he knew there was no sense in asking her to describe the picture further.

'What did you do, Signorina?'

'I put the magazine in the garbage. He never asked about it.'

'And the next month, when it came again?'

'I put that in the garbage, too, and the next one. And then they stopped coming, so I guess he knew what I was doing.'

'Was there only the one magazine, Signorina?'

'Yes, but there were envelopes, too. The kind with "Photo" on the outside, telling you not to bend them.'

'What did you do with them?'

'After I saw the magazine, I always bent them before I pushed them into the letterbox,' she said, anger mingled with pride.

He could think of no more questions, but she said, 'Then he died, and after a while the mail stopped coming.'

Brunetti put out his hand. She took it. He said, speaking as a policeman, 'Thank you for talking to me, Signorina,' and then couldn't help but add, 'I understand.'

She smiled nervously, and again her face grew red.

At the Questura, he left a note on Vianello's desk, asking him to come up as soon as he got in. It was Wednesday, and Signorina Elettra seldom reached the office before noon on Wednesdays during the summer, a fact which the entire Questura had come to accept without expression of curiosity or disapproval. During the summer, her skin grew no darker, so she was not on the beach; she sent no postcards, so she was not away from the city. No one had ever come across her in the city on Wednesday morning; had this happened, the entire Questura would certainly have heard. Perhaps she simply stayed at home and ironed her linen shirts, Brunetti decided.

His thoughts kept returning to Signora Battestini's son. Even though he knew the man's name was Paolo, Brunetti kept thinking of him as Signora Battestini's son. He had been forty when he died, had worked for a city office for more than a decade, yet everyone Brunetti spoke to referred to him as his mother's son, as if his only existence were through her or by means of her. Brunetti disliked psychobabble and the quick, easy solutions it tried to provide to complex human tangles, but here he thought he detected a pattern so obvious it had to be mistaken: take a domineering mother, put her in a closed and conservative society, and then add a father who liked to spend his time in the bar with the guys, having a drink, and homosexuality in the only son is not the most unlikely result. Instantly Brunetti thought of gay friends of his who had had mothers so passive as almost to be invisible, married to men capable of eating a lion for lunch, and he blushed almost as red as had the woman from the post office.

Wishing to learn if Paolo Battestini had indeed been gay, Brunetti dialled the office number of Domenico Lalli, owner of one of the chemical companies currently under investigation by Judge Galvani. He gave his name, and when Lalli's secretary proved reluctant to pass on the call, said it was a police matter and suggested she ask Lalli if he wanted to speak to him.

A minute later he was put through. 'What now, Guido?' Lalli asked, having served Brunetti in the past as a source of information about the gay population of Mestre and Venice. There was no anger in the voice, simply the impatience of a man who had a large company to run.

'Paolo Battestini, worked for the school board until five years ago, when he died of AIDS.'

'All right,' Lalli said. 'What, specifically, do you want to know?'

'Whether he was gay, whether he liked adolescent boys, and whether there was anyone else he might have shared this taste with.'

Lalli made a disapproving noise and then asked, 'He the one whose mother was murdered a few weeks ago?'

'Yes.'

'These things connected?'

'Maybe. That's why I'm asking you to see what you can find out.'

'Five years ago?'

'Yes. It seems he subscribed to a magazine that had photos of boys in it.'

'Unpleasant,' came Lalli's unsolicited comment. 'And stupid. They can get all they want on the Internet now, though they still all ought to be locked up.'

Lalli, Brunetti knew, had been married as a young man and now had three grandchildren in whom he took inordinate pride. Fearing that he would now have to listen to an account of their latest triumphs, Brunetti said, 'I'd be grateful for anything you could tell me.'

'Hummm. I'll ask around. The school board, huh?'

'Yes. You know someone there.'

'I know someone everywhere, Guido,' Lalli said tersely and without the least hint of boasting. 'I'll call you if I learn anything,' he said and, not bothering to say goodbye, hung up.

Brunetti tried to think of anyone else he could ask about this, but the two men who might have been able to help were on vacation, he knew. He decided to wait to see what information Lalli could provide before trying to get in touch with the others. That decision made, he went downstairs to see if there were any sign of Vianello.

15

Vianello had not yet come in. And as he was leaving the officers' room, Brunetti found himself face to face with Lieutenant Scarpa. After a significant pause, during which his body effectively blocked the doorway, the lieutenant stepped back and said, 'I wonder if I might have a word with you, Commissario.'

'Of course,' Brunetti said.

'Perhaps in my office?' Scarpa suggested.

'I have to get back to my own office, I'm afraid,' Brunetti said, unwilling to concede the territorial advantage.

'I think it's important, sir. It's about the Battestini murder.'

Brunetti manufactured a noncommittal expression and asked, 'Really? What about it?'

'The Gismondi woman,' the lieutenant said and then refused to say more.

Though the mention of her name stirred Brunetti's curiosity, he said nothing. After a long time, his silence won, and Scarpa went on, 'I've checked the recordings of phone calls made to us, and I've found two calls in which she threatens her.'

'Who threatens whom, Lieutenant?' inquired Brunetti.

'Signora Gismondi threatens Signora Battestini.'

'In a phone call to the police, Lieutenant? Wouldn't you say that was a bit rash of her?'

He watched Scarpa maintain control of himself, saw the way his mouth tightened at the corners and how he rose a few millimetres on the balls of his feet. He thought of what it would be like to be the weaker person in any exchange with Scarpa and didn't like the thought.

'If you could spare the time to listen to the tapes, sir, you might understand what I mean,' Scarpa said.

'Can't this wait?' Brunetti asked, making no attempt to disguise his own irritation.

As if the sight of Brunetti's impatience were enough to satisfy him, a more relaxed Scarpa said, 'If you'd prefer not to listen to the person who admits that she was probably the last one to see the victim alive threaten her, sir, that is entirely your own affair. I had, however, thought it would warrant closer attention.'

'Where are they?' Brunetti asked.

Feigning incomprehension, Scarpa asked, 'Where are what, sir?'

As he resisted the impulse to hit Scarpa, Brunetti realized how frequently this desire overtook him. He considered Patta a complacent time-server, a man capable of almost anything to protect his job. But it was the existence of the human weakness implicit in that 'almost' that kept Brunetti from disliking Patta in any but a superficial sense. But he hated Scarpa, shied away from him as he would from entering a dark room from which emerged a strange smell. Most rooms had lights, but he feared there existed no way to illuminate the interior of Scarpa, nor any certainty that what lay inside, if it could be seen, would provoke anything other than fear.

Brunetti's unwillingness to respond was so evident that

Scarpa turned, muttering, 'In the lab,' and started towards the back stairway.

Bocchese was nowhere evident in the laboratory, though the prevailing odour of cigarette smoke suggested that he was not long gone. Scarpa went over to the back wall, where a large cassette player sat on a long wooden counter. Beside it lay two ninety-minute tapes, each bearing dates and signatures.

Scarpa picked one up, glanced at the writing, and slipped it into the machine. He picked up a pair of headphones and placed them over his ears, then pressed the PLAY button, listened for a few seconds, pushed STOP, fast-forwarded the tape and played it again. After three more attempts to find the right spot, he stopped the tape, rewound it a little, then handed the headphones to Brunetti.

Strangely reluctant to have anything that had been in such intimate contact with Scarpa's body touch his own, Brunetti said, 'Can't you just play it?'

Scarpa yanked the headphones from the socket and pressed PLAY.

'This is Signora Gismondi, in Cannaregio. I called before.' Brunetti recognized her voice, but not the tone, tight with anger.

'Yes, Signora. What now?'

'I told you an hour and a half ago. She's got the television on so loud you can hear it from here. Listen,' she said. The voices of two people who sounded as if they were having an argument drew close, then moved away. 'Can you hear that? Her window is ten metres away, and I can hear it like it's in my own house.'

'There's nothing I can do, Signora. The patrol is out on another call.'

'Has the call lasted an hour and a half?' she asked angrily.

'I can't give you that information, Signora.'

'It's four o'clock in the morning,' she said, her voice

moving close to hysteria or tears. 'She's had that thing on since one o'clock. I want to get some sleep.'

'I told you the last time you called, Signora. The patrol's been given your address and they'll come when they can.'

'This is the third night in a row this has happened, and I haven't seen any sign of them,' she said, her voice shriller.

'I don't know anything about that, Signora.'

'What do you expect me to do, go over there and kill her?' Signora Gismondi shouted down the phone.

'I told you, Signora,' came the dispassionate voice of the police operator, 'the patrol will come when it can.' One of them hung up the phone and the tape wound on with a soft hiss.

An equally dispassionate Scarpa turned to Brunetti and said, 'In the next one, she actually threatens to go over and kill her.'

'What does she say?'

'"If you don't stop her, I'll go over there and kill her."'

'Let me hear it,' Brunetti said.

Scarpa inserted the other tape and fast-forwarded it to the middle, hunted around until he found the right place, and played the call for Brunetti. He had quoted Signora Gismondi exactly, and Brunetti shivered when he heard her, voice almost hysterical with rage, say, 'If you don't stop her, I'll go over there and kill her.'

The fact that the call was made at three-thirty in the morning and was the fourth she had made in the same night suggested clearly to Brunetti that it was rage, not calculation, animating her voice, though a judge might not see it quite like that.

'There is also her history of violence,' added Scarpa casually. 'When that is added to these threats, I think it makes a strong case for us to question her again about her movements that morning.'

'What history of violence?' Brunetti asked.

'Eight years ago, while she was still married, she attacked her husband and threatened to kill him.'

'Attacked him how?'

'The police report says she threw boiling water at him.'

'What else does the report say?' Brunetti asked.

'It's in my office if you care to read it, sir.'

'What else does it say, Scarpa?'

The surprise in Scarpa's eyes was evident, as was his instinctive step back from Brunetti. 'They were in the kitchen, having an argument, and she threw the water at him.'

'Was he hurt?'

'Not badly. It landed on his shoes and trousers.'

'Were charges pressed?'

'No, sir, but a report was filed.'

Suddenly suspicious, Brunetti asked, 'Who decided not to press charges?'

'That's hardly important, sir.'

'Who?' Brunetti's voice was so tight it sounded almost like a bark.

'She did,' Scarpa said after a pause he deliberately made as lengthy as possible.

'What charges didn't she press?'

Brunetti watched as Scarpa considered mentioning the report again and made note of the instant when he decided not to bother. 'Assault,' the lieutenant finally said.

'For what?'

'He broke her wrist, or she said he did.'

Brunetti waited for Scarpa to elaborate. When he failed to do so, Brunetti asked, 'She managed to throw a pot of boiling water with a broken wrist?'

It was as if he had not spoken. Scarpa said, 'Whatever the reason, it establishes a history of violence.'

Brunetti turned and left the laboratory.

His heart was pounding with unexpressed rage as he walked up to his office. He understood the what, that Scarpa wanted to rearrange things to make Signora Gismondi look like the murderer: however clumsily he went about it, that was what he was trying to do. What Brunetti didn't understand was the why. Scarpa had nothing to gain from making it look as if Signora Gismondi was the killer.

His step faltered as he suddenly saw it and his foot came down heavily on the next step, causing him to lurch towards the wall. It wasn't that Scarpa wanted her specifically or individually to appear to be the killer. He wanted someone else not to. But as Brunetti continued up the staircase, good sense intervened and offered him a less outrageous explanation: Scarpa wanted nothing more than to obstruct Brunetti and his investigation, which he could do best by creating a false trail that led to Signora Gismondi.

So troubling was this thought that Brunetti found it impossible to sit still in his office. He waited a few minutes, giving Scarpa enough time to remove himself to somewhere other than the staircase, and then he went down to Signorina Elettra's office, but she still wasn't in. Had she walked in at that moment, he would have demanded, to the point of shouting, where she had been and by what right she absented herself half the day on Wednesday when there was work that needed to be done. On the way back to his office, he found himself continuing his tirade against her, dredging up past incidents, oversights, excesses that he could hurl at her.

Inside, he yanked off his jacket and hurled it on to his desk, but he threw it with such force that it slid across the top and landed on the floor, taking with it a pile of loose papers that he had spent the previous afternoon arranging in chronological order. His mind tight with anger, Brunetti gave voice to serious doubts as to the virtue of the Madonna.

Vianello chose this moment to arrive. Brunetti heard him at the door, turned, and gave a grumpy 'Come in.'

Vianello looked at the jacket and the papers and passed silently in front of Brunetti to take a seat.

Brunetti studied the back of Vianello's head, the shoulders, the unwarrantedly stiff posture, and his mood lightened. 'It's Scarpa,' he said, walking to his desk. He bent and picked up the jacket and hung it on the back of his chair, then gathered up the papers and tossed them on the desk and sat down. 'He's trying to make it look as though Signora Gismondi killed her.'

'How?'

'He's got the tapes of two calls she made to us, complaining about the television. In both of them, she threatens to kill the old woman.'

'Threatens how?' Vianello asked. 'Seriously or out of anger?'

'You think they're different?'

'You ever yell at your kids, Commissario?' Vianello asked. 'That's anger. Serious is when you hit them.'

'I never have,' Brunetti said instantly, as though he had been accused.

'I did,' Vianello said. 'Once. About five years ago.' Brunetti waited for the inspector to explain, but he did not. Instead, he said, 'If you talk about it, it means you're just talking.' Vianello turned his attention from the theoretical to the practical and asked, 'Besides, how would she get in?' Brunetti watched Vianello consider and exclude the various ways this might have been done. He finally said, 'No, it doesn't make any sense.'

'Then why's he doing it?' Brunetti asked, waiting to see if Vianello would come up with the same explanation he had.

'May I speak frankly, sir?' Vianello asked.

'Of course.'

The inspector looked at his knees, brushed away an invisible speck of something, and said, 'It's because he hates you. I'm not important enough for him to hate, but he would if he thought I was. And he's afraid of Elettra.'

Brunetti's first impulse was to object to this interpretation, but he forced himself to think it through. He realized that he found it unsatisfactory because it made Scarpa out to be less of a villain than he wanted him to be: guilty only of spite, not of conspiracy. He pulled the papers towards him and once again began to arrange them in chronological order.

'Should I go, sir?' Vianello asked.

'No. I'm thinking about what you just said.'

Whatever satisfied the criteria of possibility most simply was probably the correct explanation: how many times had he invoked this rule? Malice only, and not complicity. Even though he believed this was more likely, he could not deny the satisfaction he would derive were Vianello also to believe Scarpa might be guilty of some baser, more criminal motive.

He looked at Vianello. 'All right,' he finally said. 'It's possible.' For a moment, he considered the consequences: Scarpa would plant the idea of Signora Gismondi's guilt in Patta's mind; this meant Brunetti would have to pretend to go along with it so as not to alarm Patta and be removed from the case; more time would be spent examining Signora Gismondi's life, no doubt with sufficient heavy-handedness to turn her into a reluctant witness; and once she had been badgered into altering or retracting her statement about Flori Ghiorghiu, Patta would return to his now-confirmed conviction that the Romanian woman had been the murderer, and the case could once again be considered as solved.

'I have measured out my life with coffee spoons,' Brunetti said in English. Vianello gave him such a strange look that Brunetti immediately said, 'It's something my wife says.'

'Mine says we should look at the son,' said Vianello.

Brunetti decided to hear what Vianello had to say about Paolo Battestini before telling him about his conversation in the post office and so contented himself with a mere, 'Why?'

'Nadia says she doesn't like the feel of him or at least the feel of the way people talk about him. She thinks it's strange that so many people knew him for so long, lived near him, watched him grow up, and still had almost nothing to say about him.'

Brunetti, who was of much the same opinion, asked, 'Did she say what she thought this might mean?'

Vianello shook his head. 'No, just that it wasn't normal that no one wanted to talk about him.'

Brunetti saw the expression on Vianello's face, a low-level satisfaction, and interpreted it to mean that the inspector had learned something that confirmed his wife's analysis. In order to urge him towards the pleasure of revelation, Brunetti asked, 'What happened at the school board offices?'

'Same old thing,' Vianello said.

'Same old what?' Brunetti inquired.

'Same old office of a city bureaucracy. I phoned and explained that I wanted to speak to the Director in connection with a criminal investigation. I thought it would be better not to explain which. But he was in Treviso for a meeting, as was his assistant, and the person I eventually spoke to had been there only three weeks and said he couldn't be of any help.' Vianello grimaced and added, 'Probably won't be of any help after three years.'

Brunetti waited, familiar with the inspector's style. Vianello flicked away another invisibility from his trousers and went on, 'So I finally agreed to speak to the head of personnel and went to their offices to see her. They've modernized everything and now they've all got new computers and desks.

'The woman I spoke to is the head of a department that is now called Human Resources,' Vianello began. Brunetti was struck by how cannibalistic the term sounded but said nothing. 'I asked her if she could provide records of the employment of Paolo Battestini, and she asked when he worked there. When I told her, she said it would be difficult to find records for certain periods because they were now in the midst of the process of transferring some employment information on to their computer system.' Seeing Brunetti's expression, Vianello said, 'No, I didn't even bother to ask how long it would take, but I did ask her which years were affected.' He looked up in search of Brunetti's approval, and when he saw it, he went on. 'She looked him up on the computer and said that the last five years he was there were already in the system, so she printed out a copy for me.'

'What sort of information was it?'

'Reports from his superiors on his work performance, dates of his holidays, sick-days, things like that.'

'And did you get it?'

'Yes. I gave it to Signorina Elettra when I came in.' Brunetti registered that she had finally arrived as Vianello said, 'There were long periods of sick-leave towards the end, and she's checking the hospital records to see if he was there and, if so, why.'

'I'll save her the trouble,' Brunetti said. 'He died of AIDS.' When he saw Vianello's surprise, he summarized his conversation with Dottor Carlotti the previous afternoon and half apologized for not having called Vianello to tell him this before he went to the school board offices. But he made no mention of his conversation with the *postina*.

'Better to have it confirmed by two sources,' Vianello said.

Brunetti felt a flash of anger at the suggestion that what he had discovered needed confirmation but controlled the feeling and asked, 'Did you manage to talk to anyone who worked with him?'

'Yes. After I got the print-out, I hung around in the corridor until about ten, when two of the men who worked there – I figured they might have worked with him – said they were going to the bar across the street for a coffee. I folded the papers so that their letterhead showed and followed them over.'

Brunetti marvelled at how this man, taller and larger than he, so easily rendered himself invisible once he started to talk to people. 'And?' he prompted.

'I said I was from the Mestre office, and they believed me, had no reason not to. They'd seen me there in their office, and they'd seen the woman give me the print-out, so they'd figure I had some reason to be there.

'I'd had a look over the woman's shoulder when she called up the personnel files and seen the names of a few people who still worked there, so I ordered a coffee and asked these two guys about one of them, said how long it was since I'd seen him. And then I asked about Battestini, if it was his mother who had been killed, and how he'd taken it because he'd always seemed so devoted to her.'

No wonder Vianello had seemed proud of what he had done. 'The cunning of the snake, Vianello,' Brunetti said in open praise.

'That's when things changed, though. It was very strange, sir. It was as if I'd taken that same cunning snake and tossed it on the floor at their feet. One of them even stepped back and put his money on the counter and left. There was a long silence, then the other one finally said he thought it was, but that Battestini didn't work there any more. Didn't even mention that he was dead. And then he just sort of disappeared. That is, I asked to pay for our coffees, and when I turned back, the guy wasn't there – not where he'd been beside me and not in the bar.' He shook his head at the memory.

'Did you get a sense of what it was about him, about Battestini?' Brunetti asked.

'Twenty years ago, it would have been because he was gay, but no one really cares about that now,' Vianello said. 'And most people feel pity for anyone who dies of AIDS, so I'd say it was something else, and the something else would probably have to do with the office. But whichever it was, they didn't like it that someone they didn't know was asking questions about him.' He smiled and added, 'At least that's the way it looked to me.'

'He subscribed to a magazine with photos of boys,' Brunetti said and watched this information register on Vianello's face. Then, for clarity's sake, he added, 'Adolescents, not little boys.'

After a moment, the inspector said, 'I'm not sure that's the sort of information people at his office would have had.'

Brunetti had to admit that this was true. 'Then it probably was something to do with his job at the school board.'

'Looks like,' Vianello said.

16

Brunetti and Vianello were on their way down to Signorina Elettra's office to save her the effort of – Brunetti didn't know whether to say 'accessing' or 'breaking into' the hospital patient files – when he realized he no longer cared how she got the information she gave him. That in its turn provoked a flash of shame at the moment's rage he'd felt at her absence. Like Otello, he had a lieutenant who could corrupt his best feelings.

As though forewarned that today she was to play Desdemona, Signorina Elettra wore a long dress of gossamer white linen, her hair hanging loose down her back. She greeted their arrival with a smile, but before she could say anything, Vianello asked, 'Any luck yet?'

'No,' she apologized. 'I had a phone call from the Vice-Questore.' As if that were not sufficient justification, she explained, 'He wanted me to write a letter for him, and he was very particular about the wording.' She paused, waiting to see which one of them would be the first to ask.

It was Vianello. 'Are you at liberty to reveal the nature of the letter?'

'Good heavens, no. If I did, people here would know that he's applying for a job with Interpol.'

Brunetti recovered first and said, 'Of course, of course. It had to be.' Vianello failed to find words with which to do justice to his feelings. 'Are you at liberty, perhaps, to tell us to whom the letter is addressed?' Brunetti asked.

'My loyalty to the Vice-Questore would not permit that, sir,' she said, voice rich with the sort of pious sincerity Brunetti associated with politicians and priests. Then, thrusting her forefinger towards a sheet of paper which lay on her desk, she asked idly, 'Do you think a request to the Mayor for a letter of recommendation should go through the internal post?'

'It might be faster to email it, Signorina,' Brunetti suggested.

Vianello interrupted them. 'The Vice-Questore is a traditionalist, sir. I think he'd like to sign the letter himself.'

Signorina Elettra nodded in agreement and said, turning their attention back to Vianello's original question, 'I thought I might have a look at his medical records.'

Brunetti said, 'It's not necessary. Battestini died of AIDS.'

'Ah, the poor man,' Signorina Elettra said.

'He also subscribed to magazines with photos of boys,' Vianello interrupted, his tone savage.

'He still died of AIDS, Inspector,' she said, 'and no one deserves that.'

After a very long pause, Vianello gave a grudging, 'Perhaps,' reminding them that he had two children who were barely into their teens.

An uncomfortable silence fell. Before it could do some sort of damage, Brunetti said, 'Vianello spoke to people in the neighbourhood and people where he worked, and everyone responded the same way: as soon as his name was mentioned, no one knew anything about him. There's general agreement that the mother was a nasty piece of work, that the father was *"una brava persona"* who liked a drink, but when Paolo's name is mentioned, everyone goes mute.' He gave her a moment to consider this and then asked, 'What would you make of that?'

She sat and pushed a button on her computer that darkened the screen. Then she propped her elbow on the desk and cupped her chin in her palm. Sitting like that for some time, she seemed almost to disappear from the room or at least to leave her white-clothed body there while her attention went elsewhere.

Finally she looked at Vianello and said, 'The silence could be respect. His mother's just been the victim of a horrible crime, and he died what was probably a horrible death, so no one will say anything bad about him, probably never will.' She raised the other hand to her forehead and scratched idly at it. 'As to the people where he worked, if he's been dead five years, they've probably forgotten about him.'

Vianello interrupted her. 'No. It was much stronger than that. They didn't want to talk about him at all.'

'Talk about him or answer questions about him?' Brunetti asked.

'I didn't have a pistol to their heads,' said an affronted Vianello. 'They did not want to talk about him.'

'How many people work there?' Brunetti asked.

'In the whole place?'

'Yes.'

'I've no idea,' Vianello said. 'The office is on two floors, so perhaps thirty people. In his section it looked as though there were only five or six.'

'I could easily find out, sir,' Signorina Elettra offered, but Brunetti, intrigued by the general reluctance to discuss Signora Battestini's son, thought he might stop by the office himself in the afternoon.

He told them then about his call to Lalli and said that he'd let them know as soon as he had an answer. 'Until then,

Signorina, I'd like you to take a look at Luca Sardelli and Renato Fedi. They're the only living former heads of the school board.' He did not confess to them that he suggested this because it was the only possibility he could think of.

'Do you want to question them, sir?' Vianello asked.

Glancing at Signorina Elettra, Brunetti asked, 'Would you have a look first?' When she nodded, he said, 'I'm pretty sure Sardelli's at the Assessorato dello Sport, and Fedi runs a construction company in Mestre. He's also a *Eurodeputato*, though I don't know for which party.' She had not heard of either man, so she took notes of what he said about them and told them she would have a look immediately and should have something for them after lunch.

Because he thought it would be quicker not to go all the way home if he planned to show up at the school board after lunch, Brunetti asked Vianello if he had plans for lunch and, after only a moment's hesitation, the inspector said he had none. They agreed to meet at the front entrance in ten minutes. Brunetti picked up the phone and called Paola to tell her he would not be home.

'Pity,' she said when he told her, 'the kids are here and we're having . . .' she began and then stopped.

'Go ahead,' he said, 'I'm a man. I can stand it.'

'Grilled vegetables for antipasto, then veal with lemon and rosemary.'

Brunetti gave a theatrical moan.

'And fig sauce on home-made lemon sorbetto for dessert,' she added.

'Is this the truth?' he suddenly asked, 'or your way of punishing me for not coming home?'

Her silence was long. 'Would you prefer it if I told you I'm taking them over to McDonald's for a Big Mac?' she asked finally.

'That's child abuse,' he said.

'They're teenagers, Guido.'

'It's still abuse,' he said and hung up.

He and Vianello decided to walk to da Remigio, but when they got there, they discovered that it was closed until the tenth of September. That also proved to be the case at the next two places they tried, leaving them with the choice of a Chinese restaurant or the long walk to Via Garibaldi to see if anything was open down there.

Neither said anything, but by silent consent they headed back to the bar at Ponte dei Greci, where at least the *tramezzini* and wine were acceptable. Keeping his mind clear of the veal roast, Brunetti asked for a *prosciutto e funghi*, a *prosciutto e pomodoro*, and a simple *panino con salami*; Vianello, no doubt in response to the belief that, if it was not going to be a proper lunch, it didn't matter what he ate, asked for the same.

Vianello brought a bottle of mineral water and a half-litre of white wine to the table and sat opposite Brunetti. He looked at the plate of sandwiches that lay between them, said, 'Nadia made fresh pasta,' and reached for a *tramezzino*.

The inspector finished his first sandwich and two glasses of mineral water before speaking again. He set down his water glass, poured wine for both of them, and said, 'What do we do about Scarpa?'

The fact that he failed to use the lieutenant's title was sufficient to inform Brunetti that this was an entirely unofficial conversation.

Brunetti took a sip of wine. 'I think the only thing we can do is let him go ahead with his investigation, if that's the right word, of Signora Gismondi.'

'But it's nonsense,' Vianello said angrily. He had not met her, had done nothing more than read the file in the case and spoken to Brunetti about his conversation with her, but that had served to convince him that her only involvement in the crime had been helping the Romanian woman to leave the country. As that thought suddenly took on darker impli-cations, he asked, 'Do you think he's capable of saying that she's an accessory because she gave her the money and bought her the train ticket?'

Brunetti no longer had any idea of what Scarpa was or was not capable of doing. He regretted that a woman as apparently decent as Signora Gismondi should have become a hostage in Scarpa's guerrilla war against him, but he knew that any attempt to rescue her would only increase the risk of reprisals from Scarpa.

'I think the only thing we can do is let him pursue this. If we try to stop him, he'll say we've got some secret motive for protecting her, and God knows where that will lead.' It was difficult for him to anticipate Scarpa's actions because he felt so incapable of understanding his motives. That is, he could understand them, grasp them intellectually, but he lacked the mechanism that would have allowed him to follow them through by mere instinct. He realized how much better Paola was at this sort of thing or, for that matter, Signorina Elettra. Female cats, he found himself thinking, were said to be much better hunters and seemed to take more delight in torturing their prey to death.

Vianello's question brought him back from these reflections. 'Does any of this make any sense to you, sir?'

'What, the murder? Or Scarpa?'

'The murder. Scarpa's easy enough to understand.'

Wishing that were indeed the case, Brunetti said, 'She was killed by someone who hated her or wanted it to look like they did. Which means the same thing.' Catching Vianello's look, he answered, 'I mean that whoever did it is capable of that sort of violence, either out of rage or out of calculation. I didn't see the body, but I saw the photos.' He decided there was no sense in saying how much he regretted, now, not having come back from his vacation when he had read about the murder. He should have been suspicious of the reports in the newspapers, even more so of the answers he had been given when he phoned the Questura to ask about the case and was told it was already solved. They had been on the coast of Ireland, all four of them, Raffi and Chiara spending half their time sailing and exploring tide pools, the other half eating, while he and Paola reread their patient ways, respectively, through Gibbon and the Palliser novels, and he had lacked the courage to broach the idea of returning to Venice.

While he waited for his superior to continue, Vianello ate his remaining sandwich and finished the water. He waved to the man behind the counter and held up the empty bottle.

Brunetti said, 'Both our wives would say this is simply sexist prejudice, but a woman didn't do that.' Vianello nodded in approval of simple sexist prejudice and Brunetti continued, 'So we have to find a reason a man would want to kill her, and it would have to be a man who either had access to the apartment or whom she would allow into the apartment.' The barman set the water on the table, and Brunetti filled both glasses before continuing, 'The only thing we've found so far that doesn't fit is the money: it stopped coming when she died, and her lawyer made no mention of it. We don't know how much the niece knew about it, or even if she did.' He poured some of the wine into his glass, but left it untouched. 'Not that there's any reason Marieschi should tell me, even if she did know about it,' he added.

'Could she have taken it?' Vianello asked.

'Of course.'

Brunetti had told him about Poppi, so Vianello said, 'Isn't it strange, that I'm reluctant to think a person with such a dog could be dishonest?' He sipped at his wine, turned to the barman and held up the empty sandwich plate, set it down, and said, 'How strange. Most of the people we arrest have children, but it would never occur to us to think that's a reason they wouldn't commit a crime.'

When Brunetti made no comment upon this observation, Vianello returned his attention to the matter at hand and said, 'The niece might just as easily have moved the money.'

Reflecting upon what he knew of the professional classes, Brunetti added, 'Or someone in the bank might have done it, once he knew she was dead.'

'Of course.'

The sandwiches came, but Brunetti could eat only half of one and set the rest of it back on his plate.

Not having to clarify that he was speaking of Signorina Elettra, Brunetti asked, 'Do you think she'll be able to find out who made the transfers?'

Vianello finished his wine but made no move to refill his glass. After a contemplative pause, he answered, 'If there are any records, anywhere in their files, she'll probably find them.'

'It's terrifying, isn't it?' Brunetti asked.

'If you're a banker, yes,' Vianello agreed.

They returned to the Questura, oppressed by the still-growing heat and their mutual resentment at having had to lunch on sandwiches. In her office, looking as though she'd spent her lunchtime in an air-conditioned environment waiting while the creases were pressed out of her dress, Signorina Elettra greeted them with an expression which seemed unusually sombre.

Sensitive to the difference in her mood, Vianello asked, 'The transfers?'

'I still can't find out,' she answered tersely.

Brunetti found his mind suddenly filled with random memories of the lawyer: she was tall, athletic of build, and her grasp was firm. He tried to picture her poised over the old woman, hand raised high, but when he did, his vision was interrupted by the memory of the puzzle books he used to help Chiara with: 'What's Wrong with this Picture?' He had seen Avvocatessa Marieschi's hands on Poppi's ears. He called himself a sentimental fool and found his attention returning to Signorina Elettra's voice.

'. . . been either of them,' she concluded, pointing to the screen of her computer.

'What?' Brunetti asked.

'The transfer,' Signorina Elettra repeated, 'could have been made by either one of them.'

'The niece?' Vianello asked.

She nodded. 'All the person needed was the account number, power of attorney, and the code number: the transfer would be automatic. All they had to do was fill out the form and hand it to a teller.' Before he could ask if it would be possible to check the signature on the form, she said, 'No, the bank would never give it to us without an order from a judge.'

Brunetti followed this trail to its inevitable conclusion. 'And the banks in the Channel Islands?' he asked.

She shook her head. 'I've tried in a number of ways, but I've never been able to get anything from them.' Her respect was grudging, but it was still audible.

Brunetti felt the temptation to ask if she kept her money there, but he resisted and, instead, asked, 'Can you think of any way to trace the request?'

'Not without an order from a judge,' she repeated. All of them knew the likelihood of this.

'Have you been able to find out anything about the niece?' Brunetti asked.

'Very little. Birth, school records, medical file, taxes. Just the usual things.' She was not being ironic, Brunetti realized: finding these details of a person's life was as easy for her as consulting the phone book.

'And?' Brunetti asked.

'And she seems as inconsequential as her aunt,' Signorina Elettra answered.

'Where does she work?'

'She's a baker's assistant at Romolo,' she answered, naming a *pasticceria* on the other side of the city, where Brunetti sometimes went on Sunday morning to get fresh pastries.

Brunetti's thoughts were diverted from the pastries by the arrival of Alvise, who ran into the office, preventing himself from catapulting into Vianello only by grabbing the frame of the door with one hand and pulling himself to a sudden stop, breathing heavily. 'Sir,' he gasped, looking at Brunetti. 'I just had a call for you, from a woman.'

'Yes?' Brunetti asked, alarmed at the expression on the face of the usually phlegmatic officer.

'She said you had to come immediately.'

'Come where, Alvise?' Brunetti asked.

It took Alvise a moment to answer. 'She didn't say, sir. But she said you had to come now.'

'Why?' Brunetti asked.

'She said they killed Poppi.'

17

The name galvanized Brunetti. Forcing his voice to remain calm, he asked Alvise, 'Did she say where she was calling from?'

'I don't remember, sir,' Alvise said, confused that his superior should ask for such a detail in the face of such an urgent message.

'What, exactly, did she say, Alvise?' Brunetti asked.

At the new tone in his superior's voice, Alvise released his hold on the door jamb and stood up straighter. With an effort that was visible in his face, he recalled the conversation. 'The call got transferred to the switchboard when you didn't answer, sir, and Russo thought you might be with Vianello, so he transferred the call to our office, and I picked it up.'

Once again wanting to hit the person in front of him, Brunetti said only, 'Go on.'

'It was a woman and she was crying, I think, sir. She kept asking to talk to you, and when I said I'd find you, she said to tell you to come now because they killed Poppi.'

'Did she say anything else, Alvise?' Brunetti asked with iron calm.

As if being asked to recall a conversation that had taken place some weeks before, Alvise closed his eyes for a moment, opened them and stared at the floor, then said, 'Only that she just got there and found her. Poppi, I suppose.'

'Did she say where she was, Alvise?' he repeated, voice tight.

'No, sir,' the officer insisted. 'She said only that she just got back from lunch, and she was there.'

Brunetti relaxed his hands, which were clenched into tight fists at his sides, and told the officer, 'You can go now, Alvise.' Turning back to Vianello and Signorina Elettra and ignoring the sound of Alvise's departure, Brunetti said, 'Find out where she lives. Vianello, you go over and see if she's there. I'll go to the office.'

'And if she is, sir?' Vianello asked.

'Find out who "they" are and why she thinks they killed the dog.'

Brunetti turned away and was out of the office even before Signorina Elettra reached for the phone book. Checking that his *telefonino* was in the pocket of his jacket, he ran down the steps and out of the Questura. An empty launch was tied to the dock, but he didn't want to go back inside and look for the pilot, so he set off towards Castello.

By the time he got to the end of Salizada S. Lorenzo, his shirt and jacket were clinging to his back and his collar was sodden with sweat. When he left the protective shadows of the *calli* and walked out on to Riva degli Schiavoni, the afternoon sun blasted him. At first he thought the faint breeze coming off the water would help, but it did nothing more than cast a sudden chill as it rolled across his damp clothing.

He hurried down the last broad bridge and turned into Via Garibaldi. The sun had driven almost everyone indoors: even the shade under the umbrellas of the bars that lined the street was empty as people waited for the sun to move westward and put at least one side of the street in the shade.

The outside door was open so he ran up the steps to her office. In front of the door there was a puddle of slimy yellow liquid that could have been vomit. Stepping over it, he pounded on the door with his fist and shouted, 'Signora, it's me. Brunetti.' He tried the handle and found the door open. He stepped inside, shouting out again, 'I'm here, Signora. Brunetti.' He registered a faint, sour smell, and saw more signs of the yellow liquid, this time splashed on the wall to the left of the secretary's desk and puddled on the floor below.

He thought he heard some faint noise from behind the door of her office. Not even thinking of his pistol, which was in a locked drawer in his desk, Brunetti crossed the room and opened the door to Marieschi's office.

The lawyer sat at her desk, her left hand cupped over her mouth as if to stifle a cry of panic at the sight of the opening door. He thought she recognized him, if only because the terror in her eyes diminished, but her hand remained firmly clasped over her mouth.

Brunetti said nothing but cast his eyes around the room. And saw the dog, lying on the floor a bit to the left of the desk. The entire area around her was splashed with the same stinking yellow mess. Poppi's jaws were open, her tongue extended beyond the limits of the possible. Jaws and tongue were covered with a thick whitish froth; in death one liquid eye looked up at her mistress as if in accusation or appeal.

The sudden chill that came over Brunetti was caused as much by the knowledge of what he had to do as by the air conditioning in the room. Decades ago, when he had been told always to strike a witness at the moment of greatest weakness, it had been easy to write it down as a rule; it was the practice that was difficult.

He drew closer to her desk, paused a moment, then extended a hand to the silent woman. 'I think you'd better come with me, Signora,' he said, moving no closer and keeping his voice calm.

Hand still pressed to her mouth, she shook the idea away.

'There's nothing you can do for her now,' he said, making no attempt to disguise the sorrow he felt at the ending of such beauty. 'Come out into the other room now. I think it would be better.'

Keeping her eyes away from the body of the dog, she said, 'I don't want to leave her alone.'

'It's all right, Signora,' he assured her, having no idea at all what he meant by that. He made a small summoning gesture with the fingers of his hand, and said, 'Come on. It's all right.'

She took her hand from her mouth and placed it squarely on her desk, put the other beside it and pushed herself to her feet like a woman twice her age. Not looking at the dead dog, she came around to the other side of the desk, towards Brunetti. When she reached him, he took her arm and led her from the room, careful to close the door behind them.

He pulled the secretary's chair from her desk and, placing it so that it faced away from the splashed liquid, helped the lawyer into it. He took one of the other chairs and placed it about a metre from hers, facing her, and sat down.

'Can you tell me about it, Signora?' She said nothing. 'Tell me what happened.'

Signora Marieschi started to cry. She did so softly, the only sign being her tightened lips and the tears spilling from her eyes. Her voice, when she finally spoke, was surprisingly calm, as if she were speaking about things that had happened somewhere else or to other people. 'She was only two. Still a puppy, really. She loved everyone.'

'It's in the breed, I think,' Brunetti agreed, 'to love everyone.'

'And she trusted everyone, so anyone could have given it to her.'

'Do you mean poisoned her?' Brunetti asked.

She nodded. Before he could ask how this could happen, she said, 'There's a garden out in the back, and I leave her there all day, even when I go to lunch. Everyone knows that.'

'Everyone in the neighbourhood or all of your clients?' he asked.

She ignored the question and said, 'When I got back, I went to get her to bring her up here. But I could tell when I saw her. There was . . . there was vomit all over the grass, and she couldn't walk. I had to carry her up here.' She looked around the office, saw the stain on the wall but appeared not to notice those on her skirt nor the one on her left shoe, and said, 'I put her down in here, and then she was sick again. So I took her inside and tried to call the vet, but he wasn't there. But then she got sick again. And then she was dead.' Neither of them spoke until Signora Marieschi said, 'So I called you. But you weren't there, either.' She said it so that he would sense the same futile reproach she felt towards the vet.

Ignoring her tone, Brunetti said, leaning slightly towards her, 'The officer who gave me the message said you said someone killed her, Signora. Can you tell me who you think did it?'

She clasped her hands together and, leaning forward, pushed them between her knees. He saw only the top of her head and her shoulders.

Both of them remained like that for a long time.

When she spoke, her voice was so soft that Brunetti had to lean even closer to her to hear what she said. 'Her niece,' she said, and then again, 'Graziella.'

Brunetti removed some of the sympathy from his voice and asked, 'Why would she do that?'

Her shrug was so strong that Brunetti felt pushed away by it. He waited for further clarification, and when it was not forthcoming, he asked, 'Was it about anything concerning the estate, Signora?' unwilling to let her know that he was aware of the bank accounts.

'Perhaps,' the lawyer answered, and his practised ear detected the first traces of equivocation, as though the shock of the dog's death was beginning to wear off.

'What is it she thinks you did, Signora?' he asked.

He was prepared for her to shrug this off, but he was not prepared for her to look him in the face and lie. 'I don't know,' she said.

This, he realized, was the crucial point. If he allowed the lie to pass, then there would be no more truth from her, no matter how long he questioned her or how many times he questioned her again. Casually then, as though he were a trusted old friend asked in to sit at the fireside and talk of familiar things, he said, 'We'd have very little trouble proving that you moved her money out of the country, Avvocatessa, and even if we failed to get a conviction because you do have the power of attorney, your reputation as a lawyer would be compromised.' Then, as if it had just occurred to him, as a friend, to warn her of further consequences, he added, 'And I suspect the Finanza would also want to talk to you about the money.'

Her astonishment was total. All her lawyerly skills fell from her and she blurted out, 'How did you know about that?'

'It's sufficient that we do know,' he said, all compassion absent from his voice. She registered the change in his tone and sat up straight, even moved her chair a bit away from his. As he studied her, he saw her harden in much the same way he had.

'I think we had better talk about this honestly.' He watched her begin to object and cut her off. 'I don't care in the least about the money or what you did with it: all I want to know is where it came from.' Again, he saw her getting ready to speak, and he knew she would lie to him unless he managed to frighten her sufficiently. 'If I'm not satisfied with what you tell me about the money, I will file an official report about the bank accounts, the power of attorney, and the dates and destinations of the transfers.'

'How did you find out?' she asked in a voice he had not heard her use before.

'As I said before, that's irrelevant. My only interest is in finding out where the money came from.'

'She killed my dog,' she said with sudden savagery.

Brunetti lost his patience and answered, 'Then you better hope she didn't kill her aunt, too, because if she did, you're probably next on her list.'

Her eyes widened as this hit home. She shook her head once, twice, three times, as though she wanted to eradicate the possibility. 'No, she couldn't have,' she said. 'Never.'

'Why?'

'I know her. She wouldn't do it.' There was no questioning the certainty with which she spoke.

'And Poppi? Didn't she kill her?' He had no idea if this was the truth, but it sufficed that she believed it.

'She hates dogs, hates animals.'

'How well do you know her?'

'Well enough to know that.'

'That's different from knowing she wouldn't kill her aunt.'

Provoked by his scepticism, she said, 'If she did kill her, she would have taken the money before. Or the day after.'

Realizing that she must then have known about the niece's power of attorney, perhaps even prepared it herself, he asked, 'But you worked more quickly?'

If she was insulted, she gave no sign of it and answered only, 'Yes.'

'Then you might be the one who killed her,' he suggested, thinking it unlikely but curious as to how she would react to the suggestion.

'I wouldn't kill anyone for so little,' she said; he found himself unable to comment.

Instead, he returned to the bank accounts. 'Where did the

money come from?' She gave no sign that she was willing to answer, so he went on, 'You were her lawyer, and she trusted you with a power of attorney, so you know something.' When she still resisted, he said, 'Whoever killed her was someone she trusted enough to let into her apartment. Perhaps they knew about the money, or perhaps this was the person who had been giving her the money all those years.' He watched her mind run ahead of his words and saw it register certain possibilities. Without naming the worst of them, he said, 'It might be in your best interests that we find this person, Avvocatessa.'

Her voice tight, she asked, 'Could that be who killed her?' When he didn't answer, she added, 'Poppi?'

He nodded, though he thought that the person capable of such savagery against Signora Battestini was not someone who would bother to send a warning by killing someone's dog.

All resistance disappeared as she shrank back from the awareness of her own mortality. 'I don't know who it was,' she said. 'Really, I never knew. She never told me.'

Brunetti waited almost a full minute for her to continue, but when she remained silent, he asked, 'What did she tell you?'

'Nothing. Just that the money was deposited every month.'

'Did she say what she wanted the money for or what she wanted done with it?'

She shook her head. 'No, never, just that it was there.' She thought about this for some time, then could not hide her own bewilderment when she said, 'I don't think it was important to her, spending it or being able to spend it. She just liked having it, knowing it was there.' She looked up and around the room, as if seeking some explanation for behaviour as strange as this. Then she looked back at Brunetti and said, 'She didn't tell me about it until three years ago, when she started to talk about making a will.'

'And what did she tell you?' he asked again.

'Only that it was there.'

'Did she tell you who she wanted it to go to?'

The lawyer feigned confusion, and he repeated, 'Did she tell you where she wanted it to go? You were there to talk about her will, so she must have mentioned the money to some purpose.'

'No,' she said, obviously lying.

'Why did she give you power of attorney?' he asked.

Her pause was a long one, no doubt allowing her time to construct an answer he might believe. 'She wanted me to take care of things for her.' It was vague, but it appeared to be all she was willing to divulge.

'Such as?' he asked.

'Finding the women who went in to help her. Paying them. We thought it would be easier if I didn't have to keep asking her to sign cheques. By then, she wasn't leaving the house any more, so she couldn't get to the bank.' She waited to see how he would react to this, and when he said nothing, she added, 'It was easier.'

She must consider him a fool, to think he would believe a person like Signora Battestini would trust anyone with all of her money. He wondered how Marieschi had persuaded the old woman to sign the power of attorney or what it was she thought she was signing. He wondered who had been there to witness the document. As he had told her, he cared little about where the money went, wanting only to know where it had come from. 'So you used the money to pay the expenses of the women who helped her?'

'Yes. Her utility bills were paid automatically by the bank.'

'They were all illegal, weren't they?' he asked abruptly.

She feigned confusion and said, 'I don't know what you mean.'

'I confess to being amazed, Avvocatessa, that a lawyer in

this country wouldn't be familiar with the idea of illegal workers.'

Forgetting herself entirely, she said, 'You can't prove I knew that.'

He went on with studied calm, 'I think it's time for me to explain a few things to you. Whatever business it is you're running with illegal workers and fake passports is of no interest to me, not during a murder investigation. But if you continue to lie to me or evade my questions, I will see that a complete report of your activities, as well as the addresses of the women in Trieste and Milano who are also using the false papers of Florinda Ghiorghiu, goes to the Immigration Police tomorrow as well as details about your handling of Signora Battestini's bank accounts, which will go to the Guardia di Finanza.'

She began to protest, and he stopped her with an out-thrust hand. 'Further, if you lie to me again, I will today file a report about the death of your dog, making note of your assertion that Signora Battestini's niece killed her, and that will require that the woman be questioned about possible motives for having killed the dog.'

She was not looking at him, but he could tell she was attending to his every word. 'Is that clear?'

'Yes.'

'I want you to tell me everything she ever said in reference to those accounts, and I want you to tell me any thoughts you may have entertained, during the years you knew about them, of their possible source, regardless of where this information came from or how credible you think it to be.' He paused, then added, 'Do you understand?'

There was no hesitation before she answered, 'Yes.' She sighed, but she was such an accomplished liar that he paid no attention. She allowed some time to pass and then said, 'She told me about the accounts when she made her will, but she never told me where the money came from. I told you that.

173

But once, about a year ago, she was talking about her son – I told you I never met him – and she said that he had been a good boy and had provided for her in her old age. That he and the Madonna would take good care of her.' He studied her face as she spoke, wondering if she was telling the truth and wondering if he would be able to tell if she wasn't.

'She'd become very repetitive by then,' she went on, 'the way old people get, so I didn't pay much attention to what she said.'

'Why were you there this time? You said it was three years ago she wanted to make a will.'

'It was about the television. I went to ask her to try to remember to turn it down before she went to bed. The only thing I could think of to do was to tell her the police would come in and sequester the television if she didn't. I'd told her before, but she always forgot things, or else she remembered only the things she wanted to.'

'I see,' he said.

'And she told me, again, what a good boy he had been, always staying with her. And that's when she said that he had left her safe and under the protection of the Madonna. I didn't think much of it at the time – when she started to ramble, I never paid much attention – but later it occurred to me that she might have been talking about the money, that it was the son who had arranged for it or who had done whatever it was that got the money deposited.'

'Did you ask her about this?'

'No. I told you, it didn't occur to me until a couple of days later. And I'd learned by then never to ask her directly about the accounts, so I didn't.'

There were still questions he wanted to ask her: when she had begun to plan to steal the money; what made her certain the niece wouldn't bring charges against her. But for the moment, he had obtained the information he wanted. He thought she had been frightened enough to tell the truth and was neither proud nor ashamed of the techniques he had used to make her do so.

He got to his feet. 'If I have any further questions, I'll contact you,' he said. 'If you think of anything else, I want you to call me.' He took one of his cards, wrote his home phone number on the back, and handed it to her.

He turned to leave, but she stopped him by asking, 'What do I do if it wasn't the niece?'

He was fairly certain it was the niece and she had nothing to fear. But then he remembered how immediate her protestation had been that she would not kill anyone for so little, and he saw no reason to save her from being afraid. 'Try not to be alone in your office or your home. Call me if anything suspicious happens,' he said and left her office.

18

As soon as he was outside, he called Vianello, who answered his *telefonino* but was already back at the Questura, having found no one at Avvocatessa Marieschi's home address. Brunetti quickly explained what had happened at the lawyer's and told Vianello to meet him at Romolo, where he wanted, finally, to talk to Signora Battestini's niece.

'You think she could have done it?' Vianello asked, and when Brunetti was slow to answer, he clarified his question by adding, 'Poisoned the dog?'

'I think so,' Brunetti answered.

'I'll see you there,' Vianello said, and was gone.

To save time, Brunetti took the 82 at Arsenale and got off at Accademia. He crossed the small *campo* without paying attention to the long line of scantily clad tourists in front of the museum, passed on his left the gallery he always thought of as the Supermarket of Art, and headed down towards San Barnaba.

In the narrow streets, the heat assailed him. In the past, heat like this had reduced the number of tourists; now it seemed to serve the same purpose as heat in a petri dish: the alien life form multiplied under his very eyes. When he arrived at the *pasticceria*, he saw Vianello standing on the other side of the *calle*, looking into the window of a shop that sold masks.

They went into the pastry shop together. Vianello ordered a coffee and a glass of mineral water, and Brunetti nodded his request for the same. The glass cabinet was filled with the pastries Brunetti knew so well: the cream-filled puffs of pastry, the chocolate bigne, and Chiara's favourite, the whipped-cream-filled swans. The heat rendered them all equally unappetising.

As they drank their coffee, Brunetti recounted in greater detail his conversation with the lawyer, saying only that the dog had been poisoned, but giving no details of the circumstances.

'It means this woman –' Vianello said, indicating the back regions of the shop where presumably the kitchens lay – 'knew enough about Marieschi to know how to hurt her.'

'If you'd seen her with the dog, even once, you'd know that,' Brunetti said, recalling their meeting and that noble golden head.

Vianello finished his water and held up his glass to the woman behind the bar. Brunetti drank his, set the glass on the counter, and nodded when she held up the bottle and looked his way.

When she began to pour the water, Brunetti asked, 'Is Signorina Simionato here?'

'You mean Graziella?' the woman asked, evidently curious as to what these two men could want.

'Yes.'

'I think so,' she said uneasily, stepping back from the counter and turning to a door at the back of the shop. 'Let me ask.' Before she could move away from them, Brunetti held up his hand and said, 'I'd rather you didn't speak to her, Signora, not before we do.'

'Police?' she asked, wide-eyed.

'Yes,' Brunetti answered, wondering why they bothered to carry warrant cards if they were this easily recognized, even by the women behind the counters in pastry shops.

'Is she there?' Brunetti asked, indicating the open door behind the far end of the counter.

'Yes,' the young woman answered. 'What is . . .?' she left the question unfinished.

Vianello pulled out a notebook and asked, 'What time did she get here today, Signora? Do you know?'

The woman stared at the notebook as though it were a living, dangerous thing. Seeing her reluctance, Brunetti took out his wallet but, instead of showing her his warrant card, took out a five Euro note and laid it on the counter to pay their bill. 'What time did she get here today, Signora?'

'About two, maybe a little later,' she said.

That seemed like a strange time for a baker to arrive at work, Brunetti thought. But at once she explained, 'There's going to be a health inspection next week, so we have to get ready. Everybody's working an extra half-shift.' Brunetti thought it inappropriate to comment on the fact that these inspections were not meant to be announced in advance. The woman added, 'Some of the bakers are here, too, during the afternoons, getting ready.'

'I see,' Brunetti said. Then, pointing to the door, he asked, 'Through there?'

Suddenly reluctant, she said, 'I think it would be better if the owner showed you.' Without bothering to see if he agreed, she walked over to a red-haired woman who was standing behind the cash register and said a few words to her. The other woman glanced suspiciously in their direction, back at the counter-woman, then back at them. Then she said something to the first woman, who took her place behind the cash register.

The woman with red hair approached them and asked, 'What has she done?'

Brunetti smiled, he hoped disarmingly, and lied. 'Nothing that I know of, Signora. But as I'm sure you know, her aunt was the victim of a crime, and we hope that Signorina Simionato can give us some information that might help us with our investigation.'

'I thought you knew who did it,' she said, her voice just short of an accusation. 'That Albanian woman.' As she talked to them, her eyes kept moving back to the woman at the cash register each time a client approached to pay.

'So it would seem,' Brunetti said, 'but we need some more information about her aunt.'

'Do you have to do it here?' she asked truculently.

'No, Signora. Not here. I thought we could talk to her back there, in the kitchen,' he said.

'I mean here, while she's at work. I'm paying her to work, not stand around talking about her aunt.' Every so often, and always to his surprise, life brought Brunetti further evidence of the legendary venality of the Venetians. It was not the greed that surprised him so much as the lack of embarrassment in showing it.

He smiled. 'I can certainly understand that, Signora. So perhaps it would be better if I were to return later and place uniformed officers at the door while I talk to her. Or perhaps I could have a word with the people at the Department of Health and ask them how it is you know about next week's inspection.' Before she could say a word, he concluded, 'Or perhaps we could just go into the kitchen and have a word with Signorina Simionato.'

Her face reddened with anger she knew she could not display, while Brunetti entirely failed to reproach himself for this flagrant abuse of power. 'She's in the back,' the woman said and turned away from them to return to the cash register.

Vianello led the way into the kitchen, which was lit by a bank of windows set into the far wall. Empty metal racks stood against three walls, and the windowed doors of the vast ovens gleamed. A man and a woman, both wearing immaculate white coats and hats, stood in front of a deep sink from which rose the steam of soapy water. Emerging from the suds were the handles of implements and the tops of the broad wooden boards on which the dough was set to rise before baking.

Running water drowned all other sound, so Brunetti and Vianello were within a metre of the two before the man became aware of their presence and turned. When he saw them standing there, he turned back and shut off the water and, into the silence, said, 'Yes?' He was shorter than average, stocky, but had a handsome face in which only inquisitiveness was evident.

Apparently the woman had not noticed them until her companion spoke, and she turned only then. Shorter than he, she wore glasses with heavy rectangular frames and lenses so thick that they distorted her eyes, turning them into giant marbles. As she looked from Brunetti to Vianello, the focus in the lenses changed with the motion of her head, giving the sense that the marbles were rolling about under the glass. While the man's face had displayed curiosity at the sight of strangers in his kitchen, hers remained strangely impassive, the only sign of activity those rolling eyes.

'Signorina Simionato?' Brunetti asked.

Owl-like, her head turned towards the sound, and she considered the question before answering, 'Yes.'

'I'd like to speak to you, please.'

The man's glance shot from Brunetti to the woman, to Vianello, and back to Signorina Simionato, searching for the meaning of the arrival of these two strangers, but she kept her eyes on Brunetti's face and said nothing.

It was Vianello who addressed himself to the man,

'Perhaps there's a place where we might talk to Signorina Simionato in private?'

The man shook his head. 'There's nothing like that here,' he said. 'But I can go outside and have a cigarette while you talk.' When Brunetti nodded, the man removed his cap and wiped the sweat from his face with the inside of his elbow. Hitching up his jacket, he pulled a blue packet of Nazionali from the pocket of his trousers and walked away. Brunetti noticed that there was a back door into the *calle*.

'Signorina Simionato,' Brunetti began, 'I'm Commissario Brunetti, from the police.'

If it were possible for an immobile face to freeze, hers did. Even the eyes halted their busy traffic between Brunetti and Vianello and turned their attention to the windows at the back. But she said nothing. Brunetti studied her face, saw the flat nose and the frizzy orange hair that fought to escape from the white hat. Her skin was shiny, either with sweat or natural oiliness. The sight of her general blankness was enough to convince him that this woman was not capable of using a computer to make bank transfers to unnamed accounts in the Channel Islands.

'I'd like to ask you a few questions.'

She gave no sign that she heard him and did not remove her gaze from the back wall.

'You are Graziella Simionato, aren't you?' he asked.

The sound of her name appeared to make some impression, for she nodded in assent.

'The niece of Maria Grazia Battestini?' he asked.

That summoned both her attention and her eyes back to him. 'Yes,' she muttered. When she opened her mouth to speak, he saw that her two front teeth were outsized and jutted forward over the lower teeth.

'It is my understanding that you are her heir, Signorina.'

'Her heir. Yes,' she affirmed. 'I was supposed to get everything.'

Sounding concerned and puzzled, Brunetti asked, 'Didn't you, Signorina?'

As he watched her, he was struck by the way she kept reminding him of different animals. An owl. Then a caged rodent. And at this question something feral and secretive entered her expression.

She turned those magnified eyes towards him and asked, 'What do you want?'

'I'd like to talk about your aunt's estate, Signorina.'

'What do you want to know?'

'I'd like to know if you have any idea where her money came from.'

The instinct to hide all evidence of wealth overcame her. 'She didn't have much money,' she insisted.

'But she had bank accounts,' Brunetti said.

'I don't know about that.'

'At the Uni Credit and at four other banks.'

'I don't know.' Her voice was as stolid as her expression.

Brunetti shot a glance at Vianello, who raised his brows to show that he too recognized the mule-like obstinacy with which peasants have always resisted danger. Brunetti had quickly seen that sweet reason would do no more than shatter itself against the armour of her stupidity, and so he said, injecting an unpleasant severity into his voice, 'Signorina, you have two choices.'

Her eyes floated up towards his face, her attention caught by his tone.

'We can talk about the source of your aunt's wealth or we can talk about dogs.'

Her lips pulled back over her outsized teeth, and she started to speak, but Brunetti interrupted her. 'I don't think anyone who runs a business where there is food would want to continue to employ a person accused of using poison, do you, Signorina?' He watched this register and asked, his voice entirely conversational, 'And your employer doesn't seem like the kind of person who would be very patient with an employee who had to take time off to stand trial, does she? That is,' he asked, having given her a moment to reflect upon these two questions, 'if that employee still had a lawyer to help with the trial.'

Signorina Simionato took her left hand in the fingers of her right and began to rub it, as if trying to bring it back to life. Her lenses moved to Vianello's face, then back to Brunetti's. Still caressing her hand, she started to say, 'I don't . . .' but Brunetti interrupted her in a loud voice and said, 'Vianello, tell the owner we're taking her with us. And tell her why.'

Acting as if this were a command he was really expected to carry out, Vianello said, 'Yes, Commissario,' and turned towards the door that led to the shop.

He had not taken a step before she said, her voice high-pitched with terror, 'No, wait, don't do that. I'll tell you, I'll tell you.' Her speech was sloppy, as though the consonants could be produced only with the aid of large amounts of saliva.

Vianello turned back but stayed at least a metre from her, reluctant to add the threat of his size to that in Brunetti's words. Both men regarded her, saying nothing.

'It was Paolo,' she said. 'He did it. He got it for her, but I don't know how. She would never tell me that, only how proud she was of him. She said he always thought of her first.' She stopped, as if she thought this sufficient to answer their questions and counter the threat to her.

'What, exactly, did she tell you?' asked a relentless Brunetti.

'What I just told you,' she answered belligerently.

Brunetti turned away from her. 'Go out and tell her, Vianello,' he said.

Signorina Simionato looked from one to the other, seeking mercy. When she saw none, she put her head back and began to wail like an animal, howling as if wounded.

Fearful of what would happen, Brunetti took a step towards her, but stopped himself and moved back, not wanting to be seen near her when anyone came to investigate. In an instant, the owner appeared at the door and shouted, 'Graziella. Stop it. Stop it or you're gone from here today.'

Instantly, as quickly as it had begun, the noise ceased, but Signorina Simionato continued to sob. The owner looked at Brunetti and Vianello, made a disgusted noise, and left, closing the door on them.

Remorseless, Brunetti turned to the sobbing woman and said, 'You heard her, Graziella. She's not going to be very patient with you if I have to tell her about Poppi and about the poison, is she?'

Graziella pulled off her hat and wiped at her mouth and nose with it, but she seemed incapable of stopping her sobs. She took off her glasses and set them on the surface of a stove and wiped at her face, then looked at Brunetti with her naked eyes, which were crossed and virtually sightless.

He fought back pity and said, 'What else did she tell you, Graziella? About the money.'

The sobbing stopped, and she took a final wipe at her face. Blindly, she put her hand out and began to feel around for the glasses. Brunetti watched her hand come close, move away, come close; he resisted the desire to help her. Finally her hand landed on the glasses and, careful to use both hands, she replaced them.

'What did she tell you, Graziella?' Brunetti repeated. 'Where did Paolo get the money?'

'From someone at work,' she said. 'She was so proud of him. She said it was a bonus he got for being so clever. But she was nasty when she said that, like she didn't mean it and like Paolo had done something bad to get it. But I didn't care about that because she said the money was going to be mine some day. So it didn't matter how he got it. Besides, she said everything he did was under the protection of the Madonna, so it wasn't wrong, was it?'

Brunetti ignored her question and asked, 'Did you know where it was, in which banks?'

She hung her head, looking down at the floor between their feet, and nodded.

'Do you know how it got there?'

Silence. She kept her head lowered, and he wondered what sluggish assessment she was making of his question and how much of the truth she would decide to tell him.

She surprised him by answering his question literally. 'I put it there.'

This made no immediate sense to him but, displaying no confusion, he asked, 'How?'

'After Paolo died, I went to see her every month and she gave me the money, and I took it to the banks.' Of course, of course, he had never thought to ask or to wonder about the precise physical details of how the deposits were made, thinking that they had to be arcane transfers discoverable only by Signorina Elettra's arts.

'And the receipts?'

'I took them back to her. Every month.'

'Where are they now?'

Silence.

Raising his voice, he repeated, 'Where are they now?'

Her voice was low, but by bending down he could make it out. 'She told me to burn them.'

'Who?' he asked, though he had a good idea.

'She did.'

'Who?'

'The lawyer,' she finally said, refusing to give Marieschi's name.

'And did you do this?' he asked, wondering if she realized that she would have thus destroyed proof that the money had ever existed.

She looked up at him, and he saw that the lenses were soaked with the tears that had fallen while her head was lowered, and her eyes were even more out of focus.

'Did you burn them, Signorina?' he asked, no softness in his voice.

'She said it was the only way I could be sure I'd get the money because the police might be suspicious if they came and found the receipts,' she said, her sense of loss audible in every word.

'And then afterwards, Signorina, what happened when you went to the banks to try to get it?' Brunetti asked.

'The people at the banks – I knew them all – told me that the accounts had been closed.'

'And why did you think Avvocatessa Marieschi took it?' he asked, introducing the name for the first time.

'Because *Zia* Maria told me she was the only other person who knew about the money. And that I could trust her.' She said this with audible disgust. 'Who else could it be?'

Brunetti looked across at the silent Vianello and raised his chin in interrogation. Vianello closed his eyes for a moment and shook his head: that was it; there was nothing else to be learned from her.

Brunetti didn't bother to say anything to her but turned away and started towards the door.

Behind him, however, he heard Vianello's voice. 'Why did you kill the dog, Signorina?' Brunetti stopped but didn't turn around.

Such a long time passed that anyone but the stolid Vianello would have abandoned the wait and left. Finally, consonants wetter than ever, she spat out, 'Because people love dogs.' After a short pause, Brunetti heard Vianello's steps behind him and he continued walking towards the door to the shop.

19

'Well,' Brunetti asked as they stepped out into Calle Lunga San Barnaba, 'what did you think?'

'I'd say she's what my kids are being taught at school to call "differently abled".'

'Retarded, you mean?' Brunetti asked.

'Yes. There's the look of her, the way she howled when she couldn't get her way, and an almost total lack of normal human reactions or feelings.'

'Sounds like half the Questura,' Brunetti said.

It took a second for this to register, but then Vianello laughed so hard he had to stop walking and lean against the wall of a building until he stopped. Feeling not a little proud of the remark, Brunetti made a note to tell Paola and wondered if Vianello would tell Signorina Elettra.

When Vianello had regained control of himself, Brunetti continued down towards the Ca' Rezzonico vaporetto stop. 'You think she could have had anything to do with her aunt's death?'

Vianello's answer was immediate. 'I don't think so. She

started to scream when you asked her about the accounts and threatened to have her fired if she didn't answer. She didn't seem at all troubled when you talked about her aunt.'

Brunetti was of the same opinion, but he was nonetheless glad to have it confirmed by the inspector. 'We'll have to get a list of everyone who worked with him while he was at the school board,' he said, then corrected himself, 'at least who was working there when the payments started.'

'If the records have been computerized,' Vianello said, 'it ought to be easy.'

'I'm surprised she isn't giving you homework to do every night,' Brunetti said with a smile. When Vianello failed to respond, he demanded, 'She isn't, is she?'

They reached the *imbarcadero* and stepped inside, glad of the shade. Vianello scratched his head. 'Not exactly, sir. But you know she's given me a computer. That is, the Department has given me a computer. And occasionally she suggests I try certain things on it.'

'Would I understand?' Brunetti asked.

Vianello gazed across at Palazzo Grassi, where more long lines of tourists waited in front of another temple to art. 'I doubt it, sir,' the inspector finally admitted. 'She says you have to learn these things by trying different ways of doing them or different ways of thinking about them. So you really need a computer to work with all the time.' He looked at Brunetti, then dared to add, 'And you have to have a sort of feeling for computers, too.'

Brunetti wanted to defend himself by saying that his children had a computer and his wife used one, but he thought this beneath his dignity and so made no response. He contented himself with asking, 'When can we have the names?'

'At the latest by tomorrow afternoon,' Vianello said. 'I'm not sure I would be able to get them, and Signorina Elettra said she had an appointment this afternoon.'

'Did she say where she had this appointment?'

'No.'

'Then let's leave it until tomorrow,' Brunetti suggested, looking at his watch. There was no purpose to be served by returning to the Questura, and he found himself suddenly exhausted by the events of the day. He wanted nothing more than to go home, have a meal with his family, and think of things other than death and greed. Vianello was more than willing to agree and stepped on to the Number One that was going towards the Lido, leaving his superior to wait for the one that would be along in two minutes to take him to his own home.

But when the vaporetto pulled up at his normal stop, San Silvestro, Brunetti remained on board and got off at the next, Rialto. It was only a few steps back along the canal to the city hall at Ca' Farsetti and then down the *calle* beside it to the building where the school board had its offices. Brunetti showed his warrant card to the *portiere* and was told that the main office of the Ufficio di Pubblica Istruzione was on the third floor. Never comfortable in elevators, he chose to take the stairs. On the third floor, a sign directed him to the right and along a narrow corridor, at the end of which stood the glass-doored offices of the school board. Inside he found himself in a large open space, four times the size of his own office. Orange plastic chairs lined the walls on either side of him; facing the door stood a battered wooden desk, and behind the desk sat an equally battered-looking woman, though something told him that her look was the result of choice, rather than chance.

There was no one else in the room, so Brunetti approached her. She could have been any age between thirty and fifty: her make-up was applied with sufficient abandon to disguise the evidence that would have allowed him to make that distinction. Though lipstick had enlarged her mouth, it had also managed to seep into and spread out from the many thin wrinkles under her lower lip, giving her mouth the suggestion of youthful promise at the same time that it gave evidence of years of heavy smoking. Her eyes were dark green, a mysterious emerald, but they glittered so brightly as to suggest either contact lenses or drugs. She had no eyebrows, nothing more than a pair of thin brown lines arching across her forehead in steep curves seemingly chosen at random.

Brunetti smiled as he approached her desk. Her lips moved in return and she asked, 'You the water-cooler man?' Her voice was entirely without inflection or emphasis; it could as easily be coming from a machine as from that exaggerated mouth.

'I beg your pardon?' he asked.

'Are you the water-cooler man?' her voice played back.

'No. I'm here to speak to the Director.'

'You're not the water-cooler man?'

'No, I'm afraid not.'

He watched as this information was processed somewhere behind those emerald eyes. The fact that her expectation had been confounded appeared momentarily to prove too much for her, forcing her to close her eyes. He noticed that she had two tiny silver studs emerging from her left temple, but he refused to wonder about their origin, still less their purpose.

Her eyes opened. Perhaps she opened them; he was not at all certain. 'Dottor Rossi is in his office,' she said, raising a hand with long green fingernails and waving in the general direction of a door that stood behind her left shoulder.

Brunetti thanked her, decided not to tell her he hoped the water-cooler man would arrive soon, and walked to the door. Beyond it stretched a short corridor, doors to the left and a row of windows on the right giving on to a small inner courtyard, on the opposite side of which were more windows.

Brunetti walked down the hall, reading the names and

titles on the signs beside the doors. The offices were silent, apparently abandoned. At the end of the corridor, he turned right: this time there were offices on both sides, though none of them that of the Director.

He turned right again; at the end of this corridor he found a sign that read, Dottore Mauro Rossi, Direttore. He knocked. A voice called, '*Avanti*,' and Brunetti went in. The man sitting at the desk looked up, seemed puzzled at the arrival of a stranger in his office, and asked, 'Yes, what is it?'

'I'm Commissario Guido Brunetti, Dottore. I've come to ask some questions about a man who used to work here.'

'Commissario of police?' Rossi asked, and at Brunetti's nod, pointed him to a chair in front of his desk. As Brunetti approached, Rossi stood and extended his hand. When Rossi reached his full height, Brunetti saw the bulk of the man, easily half a head taller than he was himself. Though he was more heavily built than Brunetti, there was no suggestion of fat. Rossi looked in his mid-forties; his hair, still thick and dark, fell across his forehead as he moved his head. His skin was rugged with good health, and he moved gracefully for so large a man.

The office projected the same powerful sense of masculinity: a row of silver sports trophies stood on top of a glass-fronted bookcase; silver-framed photos of a woman and two children stood on the left side of the desk; five or six framed certificates hung on the walls, one of them the embossed parchment conferring a doctorate upon Mauro Rossi.

When he was seated, Brunetti said, 'It's about someone who worked here until about five years ago, Dottore: Paolo Battestini.' Rossi nodded for Brunetti to continue but gave no sign that he recognized the name.

'There are some things we'd like to know about him,' Brunetti said. 'He worked here for more than a decade.' When Rossi remained silent, Brunetti asked, 'Could you tell me if you knew him, Dottore?'

Rossi considered the question, then answered, 'Perhaps. I'm not really sure.' Brunetti tilted his head in a request for clarification, and Rossi explained, 'I was in charge of the schools in Mestre.'

'From here?' Brunetti interrupted.

'No, no,' Rossi said, smiling to excuse his oversight in not having specified. 'I was working in Mestre then. It was only two years ago that I was appointed here.'

'As Director?'

'Yes.'

'And so you moved here?'

Rossi smiled again and pursed his lips at the continuing confusion. 'No, I've always lived in the city.' It surprised Brunetti that the other man continued to speak in Italian: at this point in a conversation, most Venetians would slip into Veneziano, but perhaps Rossi wanted to maintain the dignity of his position. 'So the transfer was a double blessing because it meant I didn't have to go out to Mestre every day,' Rossi went on, breaking into Brunetti's reflections.

'The Pearl of the Adriatic,' Brunetti said with some sarcasm.

Rossi nodded in the true Venetian's dismissal of that ugly upstart, Mestre.

Brunetti realized they had wandered astray from his original question and returned to it. 'You said perhaps you knew him, Dottore. Could you explain what you mean?'

'I suppose I must have known him, actually,' Rossi answered, then added, seeing Brunetti's confusion, 'That is, in the way one knows people who work in the same office or department. You see them or read their names, but you never get to know them personally or speak to them.'

'Did you have occasion to come here, to this office while you were working in Mestre?'

'Yes. The man I replaced as Director was here, and so when I was in charge in Mestre, I had to come in once a week for conferences because the central directorship is here.' Anticipating Brunetti's next question, Rossi said, 'I don't remember ever meeting someone with that name or talking to him. That is, when you say his name, it sounds familiar, but I don't have a picture of him in my mind. And then, by the time I was transferred here, he must have already left, that is, if you say he left five years ago.'

'Have you ever heard people here speak of him?'

Rossi shook his head in silent negation then said, 'Not that I recall, no.'

'Since his mother's death, has anyone spoken of him?' Brunetti asked.

'His mother?' Rossi asked, and then his face registered the connection. 'That woman who was killed?' he asked. Brunetti nodded.

'I didn't make the connection,' Rossi said. 'It's not an uncommon name.' Rossi's voice changed and he asked, 'Why are you asking about him?'

'It's a case of eliminating a possibility, Dottore. We want to be sure there was no connection between him and his mother's death.'

'After five years?' Rossi asked. 'You say he left here five years ago?' His tone suggested he thought Brunetti might be better occupied asking questions about something else.

Brunetti ignored this and said, 'As I said, we're trying to eliminate possibilities, rather than make connections, Dottore. That's why we're asking.' He waited for Rossi to question this, but he did not. When Rossi moved back in his chair, Brunetti observed that he did not use his hands, only the strength of his legs.

Brunetti leaned back in his own chair, threw up his open palms in a gesture of defeat, and said, 'To tell the truth, Dottore, we're at a bit of a loss about him. We have no idea what sort of man he was.'

'But his mother is the one who got killed, isn't she?' Rossi asked, like one who had taken it upon himself to remind the police of what they were meant to be doing.

'Indeed,' Brunetti answered and smiled again. 'It's nothing more than habit, I suppose. We always try to learn as much as we can about victims and the people around them.'

As if remembering, Rossi asked, 'But wasn't there something in the papers when it happened about a foreign woman, a Russian or something?'

'Romanian,' Brunetti said automatically. Some sense registered that Rossi did not like being corrected, and so he added, 'Not that it matters, Dottore. We had hoped to find some reason why she might have resented or disliked Signora Battestini,' then, before Rossi said anything, he went on, 'The son might have offended her in some way.'

'She came to work for Signora Battestini after her son died, didn't she?' Rossi asked, as if to add this fact to the others that rendered Brunetti's questions futile.

'Yes, she did,' Brunetti said, repeating his open-handed gesture less dramatically, and got to his feet. 'I don't think there's anything else I need to ask you about him, Dottore. Thank you very much for your time.'

Rossi stood. 'I hope I was able to be of some help,' he said.

Brunetti's smile grew even broader, 'I'm afraid you were, Dottore,' he said, then continued seamlessly, seeing Rossi's surprise, 'in that you eliminated a possibility for us. We'll have to concentrate our attention on Signora Battestini again.'

Rossi accompanied Brunetti to the office door. He leaned down a little to reach the handle and pulled open the door. He put out his hand, and Brunetti took it: two city officials, shaking hands after a few minutes of helpful cooperation. With repeated thanks for the doctor's time, Brunetti pulled the door closed behind him and started back towards the stairway, wondering how it was that Dottore Rossi knew that Paolo Battestini, whom he said he did not know, was dead and that Flori Ghiorghiu had come to work for his mother only after that event.

It was after eight when he got home, but Paola had decided to delay dinner at least until half-past on the assumption that he would have called if he was going to be much later.

His sober mood was matched by that of the other three members of his family, at least when they first sat down. But by the time the kids had eaten two helpings of *orecchiette* with cubes of *mozzarella di bufala* and *pomodorini*, they were ready to cheer in delight as Paola broke open the salt crust within which she had baked a *branzino*, revealing the perfect white flesh.

'What happens to the salt, Mamma?' Chiara asked as she poured some olive oil on her own helping of fish.

'I put it in the garbage.'

'Is it true that the Indians used to put fish bones around corn to make it grow better?' she asked, pushing them to one side of her plate.

'Dot Indians or Feather Indians?' Raffi asked.

'Feather Indians, of course,' Chiara answered, oblivious to the racist overtones of Raffi's question. 'You know corn didn't grow in India.'

'Raffi,' Paola said, 'will you take the garbage down tonight and put it in the entrance hall? I don't want this fish stinking up the house.'

'Sure. I told Giorgio and Luca I'd meet them at nine-thirty. I'll take it down when I go.'

'Did you put your things in the washing machine?' she asked.

He rolled his eyes. 'You think I'd try to get out of this place without doing it?' He turned to his father and, in a voice that proclaimed male solidarity, said, 'She's got radar.' Then he spelled the last word out, slowly, letter by letter, just to make clear the nature of the regime under which he lived.

'Thanks,' Paola said, certain of her powers and impervious to all reproach.

When Chiara offered to help with the dishes, Paola told her she'd do them herself because of the fish. Chiara took this as a reprieve rather than as an affront to her domestic skills and went to take advantage of Raffi's absence to use the computer.

Brunetti got up as she was finishing the dishes and pulled the Moka out of the cabinet.

'Coffee?' Paola asked. She knew his habits well enough to know he usually had coffee after dinner only in restaurants.

'Yes. I'm beat,' he confessed.

'Maybe it would be better just to go to bed early,' she suggested.

'I don't know if I can sleep in this heat,' he said.

'Let me finish these,' she offered, 'and then we can go out and sit on the terrace for a while. Until you get sleepy.'

'All right,' he agreed, put the pot back and opened the next cabinet. 'What's good to drink in this heat?' he asked, surveying the bottles that filled two shelves.

'Sparkling mineral water.'

'Very funny,' Brunetti said. He reached deep into the cabinet for a bottle of Galliano way at the back. He rephrased his question. 'What's good to drink while sitting on the terrace, watching the sun fade in the west, while sitting beside the person you adore most in the universe and realizing that life has no greater joy to offer than the company of that person?'

Draping the dishtowel over the handle of the drawer where the knives and forks were kept, she gave him a long glance that ended in a quizzical grin. 'Non-sparkling mineral water might be better for a man in your condition,' she said and went out on the terrace to wait for him to join her.

*

He found himself afflicted, the next morning, with the lethargy that often came upon him when a case seemed to be going nowhere. Added to this was the penetrating heat that had already taken a grip on the day by the time he woke. Even the cup of coffee Paola brought him did nothing to lift the oppression of his spirits, nor did the long shower he permitted himself, taking advantage of the fact that both children had already left for the Alberoni, and thus there was no chance of their angry banging on the bathroom door should he use more water than their ecological sensibilities permitted. Two decades of habitual morning grumpiness had established Paola's rights to that mood, so he knew there was little joy to be had in her conversation.

He left the apartment directly after his shower, faintly annoyed with the universe. As he walked towards Rialto, he decided to have another coffee at the bar on the next corner. He bought a paper and was reading the headlines as he walked in. He went to the counter and, eyes still on the paper, asked for a coffee and a brioche. He paid no real attention to the familiar sound of the coffee machine, the thud and the hiss, nor to the sound of the cup being set in front of him. But when he looked up, he saw that the woman who had been serving him coffee for decades was gone; that, or she had been transformed into a Chinese woman half her age. He looked at the cash register, and there was another Chinese, this one a man, standing behind it.

He had seen this happening for months, this gradual taking over of the bars of the city by Chinese owners and workers, but this was the first time it had occurred in one of the places he frequented. He resisted the impulse to ask where Signora Rosalba had gone, and her husband, and instead added two sugars to his coffee. He walked over to the plastic case but saw that the brioche were different from the fresh ones with *mirtillo* he had eaten for years; the tag on the case explained that they were manufactured

197

and frozen in Milano. He finished his coffee, paid, and left.

It was still early enough for the boats not yet to be crowded with tourists, so he took the Number One from San Silvestro, standing on deck and reading the *Gazzettino*. This did little to alleviate his mood. Nor did the sight of Scarpa standing at the bottom of the stairs when he walked into the Questura.

Brunetti passed by him silently and started up the steps. From behind, he heard Scarpa call, 'Commissario, if I might have a word . . .'

Brunetti turned and looked down on the uniformed man. 'Yes, Lieutenant?'

'I'm calling Signora Gismondi in for questioning again today. Since you seem so interested in her, I thought you might want to know.'

'"Interested," Lieutenant?' Brunetti confined himself to asking.

Ignoring the question, Scarpa added, 'No one remembers seeing her at the train station that morning.'

'I dare say that could also be said of most of the other seventy thousand people in the city,' Brunetti said wearily. 'Good morning, Lieutenant.'

Inside his office, he found himself reflecting on Scarpa's behaviour. His deliberate obstructionism might be nothing more than a sign of his hatred of Brunetti and the people who worked with him, Signora Gismondi being nothing more than a tool. Not for the first time, Brunetti speculated on a further meaning, that Scarpa might be attempting to remove the focus of attention from some other person. The possibility still left him feeling faintly sick.

To distract himself from this idea, he read his way through the papers that had accumulated in his in-tray over the last few days, chief of which was a notice from the Ministero dell'Interno, spelling out the changes to law enforcement policies resultant upon, as the document would have it, the passage of recent laws by Parliament. He read it with interest, reread it with anger. When he finished it the second time, he set it down on the middle of his desk, gazed out the window, and said aloud in disgust, 'Why not just let them run the whole country?' His pronoun did not refer to the elected members of Parliament.

He busied himself with other papers that awaited his attention and successfully resisted the temptation to go downstairs to attempt to interfere with whatever was being done to Signora Gismondi. He knew that there was no way a case could be made against her and that she was nothing more than a pawn in a game even he did not fully understand, but he knew that any attempt to help her would work only to her disservice.

He passed a stupid hour, then another, before Vianello knocked at his door. When the inspector entered, Brunetti's first glance told him something was wrong.

Vianello stood in front of Brunetti's desk, a sheaf of papers in his hand. 'It's my fault, sir,' Vianello said.

'What?' Brunetti asked.

'It was right there in front of me, and I never bothered to ask.'

'What are you talking about, Vianello?' Brunetti asked sharply. 'And sit down. Don't just stand there.'

Vianello appeared not to hear this and held up the papers. 'He worked in the contracts office,' he said, waving the papers for emphasis. 'It was his job to study the building plans submitted for any work that had to be done on the schools and see if they met the specific needs of the pupils and teachers in that particular school.' He pulled out one sheet of paper and set the others on Brunetti's desk. 'Look,' he said, holding it up. 'He had no power to approve the contracts, but he did have the power to recommend.' He added the sheet to the papers on Brunetti's desk and stepped back, as though he feared they might burst into flames. 'I was in there, talking about him, and I never bothered to ask what office it was.'

'Who, the son?'

'Yes. That's where he started. The father worked in the personnel office, and God knows no one's going to ask for a bribe there.'

'And the dates?'

Vianello picked up the papers and looked through them. 'The payments started after he had been there for four years.' He looked across at Brunetti. 'That's more than enough time for him to have become familiar with the way things worked.'

'If that's how they worked.'

'Commissario,' Vianello said, an unwonted note of asperity in his voice, 'it's a city office, for God's sake. How else do you think things work?'

'Who was in charge of the office when the payments began?'

Without having to consult the papers, Vianello answered, 'Renato Fedi. He was named head of the department about three months before the accounts were opened.'

'And went on to bigger and better things,' Brunetti chimed in. But then asked, 'Who was in charge when Battestini started working there?'

'Piero De Pra was there when he started, but he's dead now. Luca Sardelli took over when De Pra died, but he lasted only two years himself before he was transferred to the Sanitation Department. Before it was privatized,' he added.

'Any idea why he was transferred?'

Vianello shrugged. 'From the little I've heard about him, I'd guess he's one of those nonentities who just gets shifted around from office to office because he's made it his business to make friends with everyone, so no one has the courage to fire him. They just keep him around until they see a convenient spot to move him, and they get rid of him.'

Resisting the strong impulse to repeat his remark about the Questura, Brunetti contented himself with asking, instead, 'And he's at the Assessorato dello Sport now?'

'Yes.'

'Any idea what he does?'

'No.'

'Find out,' Brunetti said. Before Vianello could acknowledge the command, Brunetti asked, 'And Fedi?'

'He followed Sardelli, stayed there two years, and then left the civil service to take over his uncle's construction company. He's run it since then.'

'What sort of things do they do?' Brunetti asked.

'Yes,' Vianello answered. 'Restorations. Of schools, among other things.'

Brunetti cast his memory back to his conversation with Judge Galvani, trying to remember if there had been anything in the judge's reference to Fedi that he had overlooked, some tone, or a suggestion that he take a closer look at the man, but he could remember nothing. It occurred to him then that Galvani was not a friend and owed him no favours, so perhaps he would not have made the suggestion, even if there were reason to do so. He felt a moment's hot exasperation: why did it always have to be like this, with no one willing to do anything unless there were personal gain to be had from it or because some favour had to be repaid?

He drew his attention back to Vianello, who was saying, '. . . has grown steadily for the last five years'.

'I'm sorry, Vianello,' he said, 'I was thinking about something else. What did you say?'

'That his uncle's company won a contract to restore two schools in Castello when Fedi was in charge of the school board, and that it's grown steadily since then, especially after he took over.'

'How do you know this?'

'We looked at the papers in his office and his tax returns for those years.'

For a moment, he was tempted to ask angrily if this meant Vianello and Signorina Elettra had somehow found the time that morning to go to Fedi's office and ask to please examine their client records and tax returns, and this without bothering to get an order from a judge. Instead, he said, 'Vianello, this has got to stop.'

'Yes, sir,' the inspector said perfunctorily, then added, 'My guess is that the tenders for the work that went to the uncle's company would have been evaluated by Battestini. He was working in that job then.'

With acute awareness of the hopeless irony of the question, Brunetti asked, 'Can you find out if he did examine them?'

Gracious in victory, Vianello did no more than nod. 'His signature or initials have got to be on the original bid if he was the person who checked it for the school board.' He forestalled Brunetti's next question by saying, 'No, sir, we don't have to go and look at the papers. There's a code on the offer, indicating who examined it and checked that it met the school's requirements, so all we have to do is find Fedi's bid and see who handled it.'

'Is there any way you can check the costs to see if they were . . .' Imagination failed Brunetti, and he left the sentence unfinished.

'The easiest way, I think, would be to check the other bids and compare what they offered in terms of cost and time. If Fedi's uncle's bid was much higher or provided less, then that would suggest we've found the explanation.'

From the enthusiasm with which he spoke, Brunetti had no doubt what Vianello thought the likely result would be. But Brunetti had spent many years in contemplation of the genius with which Italians robbed the state, and he doubted that someone as successful as Fedi, were he to have given this contract to his uncle by illegal means, would have been so artless as to have left an easy trail. 'Check to see about overruns, too, and whether they were ever questioned,' he suggested, displaying two decades of experience of the city administration.

Vianello got to his feet and left. Brunetti toyed for a moment with the idea of going downstairs to observe them at work – he knew better than to delude himself into thinking he could help in any way – but knew it would be better to leave them to it. Not only would it be faster that way, but it would also spare his conscience the need to contemplate the ever-expanding illegality of Signorina Elettra and Vianello's investigative techniques.

20

After more than an hour, Brunetti's impatience conquered his good sense, and he went downstairs. When he entered her office, expecting to find Signorina Elettra and Vianello peering at the computer, he was surprised to find them gone, though the blank screen still glowed with suspended life. Patta's door was closed: in fact, Brunetti was suddenly aware that he had seen no sign of his superior for some days and wondered if Patta had indeed moved to Lyon and begun working for Interpol, and no one had noticed. Once he allowed this possibility to slip into his mind, Brunetti found himself helpless to avoid considering its consequences: which of the various time-servers poised on the slippery pole of promotion would be chosen to replace Patta?

The geographical inwardness of Venice was reflected in its social habits: the web of narrow *calli* connecting the six *sestieri* mirrored the connections and interstices linking its inhabitants to one another. Strada Nuova and Via XXII Marzo had the broad directness of the ties of family: anyone could follow them clearly. Calle Lunga San Barnaba and Barbaria de le Tole, straight still but far narrower and shorter, were in their way like the bonds between close friends: there was little chance of losing the way, but they didn't lead as far. The bulk of the *calli* that made movement possible in the city, however, were narrow and crooked, often leading to dead ends or to branches that took the unsuspecting in the opposite direction to the way they wanted to go: this was the way of protective deceit, these the paths that had to be followed by those without access to more direct ways of reaching a goal.

In the years he had been in Venice, Patta had been unable to find his way alone through the narrow *calli*, but he had at least learned to send Venetians ahead to lead him through the labyrinth of rancours and animosities that had been built up over the centuries, as well as around the obstacles and wrong turnings created in more recent times. No doubt any replacement sent by the central bureaucracy in Rome would be a foreigner – as anyone not born within earshot of the waters of the *laguna* was a foreigner – and would flail about hopelessly in pursuit of straight roads and direct ways of getting somewhere. Aghast at the realization, Brunetti had to accept the fact that he did not want Patta to leave.

These reflections fell from him as the sound of Vianello's voice approached. The deep boom of his laugh was followed by the higher tones of Signorina Elettra's. Entering the office, they stopped when they saw Brunetti: the laughter ceased, and the smiles evaporated from their faces.

Providing no explanation for their absence, Signorina Elettra moved behind her computer and flicked it into life, then pressed a series of keys, after which two pages materialized on the screen, placed side by side. 'These are the bids from Fedi's uncle's company that were accepted while Fedi was in charge of the school board, sir.'

He moved to stand beside her and saw at the top of both sheets the familiar letter heading of the city administration and below it thick paragraphs of dark type. She touched a key, and two more seemingly identical pages appeared. Another key made these vanish, replacing them with two more. Lacking the letterhead, these contained, on the left, a column of words or phrases and, opposite them, a matching column of numbers.

'That's the estimate, sir.'

He looked at the last page and read some of the words, ran his eyes to the right and saw what the objects or services would cost. At sea in ignorance, he had no idea what many of them were and no idea what any of them should cost.

'Have you compared this with the other bids?' he asked, looking away from the contract and back at Signorina Elettra.

'Yes.'

'And?'

'And his was cheaper,' she said with audible disappointment. 'Not only was it cheaper, but he guaranteed that the work would be done within the fixed period and offered to pay a penalty per day if it was not.'

Brunetti looked back at the screen, as if certain that closer examination of the words and the numbers would reveal to him whatever ruse Fedi had used to win the contract. But no matter how long he studied the pages, they refused to make sense to him. Finally he turned away from the screen and asked, 'And overruns?'

'None,' she said, tapping a few words into the computer and waiting while new documents appeared in place of the others. 'The entire project was finished on time,' she explained, pointing to what Brunetti assumed were the documents which proved this. 'What's more,' she went on, 'they were finished within the projected budget, and a civil engineer I phoned said the work was done well, far above the average quality of work performed for the city.' She saw how he reacted to this, so showed some reluctance in adding, 'The same is true of the two restorations they did to schools here in the city, sir.'

Brunetti looked from the screen to her face, to Vianello's face and then back at the screen. In the past he had often told himself to look at the evidence and not at what he wanted the evidence to be, yet here he was again, confronted with information which did not support what he wanted the truth to be, and his impulse was to assume that it did not really mean what it appeared to mean or to find other evidence that would discount it.

He saw it then, the trail he had insisted they follow, the trail that had not only led to this dead end but had taken the wrong turning from the very start. 'It's all wrong,' he said. 'What we've been doing, it's all wrong.'

He recalled the title of a book he had read some years ago and said it out loud: '"The March of Folly". That's what we've been doing: lumbering around after big game when what we should have been doing was thinking about the money.'

'And isn't that the money?' Vianello asked, pointing to the screen.

'I mean the money in the accounts,' Brunetti insisted. 'We've been looking at the total, not the money.'

Their expressions suggested they still didn't follow, and Vianello's indignant, 'To some of us, thirty thousand Euro is money,' confirmed it.

'Of course it's money,' Brunetti agreed, 'a lot of money, especially ten years ago. But it's the total we've been looking at, not the actual monthly payments. Someone with a good salary could have paid it and not missed it. Even if you were still single and lived at home, you could have paid it,' he surprised Vianello by saying.

Vianello began a blustering negative, but then he considered the conditions Brunetti had imposed, paused, and said, though grudgingly, 'Yes, if I still lived with my parents and had no interests, and never wanted to go out to dinner, and didn't care what I wore, then I suppose I could have done it.' Ungracious in defeat, he added, 'But it still wouldn't be easy. It was a lot of money.'

'But not enough to pay someone to keep quiet about the way a contract was approved for the complete restoration of these buildings,' Brunetti insisted. He jabbed his finger against the computer screen, where the final sum glowed in eerie enormity. 'A job as big as this one would have earned them millions of Euros. No blackmailer,' he said, finally naming the crime, 'would ask for so little, not with a contract this large at stake.'

He looked at both of them, waiting to see signs that they agreed with his interpretation. Vianello's slow nod and Signorina Elettra's answering smile showed him that they did. 'We've,' he began, then corrected himself and confessed, 'no, I've been blinded into thinking it was a payment for something big, something important, like a contract. But what we're after here is something small, something mean and personal and private.'

'And probably nasty,' Vianello added.

Brunetti turned to Signorina Elettra. 'I've no idea what sort of information you can get about the people who were working at the school board when the payments started,' he said, judging it superfluous to add that he no longer cared how she got it, 'and I'm not sure what sort of person we're looking for. Avvocatessa Marieschi said Signora Battestini told her it was her son who took care of her old age,' he began, then, raising his eyes in a parody of belief, added, 'with the help of the Madonna.' Both of them smiled at that, and he went on, 'We're looking for someone who worked there and who could pay four hundred thousand lire a month.'

'Perhaps,' Vianello interrupted, 'they were so rich the money didn't matter to them.'

Signorina Elettra turned to him and said, 'I don't think that's the sort of person who works at the school board, Ispettore.'

For a moment, Brunetti feared that Vianello would be offended by the apparent sarcasm of her remark, but he seemed not to be. In fact, after considering it, the inspector nodded and said, 'What's strange, if you think about it, is that the amount never changed. Salaries have gone up, everything's become more expensive, yet the payments never changed.'

Interested by what he said, Signorina Elettra slid into her chair and typed in a few words, then a few more, and the pages of print on the screen were replaced by the records of the vanished bank accounts. She scrolled them down to the month of the conversion to the Euro. After she'd checked those for January, she went on to February. Looking up at Brunetti, she said, 'Look at this, Commissario. There's a difference of five *centesimi* between January and February.'

Brunetti bent to look at the screen and saw that, as she said, the payment for February was five *centesimi* more than that for January. She hit a key, and he saw March and April, both with the adjusted total. Signorina Elettra pulled a pocket calculator from her desk, the tiny one sent to every citizen in the country at the time of the Euro conversion. Quickly she did the sums, looked up, and said, 'The February total is the right amount.' She slipped the calculator back into her drawer and shut it. 'Five *centesimi*,' she said with awe, as in the face of the terrible.

'Either the person realized the error . . .' Vianello began, but Brunetti cut him off by finishing the sentence with the more likely explanation, 'or Signora Battestini corrected him.'

'For five *centesimi*,' Signorina Elettra repeated in a soft voice, still in awe of the avarice capable of that precision.

Brunetti remembered his conversation with Dottor Carlotti and blurted out, 'Her phone. Her phone. Her phone.' When he saw their looks of incomprehension, Brunetti said, 'She hadn't been out of the apartment for three years. The only way she could have told them to make the correction was by phone.' He cursed himself for not having thought to get her phone records before, cursed himself for following the path he wanted to be the right one instead of looking at what was in front of them.

'It will take a few hours,' Signorina Elettra said. Before Brunetti could ask why there was no way to get the records more quickly, she explained, 'Giorgio's wife just had a baby, so he's working only half-days and won't be in until after lunch.' Even before Brunetti could ask, she said, 'No, I told him I wouldn't try to get into the system by myself. If I make a mistake, they'll be able to see who was helping me.'

'A mistake?' Vianello asked.

A long silence followed his words, and just as it was beginning to become awkward, she said, 'With computers, I mean. But I still gave my word. I can't do it.'

Brunetti and Vianello exchanged a glance of uneasy acquiescence, both thinking of the mistake Signorina Elettra had made some years before. 'All right,' Brunetti said. 'Check incoming and outgoing calls, if you would.' He remembered the time he had met her friend Giorgio, years ago. 'Boy or girl?' he asked.

'Girl,' she said then, with a smile just short of beatific, she added, 'They named her Elettra.'

'I'm surprised they didn't call her Compaq,' Vianello said, and at her laugh, ease was restored.

As he walked back to his office, Brunetti tried to invent a scenario that would allow for blackmail, imagining all manner of secrets or vices, all manner of outrage that might have led to someone's becoming Battestini's victim. That word rang strangely out of tune in Brunetti's mind, persuaded as he was that the person being blackmailed was the same person who had killed Signora Battestini. 'Subject,' then? And what was the line that separated one from the other, what the impulse that had driven her killer to cross it?

He ran through a list of possible crimes and vices until he

found himself faced with the truth of Paola's claims: most of the Seven Deadly Sins were no longer so. Who would kill in order not to be exposed as having been guilty of gluttony, of sloth, of envy, or pride? Only lust remained or anger if it led to violence, and avarice, if it could be interpreted as meaning bribe-taking. For the rest, no one any longer cared. Paradise, he had been told as a child, was a sinless world, but this brave new, post-sinful, world in which he found himself was hardly to be confused with paradise.

21

Brunetti had passed into the phase of an investigation he hated most, when everything came to a halt while a new map was drawn. In the past, his frustration at the imposed immobility of this situation had provoked him to acts of rashness he had sometimes regretted. But now he resisted the impulse to act on impulse and hunted for something he could justify doing. He pulled out the phone book and made a note of the numbers and addresses for both the homes and the offices of Fedi and Sardelli, even as he told himself they were the least likely suspects: it didn't have to be one of the directors; if it had been, Paolo Battestini would probably have asked for more.

He pulled out the Battestini file and read through all the press clippings. And there it was, on the second day after the murder: *La Nuova* reported that the woman calling herself Florinda Ghiorghiu had worked for Signora Battestini for only five months before the crime and that the victim's only son had died five years before. So it was not only the director of the school board who had this knowledge about Signora Battestini and her family.

After an hour, Vianello came in, bringing the list Signorina Elettra had prepared – the inspector took special pains to point out that she had obtained the information by means of an official police request – of the people who had worked at the school board here in the city during the three months before the payments began. 'She's doing a cross-check on them through other records,' Vianello said, 'to see where they are now, if they've married, died, moved.'

Brunetti looked at the list and saw that it contained twenty-two names. Experience, prejudice and intuition united in him, and he asked, 'Shall we ignore the women?'

'At least for now, I think we can,' Vianello agreed. 'I saw the photos of her body, too.'

'That leaves eight,' Brunetti said.

Vianello said, 'I know. I copied down the first four names for you. I'll go back down and start calling around and see what I can find out about the other four.'

Brunetti was already reaching for the phone when the inspector left the office. He had recognized three of the names on the list, though that was due to nothing more than the presence of a Costantini and two Scarpas, all of whose names had fallen to Vianello. From memory, he dialled the office of the union to which he belonged, to which, in fact, most civil servants belonged, gave his name, and asked for Daniele Masiero.

The call was transferred, and while he waited, Brunetti was treated to one of the Four Seasons. When Masiero answered with, '*Ciao*, Guido, and the privacy of whose life do you want me to betray today?' Brunetti continued humming the main theme of the second movement of the concerto.

'I didn't choose it,' Masiero insisted. 'And luckily I never have to call, so I never have to listen to it.'

'Then how do you know about it?' Brunetti asked.

'So many people say how sick they are of hearing it.'

Ordinarily Brunetti would have observed the conventions

and asked Masiero about his family and his job, but today he lacked the patience and so asked only, 'I've got the names of four people who worked at the school board about ten years ago, and I'd like you to find out whatever you can about them.'

'Things that have to do with my job or yours?' Masiero asked.

'Mine.'

'As in?'

'Something for which they could be blackmailed.'

'Broad field.'

Brunetti thought it wisest to spare Masiero his reflections on the Seven Deadly Sins and answered only, 'Yes.'

He heard scrabbling sounds on the other end, and then Masiero asked, 'Tell me their names.'

'Luigi D'Alessandro, Riccardo Ledda, Benedetto Nardi, and Gianmaria Poli.'

Masiero grunted as Brunetti read off each of the names.

'You know any of them?' Brunetti asked.

'Poli's dead,' Masiero said. 'About two years ago. Heart attack. And Ledda was transferred to Rome six years ago. I'm not sure about the other two, what there might be to blackmail them about, but I can ask around.'

'Could I ask you to do it without calling attention to what you're doing?' Brunetti asked.

'Like going up to them and asking them if they're being blackmailed for something?' the other man answered shortly, making no attempt to disguise his irritation at Brunetti's question. 'I'm not an idiot, Guido. I'll see what I can find out and call you back.'

It came to Brunetti to apologize, but before he could say anything, Masiero was gone.

Again he called his friend Lalli at his office and, after listening to the other man explain that he had been too busy to check into Battestini, Brunetti said he had two more names to give him, those of D'Alessandro and Nardi.

'This time I'll do it. I'll find the time,' Lalli promised, and was gone, leaving it to Brunetti to wonder if he were the only man in the city not driven to distraction by the pressure of work.

Habit took him to the window, where he studied the long cloths which hung from the scaffolding on the façade of the Ospedale di San Lorenzo, site of another massive restoration project. A crane, perhaps the same one that had stood still over the church for so many years, now stood equally motionless over the old people's home. There was no evidence that work was progressing. Brunetti tried, and failed, to recall ever having seen anyone on the scaffolding; he tried to remember when the scaffolding had gone up: months ago, at the very least. The sign in front of the church, he knew, said that the work there was begun according to the law of 1973, but he had not been at the Questura then and so had no idea if that was the year in which work was meant to begin or merely the date of its authorization. Was it only in this city, he wondered, that one measured things in terms of how long the work had not been going on?

He went back to his desk and pulled out a diary from 1998 in which he kept phone numbers. He looked one up, dialled the offices of Arcigay in Marghera, where he asked to speak to Emilio Desideri, the Director. He was put on hold and learned that, straight or gay, Vivaldi was the man.

'Desideri,' a deep voice said.

'It's me, Emilio: Guido. I need to ask you a favour.'

'A favour I can do with a clear conscience?'

'Probably not.'

'No surprises there. What is it?'

'I've got two names – well, four,' he added, deciding to add Sardelli and Fedi, 'and I'd like you to tell me if any of them might be open to blackmail.'

'It's not a crime to be gay any more, Guido, remember?'

'It is to bash someone's head in, Emilio,' Brunetti shot back.

'That's why I'm calling.' He waited for Desideri to say something. He didn't, and so Brunetti went on. 'I want only for you to tell me if you know that any one of these men is gay.'

'And that will be enough to tell you that he was capable of bashing someone's head in, as you so delicately put it?'

'Emilio,' Brunetti said with studied calm, 'I'm not trying to harass you or anyone else who is gay. I don't care that you are. I don't care if the Pope is. I even like to think I wouldn't care if my son were, though that's probably a lie. I simply want to find a way to understand what might have happened to this old woman.'

'The Battestini woman? Paolo's mother?'

'You knew her?'

'I knew about her.'

'Are you at liberty to say how you did?'

'Paolo was involved with someone I knew, and he told me – but not until after Paolo had died – what sort of woman Paolo said she was.'

'Would he talk to me, this man?'

'If he were still alive, perhaps.'

Brunetti greeted this news with a long silence and then asked, 'Do you remember anything he told you?'

'That Paolo always said how much he loved her, but to him it always sounded like it was really a case of how much he hated her.'

'For any reason?'

'Greed. She lived to put money in the bank, it seems. It was her greatest joy, and it sounded like it was her only joy.'

'What was he like, Paolo?'

'I never met him.'

'What did your friend say about him?'

'He wasn't a friend. He was a patient. He was in analysis with me for three years.'

'Sorry. What did he say about him?'

'That he had acquired more than a little of her disease but that his greatest joy was in giving her money because it seemed to make her happy to get it. I always took that to mean that it stopped her nagging him, but I could be wrong. It might genuinely have made him happy to give it to her. There was little enough happiness in his life, otherwise.'

'He died of AIDS, didn't he?'

'Yes, so did his friend.'

'I'm sorry for that, too.'

'You sound like you really mean it, Guido,' Desideri said, but with no surprise.

'I am. No one deserves that.'

'All right. Give me the names.'

Brunetti read out the names of D'Alessandro and Nardi, and when Desideri said nothing, added those of Fedi and Sardelli.

For a long time, Desideri still said nothing, but the tension in his silence was so palpable that Brunetti held his breath. Finally Desideri asked, 'And you think Paolo might have been blackmailing this person?'

'The evidence we have suggests that he was,' Brunetti temporized.

He heard the rasp as Desideri pulled in an enormous breath, then he heard only, 'I can't do this,' and Desideri was gone.

Brunetti had a vague memory of hearing Paola once quote some English writer who said he would sooner betray his country than his friends. She had thought it a Jesuitical idea, and Brunetti was forced to agree, however expert the English were at making the vile sound noble. So one of the four was gay and was sufficiently a friend, or perhaps a patient, of Desideri that he could not give his name to the police, even in a murder investigation, perhaps because it was a murder investigation. The list had been narrowed, unless Vianello found someone else who was gay. Or,

Brunetti reflected, unless there were some other reason for blackmail.

Twenty minutes later, Vianello came into Brunetti's office, the list of names still in his hand. He took his usual place on the other side of the desk, slid the sheet on to it, and said, 'Nothing.'

Brunetti's question was in his glance.

'One's dead,' he said, pointing to a name. 'He retired the year after the payments started and died three years ago.' He moved his finger down the list. 'This one got religion and is living in some sort of commune or something, down near Bologna; has been for three years.' He pushed the paper a few centimetres in Brunetti's direction and sat back in the chair. 'And of the two who are still there, one's become the head of school inspections, Giorgio Costantini: he's married and seems like a decent man.'

Brunetti named two former heads of government and remarked that the same two things might be said of them.

Spurred on to the defensive, Vianello said, 'I've got a cousin who plays rugby with him at weekends. He says he's all right, and I believe him.'

Brunetti let this pass without further observation. Instead, he asked, 'And the other?'

'He's in a wheelchair.'

'What?'

'He's the guy who got polio when he went to India. You read about him, didn't you?'

The story rang a faint bell, though Brunetti had long forgotten the details. 'Yes, I remember something. How long ago did it happen, about five years?'

'Six. He got sick while he was there, and by the time they managed to diagnose it, it was too late to evacuate him, so he was treated there, and now he's in a wheelchair.' Vianello, in a tone that suggested he was still smarting from Brunetti's refusal to believe his cousin's assessment of Giorgio

Costantini, said, 'That might not be enough for you to exclude him, but I think a man might have other things to think about after landing in a wheelchair than continuing to pay blackmail.' He paused again. 'I could be wrong, of course.'

Brunetti gave Vianello a long glance but instead of rising to the bait, said, 'I'm still hoping Lalli will tell me something.'

'Betray a fellow gay?' Vianello asked in a tone Brunetti didn't like.

'He has three grandchildren.'

'Who?'

'Lalli.'

Vianello shook his head at this, Brunetti couldn't tell if in disbelief or disapproval.

'He's been my friend for a long time,' Brunetti said with steady calm. 'He's a decent man.'

Vianello knew a reprimand when he heard it and chose not to respond.

Brunetti was about to say something, when Vianello glanced away from him. It could have been his refusal to concede the point of Lalli's decency, or it could have been no more than his refusal to look at Brunetti, but whatever it was, Brunetti took it in his turn to be offended and was provoked into saying, 'I think I'd like to talk to the one who's not in a wheelchair. The rugby player.'

'As you wish, sir,' Vianello said. He got to his feet and, saying nothing else, left the office.

22

As the door closed behind Vianello, Brunetti came to his senses. 'Where'd all that come from?' he muttered. Was this the way drunks woke up, he asked himself, or the intemperately wrathful? Did they experience this feeling of having watched from the sidelines as someone disguised as themselves spoke their way through a bad script? He reflected on his conversation with Vianello, trying to pinpoint the moment when a simple exchange of information between friends had spun out of control and turned into a testosterone-charged battle over territory between rivals. To make matters worse, the territory over which they had fought was nothing more than Brunetti's refusal to accept an opinion because it had come from a man who chose to play rugby.

After he had sat at his desk for several minutes, his better self reached for the phone and called down to the officers' room, where a nervous-sounding Pucetti, after a long hesitation, told him Vianello was not there. Brunetti put the phone down, thinking of Achilles, sulking in his tent.

His phone rang and, hoping it would be Vianello, he reached out quickly to answer it.

'It's me, sir,' he heard Signorina Elettra say. 'I've got her phone calls.'

'How did you do that?'

'They decided to keep his wife in another day, so Giorgio went into the office.'

'Is there anything wrong?' asked the uxorious Brunetti.

'No, nothing. Her uncle is the *primario* there, and he thought it would be better if she stayed another day.' He heard it in her voice, the attempt to soothe away his concern for a woman he had never met. 'She's fine.'

Signorina Elettra waited a moment in case he had further questions, and when he said nothing, then went on, 'He found my email and checked her number. In the month before her death, she called the central number for the school board – it was the only call she made – and the next day she had a call from the same number. There was only one other call, from her niece. Nothing else.'

'How many days did he check?'

'The entire month up until she was killed.'

Neither of them commented on the fact that, in her eighty-fourth year, Signora Battestini, who had spent all of those years living in the city, had received only two phone calls in the course of a month. Brunetti recalled that there had been no books in the boxes stored in her attic: her life had been reduced to a chair placed in front of a television and a woman who spoke almost no Italian.

He recalled the boxes, how hurried his examination of them had been, and, thinking of this, he missed the next thing Signorina Elettra said to him. When he tuned back in, he heard her say, '. . . the day before she died'.

'What?' he asked. 'I was miles away.'

'The call that came from the school board was the day before she died.'

Her tone revealed her pride, but Brunetti could do little but thank her and hang up. While he had been speaking to her, an idea had slipped into his mind: the objects in Signora Battestini's attic needed closer attention. Blackmail had not presented itself as a motive until after he had taken his hurried look through them, but now, with blackmail as an anchor, he might pause and take a more leisurely trawl through them. Even if he still didn't know what he was looking for, he at least knew that there might be something to find.

He reached for the phone to call Vianello to ask if he would go along with him to the Battestini house, but then he remembered Vianello's departure and his absence from the officers' room. Pucetti, then. He called down and, giving no explanation, asked the young officer to meet him at the front entrance in five minutes, adding that they would need a launch.

The last time he had slipped into Signora Battestini's home like a thief, and no one had seen him: this time he would arrive like the very personification of law itself, and no one would question him, or so he hoped.

Pucetti, who was waiting just outside the door to the Questura, had learned over the years not to salute Brunetti each time he saw him, but he had not yet learned to resist the impulse to stand up straighter. They climbed on to the launch, with Brunetti determined not to ask about Vianello. He told the pilot where to take them, then went down into the cabin: Pucetti chose to remain on deck.

No sooner was he seated than the long passage describing Achilles in his tent returned to Brunetti, and memory supplied the bombastic catalogue of the offences and slights the warrior insisted he had suffered. Achilles had suffered the slights of Agamemnon: Brunetti had been slighted by his Patroclus. Brunetti's contemplation of Homer was interrupted by an expression Paola had picked up in her researches into American slang: 'dissed'. She had explained that this was the past tense of the verb 'to dis', a term used by American Blacks to refer to 'disrespect' and denoting a wide range of behaviour which the speaker perceived as offensive.

Under his breath, Brunetti muttered, 'Vianello dissed me.' He gave a quick guffaw, and he went out on to the deck, his good spirits renewed.

The launch pulled up to the *riva*, and they were quickly in front of the building. Brunetti glanced up and saw that both the shutters and the windows of Signora Battestini's apartment were open, though no televised sound poured out. He rang the bell and saw that her name had been replaced by Van Cleve.

A blonde head appeared at the window above him, and then a man's head appeared beside the woman's. Brunetti stepped back from the building and was about to call up to them to open the door, but apparently the sight of Pucetti's uniform sufficed, for a moment later both heads disappeared, and the door to the building clicked open.

The man and the woman, equally blonde and equally pale skinned and eyed, stood at the door to the apartment. Looking at them, Brunetti could not stop himself from thinking of milk and cheese and pale skies perpetually filled with clouds. Their Italian was halting, but he managed to make it clear to them who he was and where he wanted to go.

'*No chiave*,' the man said, smiling, and showing his empty hands to reinforce the message. The woman imitated his gesture of helplessness.

'*Va bene. Non importa*,' Brunetti said, turning from them and starting up the stairs to the attic. Pucetti followed close behind. At the first turning, Brunetti looked back and saw the two of them still standing outside the door to what was now apparently their apartment, staring up at him, as curious as owls.

When he reached the top of the steps, Brunetti pulled out a

twenty-centesemi coin, sure he could use it to unthread the already-loosened screws in the flange. But as he reached the door, he found that the flange was hanging at an angle, loose from the jamb. The two screws he had so carefully turned back in place were also loose, and the door stood open a few centimetres.

Brunetti put out a cautionary hand towards Pucetti, but he had already noticed and had moved to the right of the door, his hand reaching for his pistol. Both men froze, waiting for some sound from inside. They stood that way for minutes. Brunetti put his left foot in front of the bottom of the door and rested his full weight on it, thus blocking any attempt that might be made to push it open from the inside.

After another few minutes, Brunetti nodded at Pucetti, moved his foot, reached forward and pulled the door open. He went in first, calling out, 'Police,' and feeling just the least bit ridiculous as he heard himself say it.

The attic was empty, but even in the dim light they could see signs of the passage of the person who had been there before them. A trail of scattered objects told of curiosity turning to frustration and that in its turn transformed into anger, and then rage. The first boxes stood neatly unstacked near where Brunetti had left them, their flaps pulled open, contents set on the ground next to them. The next lay on their sides, their flaps ripped open. The third pile, where Brunetti had found the papers, had been pillaged: one box had been ripped in half, and a wide semicircle of papers arched over to the next pile. The last boxes, which had held her collection of religious kitsch, had suffered martyrdom: the bodies and limbs of saints lay strewed about in positions of impossible and ungodly promiscuity; one Jesus had lost his cross and stretched for it with open arms; a blue Madonna had lost her head in crashing against the back wall; another had lost her infant son.

Brunetti took it all in, turned to Pucetti, and said, 'Call

them and tell them to send the crime team. I want fingerprints taken of everything.' He placed his right hand on Pucetti's arm and pushed him towards the door: 'Go down and wait for them,' he said. Then, in violation of everything he had ever learned or taught about the need to preserve a crime scene from contamination, he added, 'I want to have a look before they get here.'

Pucetti's confusion was so strong as almost to be audible as well as visible, but he did as he was told, slipping past the attic door, careful not to touch it, and went downstairs.

Brunetti stood, studying the scene and considering the consequences of the discovery of his fingerprints on so many of the papers, boxes and documents that lay in front of him. He could, if he chose, explain their presence by maintaining that he had used this time to examine the evidence. He could, just as easily, say that he had come up to the attic and examined the contents of some of the boxes during a previous, unauthorized, visit to the apartment.

Brunetti took a step towards the boxes. In the gloom, he set his right foot on the glass ball containing the Nativity scene, slipped, and lost his footing. He landed on his other knee, landed on something that crumbled under his weight, pushing sharp fragments through the cloth of his trousers and into his skin. Stunned by the fall and the sudden pain, it took him a moment to raise himself to his feet. He looked first at his knee, where the first faint traces of blood were beginning to seep through the cloth, and then to the floor, to see what he had fallen on.

It was a third Madonna. His knee had caught her in the stomach, crushing all life out of her but sparing her head and legs. She looked up at him with a calm smile and all-forgiving eyes. Instinctively, he bent to help her, at least to put the top and bottom parts somewhere safe. He went down on his good knee, wincing at the pain this motion caused the other, and reached with both hands to pick up the fragments.

Amidst the pieces of crushed plaster was a flattened roll of paper. Puzzled, Brunetti looked at the bottom of the Madonna's feet and saw that there was a small oval opening closed with a cork, just like the bottom of a salt shaker. The paper had been rolled up into a tight cylinder and stuffed inside her.

He dropped the head and legs into the pocket of his jacket and stepped out into the hallway. He moved to the window at the end and, grasping the top left corner of the paper with the tips of his fingers, used the back of the fingernails of his right to unroll it, hoping to leave no fingerprints. But the paper kept rolling up, preventing him from seeing what was written on it.

He heard Pucetti on the stairs below him, calling out, 'They're on the way, sir.' When Brunetti saw him appear at the head of the steps, he called the young officer over. Kneeling again, he spread the paper open with the tips of the fingers of both hands and told Pucetti to put the very edge of his foot sideways on the top. When it was anchored to the ground, Brunetti used the tips of his little fingers to scroll it open again, anchoring the open sheet with his forefingers once it was done.

The single sheet of paper bore the letterhead of the Department of Economics at the University of Padova and was dated twelve years previously. It was addressed to the Department of Personnel of the School Board of the City of Venice and stated, after a polite greeting, that, 'Unfortunately, there is no mention in the records of our department of a student named Mauro Rossi as having been awarded the degree of Doctor of Philosophy in Economics; nor, in fact, do we have any record of a student of that name and with that birth date ever having enrolled in this faculty.' The signature was illegible, although there was no mistaking the seal of the university.

Brunetti stared down at it, refusing to believe what it told him. He tried to recall the documents on the wall of Rossi's office, among them the large, framed parchment which proclaimed him as a Doctor of Philosophy – Brunetti had not bothered to read the name of the faculty granting the degree.

The letter was addressed to the Director of the Personnel Department, but certainly directors did not open their own mail: that's what clerks and assistants were for. They opened, read, and made official note of the letters which certified that the claims made in a curriculum vitae were true. They filed the letters of recommendation, the marks gained on competitive exams, made note of all the pieces of the paper puzzle that, when put together, gave a picture of someone worthy of professional rank and promotion in the civil service.

Or, he imagined, they might at times verify, perhaps according to some random system, some of the claims made on the hundreds, thousands of applications made for each civil service job. And upon discovering a false claim, they could make this deceit public and disqualify the person making it, perhaps banish them absolutely from the civil service system. Or they could, instead, use the information for their own purpose, their own gain.

He had a momentary vision of the Battestini family gathered around their table or perhaps in front of the television. Papa Bear showed Mamma Bear what he and Baby Bear had brought home from work that day.

He shook away this vision, picked the letter up by a corner, and got to his feet.

'What's that, sir?' Pucetti asked, pointing to the letter.

'It's the reason Signora Battestini was killed,' Brunetti answered and went down the steps to wait for the crime team, still holding the letter by one corner.

Downstairs, he spoke to the Dutch couple, this time in English, and asked them if anyone had tried to get into the building since they had moved in. They said that the only person who had disturbed them was Signora Battestini's son, who had asked them to let him in two days ago, saying he had forgotten his keys – at least that is what they thought he said, they added with embarrassed smiles – and had to go upstairs to check on the windows in the attic. No, they had not asked for identification: who else would want to go up into the attic? He had been up there for about twenty minutes when they left to go to their Italian lesson, but he had not been there when they got back, or at least they had not heard him come down the stairs. No, they had not gone up to the attic to check: they were renting only this apartment, and they did not think it correct to go into other parts of the building.

It took Brunetti a moment to realize that they were serious, but then he remembered that they were Dutch and believed them.

'Could you describe her son to me?' Brunetti asked.

'Tall,' the husband said.

'And handsome,' the wife added.

The husband gave her a sharp look but said nothing.

'How old was he, would you say?' he asked the wife.

'Oh, in his forties,' she said, 'and tall. He looked very athletic,' she concluded, then shot at her husband a look Brunetti could not decipher.

'I see,' Brunetti said, then switched topics and asked, 'To whom do you pay your rent?'

'Signora Maries . . .' the wife began, but the husband cut her off by saying, 'We're staying here because it belongs to a friend, so we don't pay anything, just the utilities.'

Brunetti let that lie register and asked, 'Ah, so Graziella Simionato is a friend of yours?'

Both their faces remained blank at the mention of the name. The husband recovered first and said, 'A friend of a friend, that is.'

'I see,' Brunetti answered, toyed with telling them that he didn't care whether anyone paid taxes on their rent or not, but decided it was unimportant and let it go. 'Would you recognize her son if you saw him again?'

He watched the struggle on both their faces, as their instinctive Northern European honesty and respect for law struggled with everything they had ever been told about the ways of these devious Latins. 'Yes,' both of them said at the same time, an answer which cheered Brunetti.

He thanked them, said he would contact them if the identification became necessary, and then went downstairs and outside. A police launch stood at the side of the canal, Bocchese and two technicians humping their heavy equipment on to the *riva*.

Brunetti walked towards the boat, the paper still dangling in front of him, as if it were a fresh fish he had just caught and wanted to give to Bocchese. When the technician saw Brunetti, he reached down and opened one of the cases on the pavement. From it he pulled a transparent plastic sleeve and held it open while Brunetti lowered the letter into it.

'Up in the attic. Someone's gone through it and tossed things all over the place. I'd like a complete check: fingerprints, whatever you might find that would allow us to identify him.'

'You know who it was?' Bocchese asked.

Brunetti nodded. 'Can I take the boat?' he asked Bocchese.

'If you send it back for us afterwards. We've got all this stuff to carry,' he said, gesturing down at the cases at his feet.

'All right,' Brunetti said. Before he stepped aboard, he turned back to Bocchese and said, 'By the way, there are none of my fingerprints on any of the stuff in that attic.'

Bocchese gave him a long, speculative glance and then said, 'Of course.' He bent down and picked up one of the cases and started towards the door of what had been Signora Battestini's house.

23

Brunetti resisted the impulse to ask the pilot to take him to Ca' Farsetti for an impromptu meeting with Rossi. The voice of good sense and restraint told him this was not the time for cowboy theatrics, one-to-one confrontations where there were no witnesses and no one to overhear save the two men involved. He had given in to that impulse in the past, and it had always worked against him, against the police, and ultimately against the victims, who had, if nothing else, the right to see their killers punished.

The boat took him back to the Questura, where he went up to the officers' room. Vianello looked up as his superior came in, and his face broadened in a smile that at first spoke of embarrassment, but then, when he saw Brunetti's answering grin, of relief. The inspector got to his feet and came towards the door.

Signalling him to follow, Brunetti started up towards his office, then slowed his steps to allow Vianello to walk beside him. 'It's Rossi,' he said.

'The man from the school board?' a surprised Vianello asked.

'Yes. I found the reason.'

It was not until they were seated in Brunetti's office that he said, 'I went up and took another look at the junk in her attic. There was a letter from the University of Padova hidden in one of Signora Battestini's statues; rolled up and stuck inside. I stumbled on it,' he concluded, giving no further explanation. Vianello watched him but said nothing. 'It was dated about twelve years ago and said that no one named Mauro Rossi had ever studied in the Department of Economics, had certainly never earned a doctorate.'

Vianello's eyebrows pulled together in unmistakable confusion. 'But so what?'

'It means he lied when he applied for the job, said he had a doctorate when he didn't,' Brunetti explained.

'I understand that,' said a patient Vianello, 'but I don't see how it makes any difference.'

'The whole thing, his job, his career, his future, all of them would be lost if Battestini showed anyone the letter,' Brunetti explained, puzzled that Vianello seemed not to understand.

Vianello made a gesture as though he hoped to scare away flies. 'I understand all of that. But why is it so important? It's only a job, for God's sake. Important enough to kill someone?'

The answer came from his conversation with Paola, surprising Brunetti as it came back to him: 'Pride,' he declared. 'Not lust and not greed. But pride. We've followed the wrong vice throughout,' he said to a completely perplexed Vianello.

It was clear that Vianello had no idea what Brunetti meant. Finally, he repeated, 'I still don't understand,' and then, 'Are we going to go and get him or not?'

Brunetti saw no reason for haste. Signor – no longer Dottor – Rossi was not going to abandon his position and family. Instinct told him that Rossi was the kind of man who would brave it out, who would maintain up to the very last that he had no idea what any of this was about or how his name possibly came to be associated with that of an old woman who had the misfortune to be murdered. Brunetti could all but hear his explanations and was sure they would, chameleon-like, change as more and more incriminating evidence was presented by the police. Rossi had fooled people for more than a decade: surely he would try to continue to do so now.

Vianello shifted restlessly in his seat, and Brunetti attempted to calm him by saying, 'We need his fingerprints to be on the things in the attic. As soon as Bocchese has them, we can think about bringing him in for questioning.'

'And if he refuses to give us a sample on his own?'

'He won't refuse, not once we have him here,' Brunetti said with absolute certainty. 'It would create a scandal: the newspapers would eat him alive.'

'And killing the old woman won't create a scandal?'

'Yes, but a different sort, one he thinks he can talk his way out of. He'll claim that he was a victim, that he didn't know what he was doing, that he was not himself when he killed her.' Before Vianello could ask, he went on, 'Refusing to be fingerprinted, when he knows it's inescapable – that would look cowardly, so he'll avoid that.' He glanced away from Vianello and out of the window for a moment, then returned his attention to his colleague and said, 'Think about it: he created a false person years ago, this false doctor, and he won't move from that role, no matter what we do or can prove about him. He's lived within it so long he probably believes it by now or at least believes that he has earned the right to special treatment because of his position.'

'And so?' Vianello asked, apparently bored with all of this speculation and in need of practical information.

'And so we wait for Bocchese.'

Vianello got to his feet, thought about saying something but decided not to, and left.

Brunetti remained at his desk, thinking of power and the privileges many of those who had it believed accrued to them because of it. He ran through the people he worked with, hunting for this quality, and when his train of thought brought him into company with Lieutenant Scarpa, he pushed himself to his feet and went down to the lieutenant's office.

'*Avanti*,' Scarpa called out in response to Brunetti's knock.

Brunetti went in, leaving the door open. When he saw his superior, the lieutenant half stood, a movement that might as well have been an attempt to find a more comfortable position in his seat as a sign of respect. 'May I help you, Commissario?' he asked, lowering himself again into his chair.

'What's happening with Signora Gismondi?' Brunetti asked.

Scarpa's smile made a mockery of mirth. 'May I ask the reason for your concern, sir?' Scarpa asked.

'No,' Brunetti answered in a tone so peremptory that Scarpa failed to disguise his surprise. 'What's happening with your investigation of Signora Gismondi?'

'I assume you've spoken to the Vice-Questore and he's given you his permission to involve yourself in this, sir,' Scarpa said blandly.

'Lieutenant, I asked you a question,' Brunetti said.

Perhaps Scarpa thought he could stall for time; perhaps he was curious to see how far he could push Brunetti. 'I've spoken to some of her neighbours about her whereabouts on the morning of the murder, sir,' he said, glancing at Brunetti. When Brunetti failed to react, Scarpa went on, 'And I've called her employers to ask if this story about being in London at the time is true.'

'And is that how you phrased it, Lieutenant?'

Scarpa made a tentative little gesture with one hand and said, 'I'm not sure I understand what you mean, Commissario.'

'Is that how you asked them: whether the story she's been giving the police is true? Or did you merely ask where she was?'

'Oh, I'm afraid I don't remember that, sir. I was more concerned with discovering the truth than with niceties of language.'

'And what answers did you get in your attempt to discover the truth, Lieutenant?'

'I haven't found anyone who contradicts her story, sir, and it seems she was in London when she said she was.'

'So she was telling the truth?' Brunetti asked.

'It would appear so,' Scarpa said with exaggerated reluctance, then added, 'At least until I find someone who tells me that she is not.'

'Well, Lieutenant, that's not going to happen.'

Scarpa looked up, startled. 'I beg your pardon, sir.'

'It's not going to happen, Lieutenant, because you are going to stop, as of now, asking questions about Signora Gismondi.'

'I'm afraid my duty as . . .' Scarpa began.

Brunetti cracked. He leaned over Scarpa's desk and put his face a few centimetres from the lieutenant's. He noted that the younger man's breath smelled faintly of mint. 'If you question another person about her, Lieutenant, I will break you.'

Scarpa yanked his head back in astonishment. His mouth fell open.

Leaning even farther over the desk, Brunetti thumped his palms flat on its surface and again moved his face close to Scarpa's. 'If I learn that you speak to anyone about her or insinuate that she had anything to do with this, I will have you out of here, Lieutenant.' Brunetti raised his right hand and grabbed the lapel of Scarpa's jacket, tightening his hand into a fist and yanking him forward.

Brunetti's face was suffused with blood and rage. 'Do you understand me, Lieutenant?'

Scarpa tried to speak, but all he could do was open his mouth, then close it.

Brunetti pushed him away and left the office. In the corridor he almost bumped into Pucetti, who was wheeling away from Scarpa's door. 'Ah, Commissario,' the young officer said, his face a study in blandness, 'I wanted to ask you about the duty rosters for next week, but I couldn't help overhearing you settle them just now with Lieutenant Scarpa, so I won't trouble you with them.' His face sober and respectful, Pucetti gave a sharp salute, and Brunetti went back to his office.

There, he waited, sure that Bocchese would call him when he got back with news of whatever he had found in Signora Battestini's attic. He called Lalli, Masiero and Desideri and told them they could call off the dogs, for he thought he had found the old woman's killer. None of them asked who it was; all of them thanked him for calling.

He also phoned Signorina Elettra and told her the probable meaning of the phone call to the school board. 'Why would she call him out of the blue like that, that last time?' she asked when he told her. 'Things had been continuing for more than a decade, and the only other time she contacted him in all those years was when we switched to the Euro.' Before he could ask, she supplied, 'Yes, I've checked her phone calls for the last ten years. Those were the only calls between them.' She paused for a long time and then said, 'It doesn't make any sense.'

'Maybe she got greedy,' Brunetti suggested.

'At eighty-three?' Signorina Elettra asked. 'Let me think about it,' she said and hung up.

After another hour, he walked down to Bocchese's office, but one of the technicians said his chief was still out at some crime scene over in Cannaregio. Brunetti drifted down to the bar near the bridge and had a glass of wine and a *panino*, then walked out to the *riva* and looked across at San Giorgio and, beyond it, the Redentore. Then he went back to his office.

He had been back little more than ten minutes, trying to impose order upon the accumulation of objects in the drawers of his desk, when Signorina Elettra appeared at his door. Her shoes were green, he had time to notice before she said, 'You were right, Commissario.' Then in answer to his unspoken question, she explained, 'She got greedy.' And before he could ask about that, she said, 'You said all she did was sit and watch television, didn't you?'

It took him a moment to return from the consideration of that green, but when he did he said, 'Yes. Everyone in the neighbourhood talked about it.'

'Then look at this,' she said. Approaching his desk, she handed him a photocopy of the familiar television listings that appeared in the *Gazzettino* every day. 'Look at 11 p.m., sir.'

He did and saw that the local channel was presenting a documentary called, *I Nostri Professionisti*. 'Our local professional what?' he asked.

Ignoring his question, she said, 'Now look at the date.'

The end of July, three days before the murder, the day before Signora Battestini's phone call to the school board.

'And?' he asked, handing the paper back to her.

'One of our "local professionals" was Dottor Mauro Rossi, the head of the school board, interviewed by Alessandra Duca.'

'How did you find this?' His surprise did not mask his admiration.

'I did a cross-reference search with his name and the television listings for the last few weeks,' she said. 'It seemed the only way she could ever have learned anything, since all she ever did was watch television.'

'And?' Brunetti asked.

'I spoke to the journalist, who said it was just the usual puff piece: interviewing bureaucrats about their fascinating work in city administration – the sort of thing they show late at night and no one watches.'

This sounded to Brunetti like a blanket description of all local broadcasting, but he said only, 'And? Did you ask her about Rossi?'

'Yes. She said it was all predictable: he talked at great length and with false humility about his career and his success. But she did say he was so bad at disguising his arrogance that she let him talk more than she ordinarily would with one of these types, just to see how far he'd go.'

'And how far was that?'

'He talked – Duca said, with self-effacing humility – about the possibility of a transfer to the Ministry in Rome.'

Brunetti considered the implications of this and suggested, 'And with the equal possibility of an enormous increase in salary?'

'She said he only implied that. She remembered he said something about wanting to be of service to the future of the children of Italy.' She waited for a few moments, then added, 'She also said that, from what she knows of local politics, he has about as much chance of going to Rome as the Mayor does of being re-elected.'

After a long pause, Brunetti said, 'Yes.'

'Excuse me?'

'Greed. Even at eighty-three.'

'Yes,' she answered. 'How sad.'

Bocchese, who was usually not to be seen in the Questura outside of his own office, appeared at the door. 'I was looking for you,' he reproached Brunetti. With a nod to Signorina Elettra, he walked into the office and set some things on the desk. Turning back to Brunetti, he said, 'Let me get a sample.'

Brunetti looked and saw the standard piece of cardboard with spaces for the prints of the various fingers. Bocchese flipped open a flat tin and waved impatiently towards

Brunetti, who walked over and gave him his right hand. Quickly, it was done, then the left.

Bocchese slid the cardboard to one side, revealing another one beneath it. 'I might as well do you, Signorina,' he said.

'No thank you,' she answered, walking away and standing near the door.

'What?' Bocchese asked, his voice making the word something more than a question but less than a demand.

'I prefer not to,' she said, and the possibility died.

Bocchese shrugged, picked up Brunetti's card and gave it a careful look. 'Nothing like this on anything in the attic, I'd say, but there are lots of them from some other person, probably a man, and a big one.'

'Lots?' Brunetti asked.

'Looks like he went through everything,' Bocchese answered. Then, when he saw that he had Brunetti's attention, he added, 'There's a set of the same prints on the underside of her kitchen table. Well, my guess is that they're the same, but we have to send them to Interpol in Lyon to be sure.'

'How long will that take?' Brunetti asked.

Another shrug. 'A week? A month?' He put the cards in a plastic envelope and slipped the box of ink into his pocket. 'You know anyone there? In Lyon? To speed things up?'

'No,' Brunetti admitted.

Both men turned supplicating eyes towards Signorina Elettra.

'I'll see what I can do,' she said.

24

Brunetti spent the next hour alone in his office, considering the best way to confront Rossi. He moved back and forth between his desk and the window, unable to concentrate, his every thought blocked by and turned back upon the Seven Deadly Sins. None of them, he realized, was any longer against the law; at worst they might be considered flaws of character. Could this be some novel way to carbon-date between the old world and the new? For weeks, he had listened to Paola read aloud passages from the text from which his daughter was being taught religion, yet it had never occurred to him to wonder if she were being taught the concept of sin and, if so, how it was being defined.

Theft was a choice, avarice and envy merely the vices that predisposed to it. So too with the vice of sloth: experience had taught him that many criminals were led to their crimes by the slothful belief that it was easier to steal than to work. Blackmail was another choice, and the same three vices led to it.

Brunetti had seen the signs of pride in Rossi and was

persuaded that the cause of his crime lay there. Any normal person would judge that the exposure of Rossi's fraud would cost him little but embarrassment. Perhaps he would lose the directorship of the school board, but a man with his connections could easily find work; the city bureaucracy could shift him sideways to some obscure job where he could receive the same salary and continue to proceed unhindered towards his pension.

But he would no longer be Dottor Rossi, would no longer be courted by local television and asked to speak to an attentive journalist about his prospects of taking a job in Rome. The news of his exposure would not last a week and would do nothing more than cause some mild fuss in the local papers; it was hardly an event that would interest the national press. The public memory grew shorter each day, geared as it was never to exceed the length of an MTV video, so Rossi, doctor or no, would be forgotten by the end of the month. But even this his pride could not endure.

Finally curiosity overcame Brunetti and he called down to Vianello. 'Let's go and get him,' was all he said. He paused only long enough to go down to Bocchese's office and pick up one of the photocopies of the letter from the University of Padova the technician had prepared.

He and Vianello decided to walk to Rossi's office and though they talked about him on the way, neither of them seemed fully capable of understanding his behaviour. Brunetti saw their failure to understand Rossi as a manifestation of either their moral shortsightedness or their lack of imagination.

Brunetti did not stop at the office of the *portiere* but went directly to the staircase and up to the third floor. The offices were full this morning, people walking in and out with papers and folders in their hands, the busy ants that swarmed in every city office. The woman with the studs in her temple was at her desk, looking no more interested in reality than she had been the last time he saw her. Her eyes, when she saw him, registered nothing. Nor did she seem aware of any of the half-dozen people who sat on the chairs along the walls, all of whom studied Brunetti and Vianello as they came in.

'We're here to see the Director,' Brunetti said.

'I think he's in his office,' she said with an airy wave of those green-tipped fingers. Brunetti thanked her and started towards the door that led to the corridor to Rossi's office, but he had to turn around and summon Vianello, who stood transfixed in front of the receptionist.

They found the door to Rossi's office open and went in without bothering to knock. Rossi sat at his desk; the same man, but in a way Brunetti was slow to grasp, not at all the same man. Rossi looked across his office at them with eyes that seemed to have been affected by those of the woman in the reception area. The colour was the same deep brown, but they seemed to be experiencing a difficulty in focusing similar to that of the receptionist.

Brunetti walked across the room and stopped in front of Rossi's desk. By turning his head he could read the full text on the certificate in the carved teak frame, the one from the University of Padova, conveying the degree of Doctor of Philosophy in Economics on Mauro Rossi.

'Where'd you get it, Signor Rossi?' Brunetti asked, indicating the framed diploma with the thumb of his right hand.

Rossi gave a small cough, sat up straighter in his chair, and said, 'I don't know what you're talking about.'

Brunetti shrugged this off, took the photocopy Bocchese had given him from his pocket, opened it, and slid it casually in front of Rossi. 'You got any idea what this is talking about, then, Signor Rossi?' Brunetti asked with exaggerated aggression.

'What's that?' Rossi asked, not daring to look at it.

'What you were searching for in the attic,' Brunetti answered.

Rossi looked at Vianello, back at Brunetti, then down at the letter, where his eyes remained. Brunetti noticed that his lips moved as he read it. Brunetti watched the man's eyes slide off the bottom of the paper, then swerve back to the top. Rossi read it again, even more slowly this time.

He looked up at Brunetti and said, 'But I've got two children.'

For a moment, Brunetti was tempted to enter into discussion with him, but he knew where this would lead: to Rossi's weighing the happiness of his two children against Signora Battestini's life, to his defence of his reputation, no doubt his honour, against the old woman's threats to destroy him. If it were a play, or a television soap opera, Brunetti would have had no trouble writing the script, and had he been the Director, he would have known exactly what instructions to give the actor playing Rossi so as to infuse his every sentence with puzzled indignation and, yes, with injured pride.

'I'm arresting you, Signor Mauro Rossi,' Brunetti finally said, 'for the murder of Maria Grazia Battestini.' Rossi stared at him, his eyes mirrors, if not of his soul, then certainly of the blankness on view in those of his receptionist. 'Come with us,' Brunetti said, stepping back from the desk. Rossi put both palms flat on his desk and pushed himself to his feet. Before he turned away towards the door, Brunetti saw that both of his hands were set squarely on the letter from the University of Padova, but Rossi seemed not to notice.

A week later, Rossi was back at home, though he was there under house arrest. He was not back at work, though he had not been fired from his position as Direttore della Pubblica Istruzione and had been placed on indeterminate leave while his case moved slowly along.

He had admitted, during questioning in the presence of his lawyer, to killing Signora Battestini, though he maintained that he had no clear memory of the actual attack. She had called him some time before her death, he said, to tell him that she wanted to talk to him. He had at first refused, but she had threatened him, told him to call her when he came to his senses, and hung up. He had called her back the next day, hoping she would be more reasonable, but she had threatened him again, and so he had no choice but to go to see her.

She had begun by saying she wanted more money, much more, five times as much. And when he said he could not pay it, she said she had seen him on television and knew he was going to get a big government job and would be able to pay her. He tried to reason with her, tell her that the job was just a hope he had expressed rather than something he was sure of. But she had refused to listen. When he said he had two children to support, she started to abuse him, shouting that she no longer had a son, that he had died, and so he had to pay for that, too. He tried to calm her, but she had grown hysterical, he said, and tried to hit him.

Then she said she no longer wanted the money and would tell everyone about him. The windows were open, and she started to walk towards them, saying she was going to scream to the entire city that he was a false doctor. After that, he maintained, he didn't remember anything until she was lying on the floor. He said it had been like waking up from a nightmare, seeing her there. When Brunetti questioned him, he said he had no memory of hitting her, had not realized he had done it until he saw the bloody statue in his hand.

Brunetti, when he heard this, had thought it a particularly uninventive thing to say, but then the whole confession, aimed as it was at exoneration, was not much more inventive. Rossi's lawyer had sat solemn-faced through it all, had at one point even made what sounded like sympathetic noises.

Fear, Rossi said, had driven him from the house. No, he didn't remember wiping off the statue. Because he didn't remember anything, you see; he didn't remember killing her, only her screaming and hitting at him.

It was Brunetti's visit to his office that had driven him to search Signora Battestini's attic. Yes, he knew about the letter from the University of Padova: it had haunted his life for years. He had added the non-existent degree to his curriculum vitae years ago, just after the birth of his first child, when he needed a better job in order to support his family. He had paid a print shop to make the fake diploma for him to increase his chances of getting a job. He lived in fear of exposure, he said: this must have affected him when he found himself with Signora Battestini. He was a victim of his terror just as he was a victim of her greed.

The night after the questioning, when Brunetti told Paola, he used Rossi's word, 'victim,' and said it would be the key to his defence.

'He's a victim, you see,' he repeated while they sat in her study. They were inside, having left Raffi and Sara alone on the balcony to do whatever young people do together in the soft light of a late summer evening, with a view across the rooftops of Venice before them.

'And Signora Battestini's not,' Paola said. She did not phrase it as a question but as an assertion, a truth that extended to cover all those who were already dead and thus no longer of any use. Brunetti remembered then one of the grimmer remarks attributed to Stalin: 'No man, no problem.'

'What will happen to him?' Paola asked.

Brunetti could not say with any certainty, but he could make a guess, basing it on what had happened in similar cases, where the murdered person had no claim on public sympathy, and the murderer presented himself as a victim. 'He'll probably be convicted, and that means he'll be sentenced to something like seven years, maybe less, but it will take two or three years to arrive at that. Which means he'll already have served two years of his sentence.'

'Under house arrest?' she asked.

'It still counts,' Brunetti said.

'And then?'

'And then he'll go to prison until the appeal is filed, when it will all start to chug through the courts again, but because the appeal is being considered and because he won't be considered a danger to society, he'll be sent home again.'

'Until what?'

'Until the appeal is settled.' Before she could ask, he said, 'Which will take a few more years, and even if the sentence is confirmed, it will most likely be decided that he's already spent enough time under arrest, and he'll be released.'

'Just like that?' she asked.

'There will be some variations, I suppose,' Brunetti said and reached for the book he had abandoned before dinner.

'And that's all?' she asked in a voice she had to work at making sound neutral.

He nodded and pulled the book towards him. When she said nothing, he asked, 'Are you still reading Chiara's religion text?'

She shook her head. 'No, I gave up on it.'

'Perhaps you could find an answer to all of this in there.'

'Where?' she demanded. 'How?'

'By doing what you suggested to me the other day, by thinking eschatologically,' he said: 'Death. Judgement. Heaven. Hell.'

'You don't believe in any of that, do you?' asked an astonished Paola.

'There are times when it would be nice,' he said and opened his book.